The Cooperating Witness

Mike Avery

Literary Wanderlust | Denver, Colorado

Published in the United States by Literary Wanderlust LLC, Denver, Colorado. www.LiteraryWanderlust.com

ISBN Print: 978-1-942856-58-0
ISBN eBook: 978-1-942856-63-4

Cover design: Pozu Mitsuma

Printed in the United States

For Peter Limone and his family.
He served thirty-three years for a murder
that he had nothing to do with.
No one could give him, his wife, and his children
the time back.

"What do you want, tears?"

—Ex-FBI Agent H. Paul Rico, responding to the accusation by Congressman Christopher Shays that he felt no remorse for framing innocent men for murder.

Prologue

Sunday, July 7, 2004

The Accountant cracked the back door of his office and peered down the dimly lit stairway. Five flights of stairs lay between him and the exit. It was quiet. That didn't guarantee there was no one lurking in the dark to ambush him. He took off his black horn-rimmed glasses and polished the lenses with a microfiber cloth from his back pocket. Still nobody visible on the stairs.

On Friday night he'd driven from the North End of Boston to his girlfriend Rena's condo in the Seaport. Crossing the Fort Point Channel, he'd felt someone following him. He drove around the block to see if he could spot the tail. Nothing doing. Then he drove down A Street from Congress to Broadway and back, with his eyes glued to the rearview mirror. All that did was give him the sweats. By the time he got to Rena's, he was a wreck. He was shaking the same way now.

Tony Francini kept the books for the mob. He liked to say there was no bear market for vice. But lately, the income of Frank Romano's operations was down. Frank ordered him to figure out why. The money had to be going into someone's pocket. So far, he had nothing. *Niente.* He'd talked with some of the capos to see if they had any ideas, but it just pissed them off. He hoped to Christ Frank didn't believe he was the one stealing.

He'd scanned column after column in his spreadsheets, looking for patterns that might show who was skimming. It'd be much easier if he worked for an ordinary business with contracts, invoices, receipts, payroll records, W-2 forms, bank deposits, everything organized on computers. His data came from numbers jotted on the backs of envelopes that littered his desk.

At ten o'clock he'd finally given up for the day, pushed his papers into a pile, and thrown them into his safe. He took a fresh white shirt from a drawer in his desk where he kept them for when he went straight from work to see Rena. He put his pen in a pocket protector, put it in the new shirt, and ran his fingers through his hair, which felt thinner than ever. Maybe all these hours at the office were making him go bald. He was very late for dinner. He called Rena to say he was on the way.

He started down the stairs. He labored, even on a downward climb. It was so damn hard to lose weight. He was pushing fifty and it wasn't getting any easier. The doctor said he was carrying eighty pounds more than was healthy. Eighty pounds. He didn't see how he could lose half that.

Rena didn't seem to care about his weight. His niece Elena had acted in a children's theater group Rena directed in the North End and he'd donated some money. No big deal—just five hundred bucks—but it was one of the larger contributions. Rena invited him to dinner with other donors. She made tortellini pomodoro from scratch. The guests were amazed that she would do that while entertaining ten people. She explained how she'd rolled the pasta out, then stuffed the circles of dough with ricotta cheese and chives, which gives the tortellini a soft, sweet taste, with a slight accent of the flavor of onion. The other guests shook their heads. They would have opted to buy the frozen variety at the grocery store. That's when Tony started to fall for Rena.

"How do you think they came up with this shape for pasta?" a lawyer at the table asked.

"What do they look like to you?" Rena replied.

"I don't know. Maybe like belly buttons."

Everyone laughed.

"Actually," Rena said, "there's an old legend that an innkeeper was so taken by Lucrezia Borgia's beauty that he spied on her in her room at his inn one night. It was dark, and all he could see in the candlelight was her belly button. He was so mesmerized by it that he created tortellini that very night."

Tony crept down the stairs step by step until he reached the bottom. So far so good. He held his breath and eased open the back door. A dark, narrow alleyway lay between his building and the Italian grocery next door. He should've grabbed a flashlight. Empty vegetable crates were piled haphazardly in stacks, some over six feet high, along the wall on both sides.

He picked his way around the crates. He held his nose against the putrid odor of rotting scraps of tomatoes, onions, and peppers. He kept slipping, losing his footing on cobblestone bricks slimy from garbage. He grabbed at the wall to keep his balance and skinned his knuckles on the concrete. He stopped thinking about whether someone might be hiding behind the next stack and bolted toward the street, knocking crates aside, stumbling forward. Standing on the sidewalk, breathing heavily, he glanced up and down the block. No one was there.

He started walking. He'd been planning to drive to Rena's tonight. Before leaving, he'd spotted his assistant at the photocopier. That had given Tony an idea.

"Eric," he said, "you leaving soon?"

"Hey boss, yeah. This is the last batch of these reports."

"I'm staying for a while. Would you mind taking the Jag and dropping it off in the parking lot of the dealer so they can service it in the morning?"

"No problem, give me five minutes."

If anyone followed Eric, they'd be headed away from the Seaport. His assistant would be okay. Whoever was behind him would break off as soon as they realized Tony wasn't in the car.

Tony thought about his relationship with Frank and clenched his teeth. Etched into the glass on his front door was TONY FRANCINI, C.P.A. But if you dropped in to get your taxes done, you'd go away disappointed. He wasn't really open for business. He only worked for one client. He hadn't intended to get into the rackets after he'd finished school. Then he had trouble finding work. Frank hired him as a bookkeeper for his vending machine business. They'd been friends since they were kids. Frank paid well and one job led to another.

Tony wasn't stupid, and the first time Frank asked him to keep track of miscellaneous "collections," he knew where the money came from. Yet he didn't quit. He needed the job. He told himself he wasn't committing crimes. He wasn't any more involved than the banks where Frank made his deposits. As time wore on, though, he became more and more complicit. He came up with new methods for funneling income from illegal activities through legitimate businesses, exaggerated deductible expenses, and took depreciation on equipment that he knew didn't exist. Frank said he was a regular Hemingway when it came to preparing tax returns. Now, he found himself in deep enough that he couldn't get out. Not safely. Unless Frank let him leave.

Atlantic Avenue was deserted. Tony had planned to pick up some of Rena's favorite irises, but it was too late. The "Closed" sign was hanging in the window of the flower shop. At the International Place parking garage, scratching noises came from the direction of the dumpster next to the building. Could be rats feasting on the day's garbage. Or maybe someone was crouched there, waiting for him. He turned to his left and strode rapidly across the street and through the Greenway. His heart was pounding. Cutting across the grass, he was too afraid to look over his shoulder. Once he was on the sidewalk, he stopped in front of a restaurant window and checked behind him in the reflection. Nobody there. Sweat stained his fresh shirt under the arms and over his belly.

Maybe he was being paranoid. Or maybe someone was following him. This would be a shitty time to get rubbed out, just when he had a serious girlfriend for the first time. He'd never introduced Rena to Frank, but she found the boss intriguing. "Are you the one the papers call the Accountant?" she'd cocked her head and asked one of the first times they'd gone out.

"I don't like publicity, but, yeah, I'm that guy," he'd said.

"You work for Frank Romano?"

"Yeah. Does that bother you?"

She laughed. "So long as you don't get me involved, I don't care what you do. Tell you the truth, I find the dark side somewhat fascinating." Maybe so, but she didn't know everything that went down and he wasn't about to tell her.

He wanted to ask her to marry him, but right now that wouldn't be fair. A lot of the guys who worked for Frank were married and even had kids. Most of them chose women who came from the neighborhood. They knew what they were getting into. Rena was an educated woman from a good family in New York, with a great career as an actress ahead of her. He'd never forgive himself if she got hurt because he suddenly found himself targeted by a grand jury—or worse—in an underworld war. The feds were forever snooping around, and there was always a risk the Irish guys would try to muscle in on Frank's business. He couldn't propose to Rena unless Frank let him quit.

He walked down Atlantic Avenue and started across the Congress Street Bridge over the Fort Point Channel. It was just a few more blocks to Rena's building. His breathing came easier. Lights from the old South Boston warehouses danced on the water. He stopped halfway and looked around. It was pretty but dark and unnaturally quiet. He was alone on the bridge. Ahead was the giant milk bottle, the landmark in front of the Children's Museum. The thing was large enough to hide half a dozen guys behind it. The muscles in his neck tensed. He massaged them with his hand. Maybe walking wasn't such a good idea. He couldn't think of a reason why anybody would follow him unless Frank suspected him of stealing. The boss trusted him, didn't he? Tony shook his head. Christ, he'd worked for Frank for twenty years.

Tony got across the channel and came even with the museum. No one was behind the milk bottle. He sighed and took a handkerchief and wiped the sweat from his brow and his neck. He smiled at his paranoia.

Then a car engine revved. A beat-up Ford Explorer started to roll slowly across the bridge. Tony couldn't see the driver in the dark. The van stopped next to him. "Tony, c'mere a minute," said a voice from the Explorer. The street was deserted. "C' mere, we gotta tell you something." The voice was low, and he didn't recognize it. Shit. Someone had been following him. His hands started shaking. He would've been better off in his car, instead of walking through the city alone. He'd been stupid. The thing with Eric hadn't worked. Now he was fucked. He was in no shape to run. This was bad. Very bad.

The back door opened. An Irish guy he knew and didn't like slid out.

"What's this?" Tony asked.

A tall, well-built guy got out of the driver's seat and came around the rear of the Ford. A short, wiry one climbed out of the front passenger seat. They were brothers, violent, cold, two of the hardest men he knew. The tall one worked for Frank. The short one didn't.

"We hear you've been doing a little detective work, snooping around," the tall man said.

He kept his mouth shut. This must be where the money was going.

"You got nothing to say, Tony?"

"How's this? Fuck you."

The Irish guy reached back into the van and hauled out a mattress for a double bed. He dropped it on the sidewalk and it flopped open.

"What the—"

"Lie down on the mattress," the guy said.

"Are you nuts?"

"Lie down, you'll be okay."

If Tony knew anything, it was that he wasn't going to be okay. He'd put in all those years working for Frank, telling himself that if he was loyal then the boss might let him go someday. Too late now. He looked back across the channel at the Boston skyline. He'd spent his whole life in this town. He loved it. As he stood there, it was as though he could hear the Boston Pops playing the 1812 Overture on the Fourth of July and see the fireworks exploding over the river, smell the Italian sausages grilling in the kiosks outside Fenway Park, and feel the sticky powdered sugar on his fingers as he and Rena ate cannoli walking through the North End at the Feast of Saint Anthony.

A deep foghorn sounded dimly in the harbor.

He'd always known there was a risk of something like this. Didn't mean he was ready for it. He worked for gangsters, but he wasn't a tough guy. He didn't belong here, on this dark street, with these goombahs. He didn't have a gun—he'd never even fired one. He'd say a silent prayer, but he'd left God behind a long time ago. Still, if there was a God, now would be a good time to make His presence known. He'd been an acolyte as a kid. He'd lit thousands of candles for the Church. That was no help now. Maybe in the afterlife, if there was such a thing. He didn't think so.

He grabbed on to the thing he cherished the most—the last couple of years with Rena. He closed his eyes and saw her, smiling and reaching for him. Life could have been different with her. It would have been good. He might have been good.

The tall man circled around behind him and delivered a sharp blow to his kidney. Tony gasped, stumbled forward, tripped on the edge of the mattress, landed face down. He struggled to get up. The guy stomped hard on his back and Tony collapsed. Wincing with pain, he rolled over. "What's the mattress for?" he wheezed.

The guy slipped a pistol out of his belt from behind his back and racked the slide. There was a loud clack as the weapon's mechanism pushed a shell into the chamber. Tony went rigid. The man kneeled down and forced the barrel of his pistol into Tony's mouth.

"The mattress is for the bullet and the blood," he said.

1

Three years later, October 2007

On Thursday night, near the end of her shift, Susan Sorella perched on a stool at a counter in the kitchen at Gabriella's, filling saltshakers. She was wearing blue jeans and a white blouse, all the uniform the restaurant required. Her father Lorenzo emerged from the walk-in refrigerator with a towel in his hand.

"Can we talk about next week's menu?" he asked.

Mike, one of the waiters, burst through the door from the dining room with a frown on his face and grabbed Susan's father by the arm. "Enzo, there's somebody here to see you," he said.

"Who is it?" her father said.

"You better go see," Mike said.

Her dad put down the towel and entered the dining room, leaving the kitchen door ajar. Susan peered through the opening. *Jesus Christ.* Twenty feet away, alone at a table with his back to the wall, sat Frank Romano. He looked exactly like the picture *The Boston Herald* always ran of him when they did a story about organized crime. Tall and trim, he sat erect in his chair, wearing a dark gray suit, with a gray shirt and a burgundy tie. No jewelry, except for black sapphire cufflinks. Hair combed straight back. Deep-set eyes. They said Romano was a ruthless crime boss who presided over loansharking, gambling, drugs, fencing operations for major thefts, and the violence to keep everyone in line, including murder. What the hell was he doing at their restaurant?

Her father walked slowly across the room. He had a slight limp from an accident on a motor scooter when he was a teenager in Italy. "Hello, Frank, how are you," he said, as they shook hands. Susan grabbed the doorjamb. The fucking godfather walks in and her dad is like, hello Frank? Her dad was a gentleman from the old school, who addressed adults other than his close friends as mister and missus and used their last names. She didn't know he'd ever met Romano.

They lowered their voices, and she wasn't able to overhear their conversation. Her father waved Mike over. Then Mike came back to the kitchen.

"What's happening?" Susan asked.

"Your father told me to bring him an espresso and some buccellati."

"What are they talking about?"

"I couldn't hear anything."

Mike served the espresso and fig cookies. Her father sat sideways to the table, with one leg thrown casually over the other. Romano made a little tent with his hands, and then gently patted her father's arm as he spoke, like Italian neighbors. They were so familiar. Surely her father could have no connection with Romano's business. Maybe it was something personal. Maybe their families knew each other in Italy. The restaurant couldn't possibly be a front for the mob. Susan's mind raced.

Her parents started the business a few years after they came to America from San Gimignano in 1977. They didn't have enough money for her mother Gabriella to stay at home or to hire someone for more than a few hours a week to babysit. The restaurant became Susan's daycare center. As an infant, she basked in the wonderful aromas of slow-cooking tomatoes, garlic, capers, and anchovies. The smell of baking bread filled the restaurant all morning. She sat in a little corner of the kitchen that was her own, from which she safely watched the cooks preparing food and the waiters bustling back and forth from the dining room. In the early mornings, her father would take her in the stroller to the market to buy fresh fruit and vegetables. All the vendors knew her. She never left without her own little basket of treats—cherry tomatoes, bite-sized balls of mozzarella, slices of prosciutto, and always a sweet, maybe biscotti, or a little box of torrone.

Her mother died from a brain tumor when Susan was four. She grew up with her father. He moved them to the apartment upstairs from the restaurant, so he'd always be close by when Susan was home. In the afternoons after school, she'd sit at a dining room table near the kitchen in the restaurant doing her homework. Later, she worked there—at first on the door, then waitressing, and finally as a line cook during the summers when she was home from college. After she came back to Boston, she went back to waitressing all year. In her final semester at Suffolk Law, she was still at it. She needed the tip money.

Her dad got up from the table and headed her way. She stepped farther back away from the door.

"Frank Romano wants to talk with you for a moment," he said.

Her eyes widened. "What?"

"He wants to talk with you."

"You can't be serious."

"It's about some case."

Susan stepped closer to her father. "How do you know him?" she whispered.

"We can talk about that later, but go ahead and see him. I'm sure it's okay. He just wants to give you some information."

"What kind of information?"

"I didn't ask him."

Susan's head was spinning, and her hands were shaking as she approached the table. She'd never met anyone like Romano. Until this very moment, she wouldn't have been able to imagine herself speaking with him. What sort of information could he want to pass on? And why to her? She was just a law student. She couldn't believe her father was okay with this.

Romano stood up, gave a slight bow, and pulled out her chair.

"Good evening," she said quietly as she sat down. "I, uh, I don't think I've ever seen you in the restaurant before."

"Well, your father and I have known each other for a long time."

She blinked. Should she pretend that she knew that or not? Better not. She didn't have any idea how they knew each other.

"It's good to meet you," he said. "You bear such a striking resemblance to your mother. You didn't get those blue eyes from her, though."

An oil painting of her mother as a young woman hung in the entrance to the restaurant. Slender, with silky black hair and deep-set brown eyes veiled by long lashes, Gabriella Sorella had been a beauty. Susan wondered, not for the first time, what her mother would be like today if she had lived. What a weight it would have taken off her father to have his wife's help running the restaurant. Maybe Susan should have played that role. Instead, she'd gone to law school. A shadow of guilt crossed her mind.

Romano talking about how much Susan looked like her mother made her skin crawl. She had to find out what his connection was to her family.

"I hear you're doing very well in law school," Romano said. He stared directly into her eyes, taking her measure. She barely managed to meet his gaze without looking away and waited for him to speak again.

He took a small bite out of one of his cookies and sipped his espresso. "I heard you're working with Attorney Coughlin. I hear he's going to get appointed to defend Nicky Marino on the Francini murder, tomorrow. Since I know your father, I came to tell you some things you need to know."

That freaked her out. She'd read about the Francini murder and knew some defendants had recently been charged with it, but she had no idea Bobby Coughlin would do that kind of case. According to the papers, Marino was the one who shot Francini. Coughlin didn't have the skills or the balls to handle a case like that. He was a cop-out artist who never went to trial. She hated working for him.

Now she wanted to hear why Romano was here but listening to what he had to say might get her in trouble. She was about to fall down the rabbit hole. "Wouldn't it be better if you talked to one of the lawyers on the case?" she asked.

Romano shook his head. "Let's just say I think you'll be able to use what I'm about to tell you wisely. A rat named Joseph Brady has been talking to the D.A.'s office. He's admitted to Tony's murder and says he did it with Nicky Marino. He claims my friend Danny Costa ordered the hit because Francini was stealing from me. The truth is we had no problem with Francini. He worked for us, but I trusted him, and as far as I know, he wasn't stealing money from anybody. Costa had nothing to do with his murder and neither did I. If Brady is lying about Francini and Costa, then he's probably lying about Marino too."

Susan held her breath a moment. This man didn't beat around the bush. Coming right out and saying that Francini had "worked for us" was incriminating. Maybe it didn't matter. Everybody in town already assumed it to be true. More to the point, could what Romano was saying about the defendants' innocence be true?

"You understand, I can't go to court with this," Romano said. "The prosecutor would have a field day with me on the stand, and the jury wouldn't believe me anyway."

"Is Brady lying about his own involvement?" Her curiosity outpaced her fear of the rabbit hole.

"What I hear, no he's not. But he didn't do it alone. The cops found Francini's body in front of Rena Posso's condo. Brady could hardly carry it up there by himself. Coughlin has to find out who else was involved," Romano said.

"Do you know who it was?" she asked.

Romano's face remained expressionless. He stood up slowly. "You and the lawyers have to take it from here. It was a pleasure meeting you. Please tell your father the buccellati are as good as ever." Romano turned and left the restaurant.

Susan absent-mindedly picked up one of the remaining cookies and ate it. She was scared, but this could be huge. She'd been thinking of quitting Coughlin's office, but Romano's visit put a whole new spin on the internship. If Romano was telling the truth and Coughlin's client was innocent, working there would be a real crusade. She collected the dishes and headed back to the kitchen.

"Dad, how do you know Romano?"

He looked away, then back at her. "I don't want to get into that. It's nothing for you to worry about."

That didn't sound good. This was the first time she could recall that her father had refused to answer a question from her. She was going to ask again, but the look on his face convinced her not to.

"You haven't asked what he wanted to talk to me about," she said.

"It's not my business. You're going to be a lawyer. I imagine there will be a lot we can't talk about. Romano is a dangerous man, but you're my daughter. I don't think he'd get you in trouble."

"Can I ask you this? Can I trust him to tell me the truth? Should I believe what he says?"

"I think he'd tell you the truth. Maybe not the whole truth, though. Keep your eyes open."

She cleaned up and told her father good night. It was unbelievable that he knew Romano. A man like that was mythical. You heard things about him, you might read something about him in the paper, but you didn't eat cookies with him. He'd given her inside information about the Francini murder. He said it was because he knew her father. Maybe there was another reason. Maybe he knew what a wuss Coughlin was and wanted to make sure that someone else got the message. That would put her in a tricky position. She'd talk with Coughlin on Monday. Who knew what he was going to make of this?

2

"Nicholas Marino. Charge is murder in the first degree," the clerk's voice rang out on Friday morning in the Boston Superior Court. Bobby Coughlin was sitting in the jury box where the lawyers waited for their cases to be called when there was no trial in progress. The hardwood benches were like church pews without cushions. Some genius probably thought this would keep jurors awake.

Two court officers ushered the prisoner into the room through the side door that led to the lockup. Marino's clothes were dirty, his shirt torn, his eyes bloodshot. The officers took off Marino's handcuffs and he rubbed his wrists. A stir ran through the seats. The defendant's eyes darted around the courtroom and settled on a pretty redhead who was crying softly in one of the back rows. He attempted a smile, but failed. His shoulders sagged.

The Honorable Michael P. Morgan sat on the bench. What a joke. Wearing a black robe, with his white hair parted and combed smartly to the side, he looked distinguished, even judicial. Bobby bet if Morgan didn't have his job as a judge, he couldn't have made a living as a lawyer. His best days, such as they were, were long gone. Morgan got the appointment thirty years ago, friendly with a former governor before the bar association started reviewing judicial nominees.

Morgan's job was pretty simple. Keep the assembly line for criminal justice moving by processing the cases—taking pleas, appointing lawyers, and scheduling hearings. The defendants were just docket numbers to him. The clerk may as well not even tell him their names. The accused shuffled forward one at a time, eyes vacant, mostly clueless about the procedure.

Bobby Coughlin was there to catch a new case. He took court appointments to represent indigent defendants. It supplemented his income from his private practice. The Public Defender's Office couldn't handle everyone who couldn't afford a lawyer. The state paid Bobby by the hour at a fraction of the rate a decent lawyer would charge a private client. The judges reviewed his time sheets; supposedly to make sure he wasn't padding his bills. They were cheap bastards and routinely cheated him out of some of the money he deserved. He didn't dare to complain, or he'd stop getting appointments.

Bobby didn't make loads of money practicing law, but together with his wife Marie, they did okay. She was a dental hygienist in a Boston suburb. They had no children. He had a nice house, no debts other than the mortgage, wore decent suits. He stayed in shape with weights at the gym. Compared to other trial lawyers in Boston, work didn't stress him out. He kept things simple and accepted his own limitations. When his clients went to jail, he slept comfortably, figuring it was out of his control. He didn't need medication to keep his blood pressure in check, didn't drink too much to take the edge off, rarely let work interfere with his marriage. Not to say his marriage was in good shape—it wasn't.

Bobby continued to wait. Nicky Marino featured in the lead story in *The Boston Herald* on Bobby's lap. Above the fold was a picture of the D.A. at a press conference, announcing the indictments of three men for the Accountant's murder. One of the accused, Danny Costa, was still at large.

There didn't seem to be anyone waiting in the courtroom to represent Marino. It sure as hell wasn't anything that Bobby would want. He stuck with more modest crimes—unlawful possession of a firearm, a drug sale, maybe a mugging. He didn't go anywhere near murder. Or organized crime.

The Boston Herald said Francini's killers had propped his dead body up against the front door of his girlfriend Rena Posso's penthouse on the South Boston waterfront. There was a single exit wound on the back of his head and "oracular fouling," as the crime scene techs put it—black gunpowder residue in his mouth. It didn't take CSI to figure out that someone shot him with the gun barrel crammed between his teeth. The killers hacked off all five fingers from his right hand and stuffed them in the pocket protector Francini invariably wore in his white shirt. The rumor was that he was stealing money from the mob to keep the girlfriend in a luxury condo.

Bobby thought it'd be nice to have a mistress on call in fancy digs with a view of the water. On a stormy day, with the wind whipping up the waves in the harbor, rain pelting hard against the windows, slipping under the covers with a fashion model like Rena Posso would be pretty cozy. At least until you showed up dead on her doorstep.

The clerk's words, "Murder in the first degree," left Bobby short of breath. As a young lawyer, he'd represented a fourteen-year-old boy in Juvenile Court. Jamie Walker's old man came home drunk one night and shouted that the kid was going to get what was coming to him. Jamie loaded a shotgun, staggered down the stairs from his bedroom in tears, and blew his father away from a distance of three feet. Bobby's investigation disclosed a long history of abuse by the father against his wife and son.

Bobby had been convinced the case would be resolved in

Juvenile Court. Together with the social worker at the clinic, he put together a binder that included medical records, photographs, and statements from Jamie's teachers. He worked up a solid treatment plan that could be implemented in a juvenile facility. He thought he had the bases covered.

The D.A., however, argued that taking the shotgun and shells to his room demonstrated premeditation. He surprised Bobby by asking the judge to transfer the case to adult court. After a brief hearing, she did. Before a more senior lawyer was appointed to represent Jamie in Superior Court, the boy hanged himself in his cell. He left a note that read simply, "I never had a chance."

Marino was standing in front of the judge, but no lawyer had come forward to represent him. Bobby started to sweat. What if Morgan asked him to do it? Jamie's suicide had driven him out of the law for years. He'd been in front of Morgan enough— surely, the judge knew that he didn't take this type of case. Yet in the last case Morgan had appointed Bobby to, Bobby's client had refused to take the plea the prosecutor had proposed. The case had dragged on. Morgan had been pissed off. What if the judge wanted to show Bobby who was the boss?

The clerk turned from his desk toward the bench. "Marino needs appointed counsel, your Honor." The judge hooked his finger at the clerk to come closer and they conferred in voices too low to be heard in the rest of the courtroom. The clerk went back to his desk and opened a file and leafed through the papers. The clerk's head came up and nodded at the judge.

"Mr. Coughlin, please approach the bench," Morgan said. The judge's voice jerked Bobby out of his seat. His briefcase fell out of his lap. Papers flew, under the bench and into the aisle. He knelt to pick them up, then stood and mumbled, "Excuse me, your Honor." He reached down and wiped the dust from the courtroom floor off the knees of his trousers, then walked to the side of the bench.

Morgan looked him over. "Mr. Coughlin, Mr. Marino is

employed, but can't afford to hire a lawyer for a murder case. The P.D.'s Office can't take this case. You're on the list of private lawyers qualified to handle murders. Is there any reason you can't represent this defendant?"

"They put me on that list years ago, Your Honor. I'd completely forgotten about it."

"You never took yourself off."

"That was an oversight on my part. I've never tried a murder case, and I can't try this one. I don't have the resources to do it." Bobby didn't have an associate to write the legal briefs that might be required or an investigator to do the necessary foraging for the facts. If he devoted all his time to this, there was no one to cover the rest of his practice. But mostly, the very idea of doing a murder case scared the crap out of him.

"You're experienced, Mr. Coughlin. You can handle it."

"Your Honor, I'm sorry, but —" Bobby said.

Morgan held up his hand and looked at the court reporter sitting below the bench. She lifted her fingers off her stenotype machine. She'd worked in Morgan's courtroom long enough to know when he wanted to go off the record.

"Mr. Coughlin, I know you always do your best. In this instance, I doubt if Marino will go to trial. I can't say for sure, but I suspect the D.A. is more interested in the co-defendant Danny Costa than this man, even though he was allegedly the shooter. Marino still needs competent representation. The Court would appreciate it if you would perform this duty. I'll be very disappointed if you don't."

Bobby looked back at the bar and struggled to clear his mind. He understood what the judge was getting at. Morgan expected that to avoid a life sentence Marino would plead guilty and testify against Costa. The judge wasn't giving Bobby any choice.

"Yes, your Honor."

Bobby thought about those old movies, where someone in the jungle comes around a corner and stumbles into quicksand

and slowly sinks until his head disappears under the ooze. Was quicksand really a thing that existed? It didn't matter. He was going under.

The defendant standing next to him was shivering, even though the clanging radiators in the old courthouse drove the room temperature to close to 80 degrees. The clerk read out the charge. Marino pleaded not guilty. The judge scheduled a status conference in one week and set bail in the amount of one million dollars. The court officers began to lead Marino from the room. "When are you coming to talk to me?" he asked Bobby.

Bobby wanted to hear Marino's story, but no way was he going to get hung up at the jail and risk disrupting Friday night with his wife. He was in enough trouble with her already and he'd promised to cook dinner. He'd found a new recipe for veal scaloppini in a mustard sauce that he hoped would help get him out of the doghouse.

"I'll see you Monday," he said.

Marino's shoulders slumped and he hung his head. He shuddered as the court officer put the handcuffs back on him and took hold of his elbow. The officer led him toward the door to the lockup. At the last second, Marino turned toward Bobby. His eyes were wide with fright. "Please," he mouthed. Then they were gone.

3

Monday afternoon, Susan walked through the atrium at Suffolk Law School and out the door into the rain. For the first time in weeks, she was eager to get to Bobby Coughlin's office. She pulled the hood on her purple anorak up over her head and tucked her hair behind her ears. She'd recently had it cut much shorter, so it fell just to the bottom of her neck. She didn't have time for the hassle of long hair, and she wasn't the kind of woman who liked to fuss with her appearance. This made life easier for her in the wind, rain, and snow of Boston winters. She took secret pride in the casual, tousled look she was now able to affect.

What a weekend! She loved the Red Sox three-game sweep of the Angels that sent them to the ALCS. Susan watched the game at the Beantown bar, half a block from school. The Angels, in the bottom of the ninth, with the game tied three to three, intentionally walked Ortiz, only to have Ramirez crush a three-run homer over the Green Monster. Hello? Didn't they know who was on deck? Ortiz and Ramirez were the best three/

four hitters since Gehrig and Ruth. When the Angels' catcher signaled for the intentional walk, she'd shouted out, "You're going to pay!" Then everyone started chanting, "You're going to pay! You're going to pay!" And the Angels did, big time.

As much as she loved baseball, the Sox win was nothing compared to Romano's Thursday night visit. Susan couldn't wait to see Coughlin's face when she told him about it. The more she thought about what Romano had said, the more excited she got about the possibility that Marino could be innocent.

How she'd ended up with Coughlin was a mystery. Most trial lawyers never got all their work done. They routinely worked late and went to the office on Saturday. Not Coughlin. He was often out the door by three or four. Given her record, the placement office should've put her with one of the better criminal lawyers in Boston. She'd talked her way into Suffolk's criminal clinic when she was only a 2L. That was rare. There was a limited number of slots and a lot of students wanted to do it. In the clinic, she got two not guilty verdicts in jury trials, which was even more unusual.

Susan entered Coughlin's private office. He was leaning back in his chair reading with his foot propped against the file drawer. He looked up. "I've been appointed to represent Nicky Marino. Do you know who that is?" he asked, without so much as a greeting.

"One of the guys charged with the Francini murder," she said. "How did *you* land his case?"

"It's not anything I wanted. Morgan put me on it."

Susan sat down. "Should be a lot of publicity."

"Yeah, who needs it? The vultures in the media are going to be second-guessing my every move."

"It so happens I've got some information about that case," she said.

"How would you know anything about it?"

"Somebody who knew I was working for you came to see me." Susan crossed her legs and Coughlin's eyes darted from her face to the hem of her skirt as it rode up above her knee. Good god, it didn't take much, and it never stopped. She shifted slightly in her chair and let the skirt ride up a couple more inches just to torment him. She felt a little cheap but messing with her boss's head gave her some revenge for all the boring jobs he'd given her.

He tore his glance away from her legs. "Someone came to see you? Who?"

"Frank Romano."

"What?" He shot forward in his chair and his foot kicked the file drawer closed with a loud bang.

"Romano," she said.

"You're kidding me."

"No, he knows my father, and he came to the restaurant to talk to me."

"Why didn't he just come—wait, what do you mean he knows your father?"

She wasn't sure how to answer that. She didn't want to say anything that would imply that her father was connected. "I think he knows him through the restaurant. Most of the people in the North End have eaten there." Maybe Coughlin would let that slide.

"I don't get why Romano would talk to you instead of me," he said.

Ah, that was his main concern. Of course. Well, she wasn't about to speculate on that subject. She'd try to keep him focused on the story itself.

"He said that he and Danny Costa didn't have anything to do with Francini's murder."

"Big surprise."

She uncrossed her legs and sat forward. "There's more. Francini hadn't been taking money. Romano had no problem with him. Costa wasn't involved, and it's likely that Brady is lying about Nicky Marino."

"What do you expect him to say? Of course, he denies it."

It was obvious that Coughlin was offended that Romano had come to her. These male ego-driven power plays were exhausting. So much extra work—the interruptions, the put-downs, the mansplaining. She shouldn't have to sell Romano's information. Any halfway intelligent lawyer would realize it was worth investigating.

"If someone accused a man like Frank Romano of murder, of course, he'd deny it, even if he was guilty," she said. "I hadn't accused him of anything. He sought me out. He wanted me to give you some very specific information—that Francini wasn't stealing from him."

"So what? Nobody can prove whether he was or not. Suppose the D.A. subpoenaed Romano's books—they were kept by Francini. They wouldn't show much. And I don't suppose he offered to testify that Francini wasn't stealing."

"That's true. He admitted there was no point in his coming to court with this."

"This doesn't really amount to anything, certainly nothing we can use." Coughlin shook his finger at her. "In the future, you are to leave interviews with potential witnesses up to me."

"Isn't the prosecution going to claim that the motive for the murder was that Francini was stealing from Romano?" she said. "Romano contradicts that and—"

"As I said, that's nothing that can be proved one way or the other," Coughlin said. "We have to be realistic and look at the evidence. I saw the prosecutor Tom Flanagan this morning and he has a cooperating witness. One of the killers, Brady, has flipped and given up the whole story."

Susan grimaced. If Romano had no motive to kill Francini, maybe they should be looking for someone who did have a motive. That was certainly worth looking into. Why couldn't Coughlin see that? He wasn't taking her seriously. He probably thought of her as nothing more than a pretty girl who was still a student. He didn't know anything about her. When she applied for the job, he hadn't even requested her transcript. He'd never asked her about her experience in the clinic. They'd never talked about any serious legal questions.

Maybe, though, she should consider the possibility that she was too gullible. She'd been flattered that Romano came to see her. Maybe his claims really didn't amount to anything. She shook her head. No. Just because her boss dismissed what she said didn't mean that she should put herself down. She'd worked as a paralegal for a law firm in Chicago after college and had fallen into that trap with a couple of the male partners. She came up with a new method for coding the data in one of their environmental cases. She started to tell the lawyers about it, but they cut her off without listening to any details. "Look," one of them said, "We know what we're doing. You're a new girl so don't rock the boat. Just follow instructions." She felt stupid for trying to change things and abandoned the idea. Later, Susan mentioned it in passing to one of the few women partners at the firm, a nationally recognized expert in environmental law. She said Susan's idea would save the firm hundreds of hours in data analysis. Two weeks later the lawyers implemented her coding scheme. That woman wouldn't have ignored Romano's information, but now Susan didn't have someone like that to help her.

Coughlin looked away from her and started to thumb through the papers on his desk.

"Can I work on this case?" she asked.

"Yeah, I'm counting on it."

"What would you like me to do?"

"You can start by drafting some discovery motions to find out what evidence the prosecution has."

Coughlin handed Susan a copy of the indictment and described what the prosecutor Flanagan had said about Brady and his expected testimony. "Flanagan also said he has some physical evidence," he said.

"We'll have to find out what that is. I'll include requests for that and any forensic reports in the motions I'm drafting."

"You can get started on the motions. I'm going to the jail to see the client," Coughlin said.

She went to the conference room. The story Flanagan told suggested that there might be some trace evidence in Brady's trunk from transporting Francini's body. She hoped they wouldn't have Marino's fingerprints, much less DNA, on anything incriminating.

She'd love to tear apart the evidence of the Boston Police crime lab experts. She'd learned a lot in her Scientific Evidence class last semester about forensic evidence. Most defense lawyers were poorly trained and unprepared to challenge scientific witnesses. Forensic experts had been getting away with murder. Bogus evidence had put too many innocent people on death row. She'd relentlessly force witnesses to concede the scientific limitations of their fields. She'd show up experts that gave opinions about probabilities that weren't based on the existence of a real database. DNA had one, but not most fields. She'd ask every witness what her error rate was. Every forensic methodology had some rate of error, but expert witnesses didn't like to admit that. She'd ask them how they did on proficiency tests administered by outside evaluators. She'd conclude in her final argument that there was a reasonable doubt about whether the forensic evidence should be relied upon, and the jury would discount it altogether. Well, that might be a stretch. Nothing was that easy.

She photocopied the press clippings in the file and read through them. This case had a little bit of everything. The mob, a murder, and a moll. The picture of Francini's girlfriend was captivating. Rena Posso was gorgeous, talented, and successful as an actress and a model. The Accountant enjoyed some local notoriety, but judging from his picture, he was no lothario. It might not have much to do with the case, but she'd like to know what that was about. Maybe she could find out.

4

The waiting room at the Plymouth jail was a cheerless corner of the world. The plastic furniture, bolted to the floor, was scarred with the initials of visitors who'd felt compelled to mark their territory. The linoleum was coming up in places, and it was impossible to tell when the walls had last been painted. Wives and girlfriends slumped in their seats. Kids, too young to understand where they were and how often they'd be back, ran in circles around their mothers until they were stopped with a holler or a slap. It wasn't the first time their husbands had brought these women to this place. Their half-closed eyes and sour, downturned mouths told the story. The waiting room was a scene from the war on crime that didn't make it onto the evening news. A hidden cost of over-incarceration.

Bobby walked past the women and approached the guard on duty behind a Plexiglas screen. He slid his bar card and driver's license through the slot. "Attorney Coughlin to see Nicky Marino." The guard gave him only a brief glance, comparing his face with the picture on the license. He checked his computer, filled out his logbook, and gave Bobby a pass and a key.

Bobby went to the metal lockers against the wall. He knew the drill. He put his keys, watch, wedding ring, and wallet inside. This left him with only a pen, a yellow pad, and one business card for the client. He sat down to wait.

Bobby wondered what sort of man Nicky Marino was. This morning's paper said that he worked construction. So, maybe a tough guy. He hadn't looked that tough at the arraignment. Scared shitless is what he was. Granted, who wouldn't be in his situation? Frank Romano must think Marino had some balls if he sent him out there to shoot Francini. And it would take some sand to stand there while his fucking partner cut off the guy's fingers and stuffed them in his pocket protector. Bobby shuddered.

He'd been able to put the case out of his mind Friday night. The veal was great. The mustard sauce was terrific. After dinner, he and Marie started watching *Casablanca* on television. They drank a little more wine. Ingrid Bergman showed up on the screen and Bobby put his arm around Marie. Sam started playing *As Time Goes By,* and Marie turned off the TV. They headed for the bedroom. They kissed awkwardly and fumbled while getting their clothes off, but by the end, it felt like old times. It was the first time they'd made love since he'd admitted to having an affair with Gina. Maybe, eventually, he and Marie might put things back together.

Gina was a stenographer who worked freelance for civil lawyers. Bobby met her at a deposition he was covering for a friend. The witness was a goofball, and they got to laughing about it after the session was over. The next week they met for coffee, which the following week turned into wine, then eventually romance. He hadn't started out to have an affair, but she kept proposing new things. He'd been married to Marie for twenty years, and only had a couple of girlfriends before that. Nothing had prepared him for someone like Gina. She had her own business and flaunted her independence. She picked him up early from work in her red BMW. They drove to little hideaways on the North Shore for drinks. Gina would catch his eyes and hold them until he had to turn away. She held her face close to his as they talked, touching his arms and his chest with her hands. Often, sitting at a bar, she'd turn her body so no one could see what she was doing, drop her hand into his lap, and run her fingers over the top of his cock.

The first time he had sex with Gina it was like going over a waterfall in a barrel and surviving. Despite all that, it stressed him out to sneak around. One night Marie asked him about some unusual charges on his credit card bill. He'd been tempted to try to lie his way out of it, but she'd figured things out. Her face wore the pain she was in like a macabre type of makeup. He crumbled and admitted everything. He saw Gina one last time and broke up with her. He'd been trying to make things right with his wife ever since.

On Saturday morning, he told Marie that he'd been appointed to represent a defendant in the Francini murder. She started crying. She'd stuck with him as he'd battled depression after he quit practicing law in the wake of Jamie's suicide. She said she couldn't go through anything like that again. She demanded that he go back to the judge and get off the case. Short of a heart attack or a stroke, there was no way the court would let him withdraw. They'd argued all weekend. He felt like shit.

Marie was right. Taking this case put him on the brink of disaster. The shooter on a mob hit. If he had to get trapped in a murder case, why not a crackhead who shot his supplier? Maybe a drunk driver who ran over a pedestrian. Something straightforward, with lots of evidence, where the defendant would be sure to plead out. He didn't even want those cases. But he could've handled them a lot easier than Marino. If he screwed up, Marino would go away forever. And it would get a lot of ink.

"Coughlin." The guard pointed at Bobby and gestured toward the metal detector at the end of the room. He walked to it and let the second guard see his pass. Bobby removed his shoes, put his pen and the locker key in a plastic bowl, placed it on the conveyor belt, and passed through the metal detector. After a brief wait, the control room officer opened the door in front of him and he stepped into the trap, a short passage between two locked doors, only one of which opened at a time. The first door closed and then the second swung open. He walked through and presented his pass to the next guard.

Bobby followed the guard down a long hallway to a small attorney visiting room, where lawyers were free to talk to their clients without a screen between them. Marino was sitting on one of two chairs at a metal table surrounded by bare walls. The only light came from an overhead fixture shielded by steel mesh. The room was cold. The guard locked the door and left them alone.

Bobby sat down. "Mr. Marino, I'm Bobby Coughlin and I'll be your lawyer. Before we get started, let me explain the attorney-client privilege to you. Everything you say to me is confidential. I can't repeat anything you tell me without your permission, except to people in my office who are working on your case. It's like talking to a priest or a minister. You can be completely honest with me, without worrying about whether what you tell me is going to get you in more trouble," Bobby said. His stomach was sour.

"You can repeat whatever you want. I had nothing to do with this murder and don't know nothing about it. I got no idea why I'm here." Marino spoke rapidly and breathed heavily. "Did you talk to my wife?"

Bobby remembered the redhead who'd been crying in the courtroom at the arraignment. "Not yet. Tell me her name and the number. I'll call her."

"Patty. She's gotta be panicking. You have to call her right away, and tell her this is a big mistake."

Most defendants started out by trying to convince Bobby they weren't guilty. Maybe they thought a lawyer wouldn't work very hard for them unless he thought they were innocent.

"Let's start this way," he said. "Tell me a little about yourself."

"Like what?"

"You know, your age, what you do for work, your family, stuff like that."

"Well, I'm thirty-four years old. We have two kids—a girl and a boy, both in elementary school."

Bobby got their names and ages and wrote them down. "What do you do for work?"

"I'm an ironworker. I work on big construction projects."

"Union job?"

"Yeah. I've done this for about ten years."

"What about your wife, does she work?"

"Yeah, she's a waitress."

As Marino talked about his background his face softened. Bobby had established a little rapport. "Did you know Tony Francini?" he asked.

"No. I saw him once in a restaurant, but I never met him."

"You sure you never met him?"

"Never."

Bobby tapped his pen on his pad. "You know who he was?"

"Yeah, I heard. I heard he was some kind of accountant for the mob."

"What else did you hear?"

"They say that Francini was skimming, but I don't know nothing about that except what I read in *The Herald*."

"You know how much he stole?"

Marino shrugged. "I dunno. The paper didn't say."

"How much do you think?"

"I got no idea."

"You own a gun, Nicky?" Bobby thought switching to the client's first name might put a little pressure on.

"No. Why would I have a gun? I'm just a construction worker."

Marino must be connected somehow, or he wouldn't have

been chosen for the hit. Bobby leaned forward in his chair. "That's all you do? You don't do a little something on the side?"

"Look, I take sports bets at construction sites. It's no big deal. I make a few extra dollars a week. That's all."

Bobby nodded. "You know Danny Costa?"

"Everyone in the North End knows Danny Costa. He's a popular guy."

"Yeah, but you're into sports betting. You don't work with Costa?"

Marino frowned. "No. First, I don't do any business with Costa. And second, I'm not gonna talk to you about gambling. The important thing is that I don't know jack shit about this murder."

"Why do you think you've been accused of it?"

"As god is my witness, I don't know."

"Well I'll tell you," Bobby said. "I saw the prosecutor this morning, and he said that Brady told them everything. Brady confessed and he's willing to testify."

"Whattya mean, he told them everything? As far as I'm concerned, there's nothing to tell. I got nothing to do with this."

"Not according to Brady. He says Costa paid you fifteen grand to help him and that you're the one who shot Francini."

"He says what?"

Marino's mouth hung open. He seemed genuinely shocked. Maybe he was a good actor. If it wasn't that, either he didn't have anything to do with the murder, or Brady was the shooter and was shifting the blame to Marino. Technically, it wouldn't matter. They'd both be guilty of murder.

"He's lying," Marino said. "None of this makes any sense. Costa ain't gonna ask me to kill someone—he barely knows who I am."

Bobby sat quietly without speaking to let things sink in.

"What does Brady get out of playing ball with the prosecution?" Marino asked.

"He was looking at a career criminal charge. They'll drop

that and give him a deal on this murder."

"Mr. Coughlin, this is bullshit. I don't know Romano and didn't know Francini. I'm not a wise guy and there's no way I'd be messed up in anything like this."

"You've got nothing else to tell me, Nicky?"

"There's nothing to tell," Nicky said.

Bobby wrote down the name and number of Marino's boss and his union steward. They were possible character witnesses if he needed them. Other than Patty and the kids' information, that's all he had on his yellow pad.

"I'll see you in a few days and we'll talk some more," Bobby said as he got up from the table.

"You believe me, right? You're gonna prove that I didn't have anything to do with this, right? You'll tell Patty that everything will be okay?"

"It really doesn't matter what I believe. In the final analysis, it's up to the jury. My job is to give you the best defense I can, and I will." He knocked on the door for the guard to open it, nodded to Marino, and turned and left the room.

Bobby sat in his car for a minute before heading out. He'd lost his patience with Marino at the end of the interview. He should've been more supportive if he wanted the client to trust him. The problem was that every minute this dragged on, Bobby's anxiety climbed. This damn case was going to have him arguing with everyone—his wife, the client, the prosecutor, the judge. There was no safe harbor. He didn't know if he could get through this. And this was just day one.

5

On Monday night, Nicky Marino was lying on his bunk at the jail staring at the ceiling. They'd brought him in on Friday. The guards strip-searched him and sent him into the showers. They took his clothes and gave him a crummy set of prison blue jeans and a khaki shirt. Then they shoved him in this cell. That night he barely slept. He had no idea why he'd been arrested. What he did know was that there was no goddam way he could post a million-dollar bail.

His so-called lawyer had finally come to see him today. Coughlin didn't seem to know much about the case. He hadn't said one thing that gave Nicky any hope. Nicky didn't know any lawyers and didn't have the dough for his own lawyer anyway. He was stuck with this guy. Coughlin acted like he was guilty, asking him about Danny Costa. Nicky didn't have any real connection with Costa. He saw him around the North End. Had a drink with him a few times in a crowd. Costa was okay and probably wasn't the kind of guy to be mixed up with murder. But Nicky didn't know for sure.

Nicky didn't want to get into details with the lawyer about gambling. Patty didn't know about it. It was a way to pick up a few extra dollars and get things for her and the kids. There was no rough stuff. Nicky collected the cash and the bets and turned them over to somebody else. He got the money from that same guy to pay off the winners. A lot of ironworkers bet on the games. There was nothing wrong with it. Still, not to upset Patty, he'd kept it to himself.

There was no way the sports betting was related to this murder charge. Nicky didn't have any beefs with any of the men whose bets he took. He was square with the guy he gave the money to. He didn't have any enemies. All he knew was his little corner of the action. He didn't even know for sure if the people further up the chain were working for Romano or someone else.

Nicky had only seen Tony Francini once. He and Patty were drinking beer at Tangierino, a Moroccan restaurant in Charlestown. Patty worked evenings. When she had a night off, he liked to take her out. They'd gotten married a couple years after high school. After a few years, they had a girl, then a boy, a year apart. Marjorie, her mother, babysat for them. He got along good with Marjorie. His parents had been killed in a car accident when he was twenty-two. He was an only child. It'd been easy to get close to Patty's family. Her father had passed away, but she had a sister who was married and had two kids. Everyone had dinner together on Sunday afternoons at Marjorie's house. If Nicky was lucky enough to get tickets, he went to Sox games with Patty's brother-in-law. Nicky and Patty didn't have a lot of money, but they went down the Cape for two weeks every summer. They always got the same place near Falmouth. A little two-bedroom cottage not far from the water. They'd go swimming at Old Silver Beach, and he'd rent a boat, and they'd fish for striped bass and bluefish in Buzzard's Bay. The kids loved it and it gave him and Patty more time together than they ever had in the city. They'd go to Hyannis for dinner and go out dancing. He wasn't much on the dance floor, but

Patty loved him for trying.

That night at Tangierino, Patty was smiling, sitting close to Nicky with her arm slung casually over his shoulder. His work kept him in pretty good shape and she said she liked the feel of his body. He felt her breast pressed against his arm and he turned and kissed her on the cheek.

"Let's not stay out too late tonight," he said.

"See that big guy over there smoking a stogie?" the bartender said, nodding his head slightly toward the back of the room.

Nicky looked over. "Good god. He's gotta check in at about three hundred pounds. And look at the crew he's with." The guy was sitting with some tough-looking Charlestown types in a tented booth, smoking cigars.

"That's Tony Francini, the Accountant. He keeps the books for the mob," the bartender said.

Francini's face was flushed from drinking. He wore a broad smile. He was telling a story. He paused and everyone at the table burst out laughing. He called the waitress over and ordered another round. One of the other men reached for his wallet, but the Accountant waved him off.

An olive-skinned woman with dark eyes hung on Francini's left arm. She leaned toward him and whispered something in his ear. A red silk blouse with a plunging neckline revealed the swell of her breasts. Nicky couldn't keep from staring. The Charlestown guys caught him looking in their direction and he'd quickly turned away.

"Go ahead, check her out," Patty said, raising one eyebrow. "Then I'll flip a coin with those guys to see who gets to kick your ass." He turned toward her, and she gave him a long kiss on the lips. "I'm pretty sure you got all you can handle right here."

"You know what? I got all I want right here," he said.

Nicky was jealous of how comfortably Francini related to everyone. The woman on his arm was obviously his girlfriend. The way the other men looked at Francini and waited for him to speak showed respect. The waitress showed up with drinks, and he put his hand on her arm and started telling a story. Evidently, it was about one of the other guys at his table. Francini kept pointing to him as he talked. Soon they were all laughing, including the waitress.

Francini and his crowd were still at their table when Nicky and Patty left. Nicky didn't see him again until the picture of his body slumped against the condo doorway ran in *The Herald*. Lying on the thin mattress in his cell, his image of Francini didn't square with that shot in the paper. He'd been an important guy. Then suddenly he was dead.

That was three years ago. Nicky didn't have anything to do with it then, and he had no idea how he might be connected to it now. For first-degree murder, Massachusetts gave you life with no possibility of parole. You died in prison. Period. It was impossible to imagine what Patty and the kids would do if he didn't get out of this. They'd have a hard time getting by on the money she made. The idea of Sheila and Tommy growing up without him was too much to bear. He prayed that Coughlin was better than he seemed so far.

6

Pandemonium reigned when Bobby and Susan arrived in Morgan's courtroom on Friday morning. Half the reporters in the city were crowded into the place. Two sketch artists from TV stations worked on portraits of a new face sitting at the defense table. Bobby had received no warning of what was coming and approached the clerk. Bobby pointed at the new guy, a slender man, about fifty years old, with a pleasant face and dark hair combed straight back. "Who's that?" he asked.

"That's Danny Costa," the clerk said. He walked into the D.A.'s office at eight o'clock this morning with his lawyer and surrendered. No one knew he was coming."

Bobby had never seen Costa before. He didn't look like a gangster. He looked like one of the middle-aged Italian guys you'd find any day of the week playing bocce in the dirt yards outside Italian restaurants in the North End. Costa sat quietly and calmly without speaking. He turned toward a woman, probably his wife, in the gallery and flashed a wide smile. His eyes twinkled. Bobby assumed it was his family that filled most of the seats.

At the prosecution table sat the D.A. himself, a tall, distinguished-looking man with silver hair. He was beaming as though he'd personally tracked down Costa and dragged him into court. Beside him were Tom Flanagan and the two detectives that ran the investigation for the Commonwealth. Bobby had no use for the D.A., who was a politician through and through. He was decked out in a conservative herringbone suit that must have set him back six times what Flanagan was wearing. The D.A. would let Flanagan do the talking in the courtroom, but he'd address the cameras outside afterward. The asshole would want to assure the public that his office was doing a great job protecting them from crime. Several younger prosecutors stood behind the public gallery to watch the proceedings. They probably got points for showing up when the D.A. was present.

Near the back of the room, Patty Marino sat alone, twisting a handkerchief between her fingers. Bobby nodded in her direction. He turned to walk to the defense table and almost lost his balance. This circus atmosphere was just a harbinger of worse things to come.

A lawyer Bobby recognized, Richard Charles, a handsome man in his forties with short-cropped salt and pepper hair, came in and sat next to Costa. Bobby sat down next to Nicky Marino, at the other end of the table.

"Should I sit in the gallery?" Susan asked.

"Stay here, next to me," Bobby said. He'd never been on such a big stage and Susan's presence made him feel like he had a team. He introduced himself and Susan to Danny Costa and Richard Charles.

Marino grabbed Bobby's arm. "Why haven't you been to see me again?"

"I've been busy working on the case in Boston," Bobby said. In fact, the only thing he'd done was to call Patty Marino and talk with her on the phone for a few minutes. Bobby received the draft motions from Susan on Thursday, gave them a quick look, made a couple of minor changes, and asked the secretary to print them out. He hadn't devoted any more time to the case than he would have given a driving under.

"You can't just leave me alone out there at the jail. You've got to tell me what's going on."

"Look, there's a lot to do on a case like this. I can't spend all my time driving back and forth to Plymouth."

"All your time? You only came out once."

Bobby didn't need a lecture. He knew he had to do a better job of staying in touch with Nicky Marino. It had taken so long to put himself back together after Jamie's death, and now there was another poor bastard alone in a cell needing saving. He'd gotten way too close to Jamie. He wasn't going to make that mistake with Marino.

"Mr. Coughlin, we gotta talk," Marino said loudly. Costa turned and looked at Marino and put his finger to his lips. Marino opened his mouth as though to say something else, but closed it and collapsed back in his chair.

"We'll talk, but not in the courtroom," Bobby said. "I'll come and see you in the lockup after we're done here."

Bobby probably should've spent more time on those motions. Still, he wanted it to seem like he'd been doing something, so impulsively he pushed copies down the table. "I'm going to file these today," he said.

Richard Charles riffed quickly through the small stack of papers. "Why don't you hold off for a week or so? Then you and I can get together and file something for both of us." Bobby was relieved and nodded his agreement.

The court proceedings began and what little business there was moved quickly. Tom Flanagan detailed the brutal way Francini had been killed and asked the judge to set bail for Costa in the amount of one million dollars. Flanagan emphasized that the charge was first-degree murder and the defendant had every incentive to flee the jurisdiction. Richard Charles described his client's extended family and stressed that he was a life-long resident of Boston with many ties to the community. Charles reminded the judge that Costa had voluntarily surrendered. Nonetheless, it came as no surprise that Morgan went with the prosecution and ordered a million dollars bail.

The judge ordered the defendants to file preliminary motions within three weeks. He gave the prosecution three weeks after that to respond and ordered another status hearing in six weeks. With that, he adjourned court and retired to his chambers.

Bobby told Marino that he'd come to see him in the holding cells in a few minutes. Was there an outside chance the guy was innocent? Probably not. The smart move was to limit his exposure by pleading guilty. He'd like to find a way to get Marino to see that sooner rather than later.

7

Susan walked with Coughlin toward the rear of the courtroom. Patty Marino approached them, trembling.

"What's going on?" Patty asked.

Coughlin turned to Susan. "Bring her up to date." He kept walking and left the room.

Bring Patty up to date with what? There was no good news to share with her. Susan was supposed to be learning by watching Coughlin handle things. Apparently the lesson this morning was that you didn't need to treat the incarcerated client's wife like a human being. Patty was dressed well and wore makeup. No doubt she wanted to look pretty for her husband. Now tears had left her with red eyes and smeared mascara. The woman was a wreck. Susan would do her best to reassure her.

She put her arm around Patty's shoulders. "Let's take a seat in the hallway and talk for a while." They found a bench near the entrance to the courtroom. Patty clutched her pocketbook on her lap.

"My name is Susan, Mrs. Marino, and I'll be working on

your case with Mr. Coughlin." She smiled.

"Patty. Call me Patty. Are you a lawyer?"

"No, I'm in my last year of law school. I help with research and things like that."

"No offense, but I was hoping to talk with Nicky's lawyer. I'm sure you're good at your research, but my husband's charged with murder. Don't you think his lawyer should make time for me?"

"Absolutely. You're right, and Mr. Coughlin will talk with you. I'm sorry he wasn't able to stay just now, but he had to go quickly to see your husband before they send him back to jail."

She was afraid she'd be making excuses for Coughlin a lot over the course of this case. Patty was pissed. Susan would be too. Coughlin could have asked her to come into the office any time in the last week or met her earlier this morning before court. Instead, he'd ignored her.

Tears welled up in Patty's eyes. She let go of her purse and grabbed Susan's hands. "Nicky is innocent. When is Mr. Coughlin going to get him out of jail?"

Coughlin should have told Patty before this that Nicky wasn't getting out. It was possible Coughlin had said something on the phone and Patty hadn't heard it. People were easily overwhelmed by the legal system and often failed to take in negative information. Susan sometimes was forced to tell some of her clients in the clinic the same basic things over and over. Gradually she'd realized that they weren't ignoring her. They just didn't hear some of the things she told them. She didn't think that was what happened here, though. Coughlin probably just didn't want to tell Patty that the court wouldn't release her husband from jail. That was way too defensive. No one could have gotten Nicky out. Her boss must really be thrown by this case.

"I'm afraid that people charged with murder almost never get out on bail," Susan said. "Nicky will probably have to stay in jail until the trial. Mr. Coughlin will do everything he can to defend him."

That sounded so lame. Susan didn't know what else to say. She had her doubts about Coughlin's abilities. Maybe they should talk about something other than the case.

"Patty, do you have kids?"

"Two. Sheila's in fourth grade and Tommy's in third. Do you want to see their pictures?" She took a small wallet out of her purse and flipped it open. There were several photos of each child and Susan took her time looking at them.

"The kids are darling. This must be hard on them."

"It's terrible. I don't know what to tell them. Nicky told me not to bring them to the jail. They don't even know where he's at."

Susan pursed her lips. "I don't know. Maybe you should tell them the truth. You might tell them you believe Nicky is innocent, that this is a mistake."

"Do you think that's what I should do?"

"I don't know your kids. You'll have to decide. You should think about it."

Patty put her wallet away. "Sheila's going to hear something at school anyway. Maybe even the third graders will hear their parents talking about it and say something to Tommy."

"Probably better they hear it from you first. We're just getting started. We're going to file some motions to find out what the prosecution's case is based on. Then we'll do some investigating. I'm afraid the trial won't be for months."

Patty wrung her hands. "Nicky isn't the kind of man who would kill anybody."

Susan put her hand on Patty's shoulder. "He's lucky to have a wife with such faith in him. You'll have to be strong for him and the kids."

"I don't know. I've never had to deal with anything like this."

"I know it sounds trite, but the only way to get through this is one day at a time."

Patty took a tissue out of her purse and wiped her eyes.

"Thanks for sitting with me. It means a lot to have someone to talk to. I'm sorry I jumped on you about not being a lawyer."

"No worries. I understand."

Patty was going to have a tough time financially with her husband in jail. While she was digging in her purse to get the pictures, Susan had seen a nametag, like Patty'd wear on a job.

"Are you working?" Susan asked.

"Yeah. I'm a waitress at the Rosebud Diner in Davis Square—do you know it?"

"I've seen it, but I've never had a chance to eat there."

"I like the people who come in, and the tips are good for a diner."

Susan nodded. "I work as a waitress too, at Gabriella's in the North End. It's my dad's restaurant and I've worked there most of my life."

"You go to school, you waitress, and you work for Mr. Coughlin?"

"I've just been working for Coughlin for a month. I'm sure what I do is easier than working and taking care of two kids at the same time."

Patty gazed down at her shoes. "I never even went to college. I got good grades in high school, but there was no money to go on. I thought about going to community college and working at the same time. When the kids came, that was the end of that. How do you like working with your dad? Mine passed away."

"I'm sorry. I love Gabriella's. It's named after my mom, who died when I was a little kid. My father's from Italy and we serve real Italian food."

"We've both lost a parent. Now I might lose my husband." Patty teared up again.

Susan didn't know if bringing Patty up to date meant talking about Brady. Patty would ask what they were going to do about him. Susan sure as hell didn't know how to answer that one. She'd let Coughlin handle it.

What would she do in this woman's position, with a husband

in jail and two young kids at home? The pain showed in Patty's eyes. Susan wanted to talk to her longer, but it was late, and she was due in class.

She stood up slowly. "I'm afraid I've got to go now. I'm due at school. You should call whenever you have any questions. If Mr. Coughlin is tied up dealing with legal matters, ask for me. If I don't know the answer, I'll find it out and get back to you."

They took the elevator downstairs. Susan gave Patty a long hug before saying goodbye. She vowed to give Coughlin a piece of her mind for ignoring the client's wife.

8

Bobby hated going into the lockup. The place smelled of sweat and human waste and fear. Most of the prisoners were either in court or were already on their way back to the jail, so the first several cells in a long row were empty. There was nothing in them except a bench for the prisoners to sit on and a toilet with no toilet seat. The floors were littered with the wrappers from breakfast sandwiches and empty paper cups.

Bobby walked down to the cell at the end of the row, where Marino stood alone, clinging to the bars. They could talk quietly without being overheard.

"Did you have any conversation with Costa before I got here?" Bobby asked.

"No. I told you before I don't really know him."

"Costa is the one the prosecutor really wants. He doesn't care that much about you. If you can help him make his case against Costa, he'll go easy on you."

Marino threw up his hands. "How can I help him if I didn't do anything and don't know anything?"

"I can't help you if you don't level with me."

"I'm telling you the truth. I didn't do this."

Marino wasn't budging. It was still early in the case, and Bobby was getting too impatient. He twisted his wedding ring nervously on his finger. He needed to stop pushing Marino so hard or the client wouldn't listen to anything Bobby said.

"Well, let's talk for a minute about your defense. Do you have an alibi for the shooting? Do you know where you were late at night on July 7, 2004, when Francini was killed?"

"That's more than three years ago. I'm not the kind of guy who keeps a calendar."

"Is there any way you can figure it out?"

"What night of the week was that?"

Bobby consulted the perpetual calendar on his cell phone. "Wednesday."

"I must have been home with my wife and kids. I never go out during the week."

"A man's wife doesn't make much of an alibi witness, Nicky."

Marino's eyes flamed. His hands came off the bars of his cell and Bobby thought Marino was going to try to reach through them. He balled his fists and glared at Bobby. "Just a minute. You're saying my wife is lying? You're supposed to be on my side."

Bobby took a step back "Calm down. I'm not accusing her of lying. I'm just saying that jurors won't put much weight on a wife's alibi testimony."

Marino shook his head. "Whattya want from me? You said to tell you the truth—that's the truth. I'm a family man. I don't go out drinking with guys from work, I don't go bowling, I don't belong to any clubs or anything."

The veins in Marino's neck were bulging. No point talking to him now about a rational strategy to limit his exposure. Discussion of a plea would have to come later. Marino didn't trust him. To be honest, he didn't have any reason to. Bobby needed something that would show Marino he was acting in his best interests. No clue to what would accomplish that.

He didn't know how to get a handle on this case. He was worse off than he'd been on Jamie's case. At least then he'd built a theory of the defense and was able to make a presentation to the court. Here he had nothing. If the client didn't plead out, this was going to be a real disaster.

"I'll set up a meeting with Costa's lawyer to find out what Costa has to say. I'll let you know."

"Don't tell anybody I'm thinking of making a deal with the D.A., cause I'm not."

"Obviously, anything of that sort would just be between you and me."

"You don't know me," Marino said. "You don't know anything about me. If you did, you'd know—you'd know there's no way I'd be involved in murder. You gotta prove that Brady is making up this crap about me. Please. Please, you gotta work on that end of it."

"I'm going to look into every aspect of this business. I'll come out when I've got something to go over with you. In the meantime, remember what I told you. Don't talk to anyone at the jail about your case."

It didn't make sense that either the D.A.'s office or the FBI would buy a completely manufactured story from Joseph Brady. It wouldn't do any good to tell Marino that, though. Bobby turned and walked down the row of cells toward the exit.

He walked back toward his office, thinking that this would have been a good time of year to go down to the Caribbean for a couple of weeks. When he was in law school at B.U. and single, he used to love to go to Jamaica. The beat of the reggae music coursed through him now. Marie had some vacation days left. They could get a little cottage near the beach, spend a day in the rain forest, relax. Maybe smoke a little ganja. Make love whenever they wanted. That's what he'd do if he didn't have this goddam case.

9

Susan and Coughlin walked from Beacon Hill to meet with Richard Charles at his office further downtown. Coughlin marched along silently.

Susan broke the ice. "You left Patty Marino hanging the other day in court. She needs some of your time."

"I had to talk to Nicky," Coughlin said.

"Yeah, but you could have spent a minute or two with her first. She's terrified."

"Look, I've got a lot on my mind. I'll get to her, but I don't need a hard time from you about it."

Susan wanted to say more but didn't think it would get her anywhere.

"And don't mention the visit from Romano," Coughlin said.

"Okay."

"We need to be strategic about how that information gets shared."

And he's in control of the strategy, Susan thought. Coughlin was getting under her skin.

Charles decorated his office beautifully with sleek and modern furniture. Whereas Coughlin hung simple posters of reproductions from the Museum of Fine Arts on his walls, Charles displayed original oils, for the most part, expressionist works. There was what looked like a Max Pechstein in his reception area. Susan went closer. It was a Pechstein! One of the many paintings he made of bathers—nudes lying languidly on the beach, the dark blue sea behind them. The colors possessed the intensity of neon. She thought about Marcella, the girl in the yellow and black striped dress, sitting on a green couch with a cat, who'd been painted by both Pechstein and Ernst Kirchner. She'd seen the paintings at the Brücke Museum in Berlin three years ago and the oddity of both artists painting the same scene got her to research the story behind it. The fifteen-year-old model and her sister had gone on an extended vacation in the countryside with the artists. They posed for many paintings, some in the nude. Pechstein and Kirchner enjoyed a libertine lifestyle and were probably sexually involved with the girls. Kirchner had depicted Marcella in profile on the couch. The girl's mood of sadness and resignation as she sat, turned away from the viewer with only one eye visible, resonated with Susan. The artist captured a feeling of alienation that the young girl must have felt from the Bohemian scene in which she found herself. Marcella reminded her of her own feeling of vulnerability in the male-dominated world of criminal law. She wasn't cavorting at the beach or posing in the nude. The way men looked at her, however, often left her feeling exposed.

Susan and Coughlin joined Charles in his conference room. The cherry wood of the long table gleamed in the sunlight that came through the window at the other end of the room.

"Brady's the key to this case," Charles said. "He's a drowning rat that would say anything to save himself. Our best chance of beating this thing is to expose him for what he is."

"How much do you know about him?" Bobby asked.

"Brady's testifying to avoid a career criminal charge based

on having a gun in his car when he got arrested. Costa told me that Brady's committed several murders and is completely unreliable. He'd sell out his own mother if he needed to. I've hired an investigator to find out more."

Charles looked directly at Susan. "Did you prepare those motions that we got the other day? They were very good."

The heat rose on her cheeks. She'd worked hard on those papers. That Charles assumed she'd written them was rewarding, but also disconcerting. Best to be diplomatic. "Mr. Coughlin prepared the final motions, Mr. Charles, I just did the first draft."

"Please call me Richard. Bobby's lucky to have someone from Suffolk in his office. They teach you to practice law. Not like the school across the river where they spend so much time on legal theory and so little on what you need in a courtroom." He turned to Coughlin. "I've added a few things from my stock discovery motions, and some requests for information specific to this case." He passed papers across the table. "Here are my redrafts. Why don't you take a look at them later and call me tomorrow and let me know if they're okay? Then we can get them filed."

Susan leafed through the motions. Richard intended to take charge of the defense. Hopefully, Coughlin would accept his leadership.

"Costa's into gambling," Richard said. "Everyone knows that. But he's never been implicated in a murder in his life and didn't have anything to do with this one." He turned to Coughlin. "Flanagan already asked me if Costa would be interested in pleading guilty to second-degree murder, so he'd be eligible for parole at some point. I said no way. What about you, Bobby? Are you and your client prepared to go all the way with this?"

"Marino says he had nothing to do with the murder."

That didn't answer the question, but Richard didn't push it.

"Let's talk about Brady," Richard said. "We've got to get the jury into his head. It was a lizard brain decision on his part to cooperate. It runs against everything in his background to testify for the prosecution. We need the jurors to feel how desperate he was, to taste the fear, to get that this was a question of survival for him. They're not going to like him, and that's fine, but it's more important for them to understand what would drive him to rat out innocent men."

"Do you think fear is enough?" Susan asked. "Wouldn't a guy like Brady know all along there's a chance that someday he might get nailed and spend the rest of his life in prison?"

"You're saying there's something else?" Richard asked.

"Yeah," Susan said. "He's got to have a beef with Romano, or maybe these particular guys. Maybe he's angry about something and that overcame his reluctance to be a snitch."

"We've got to look for that," Richard said.

Susan was dying to see Richard question witnesses in the courtroom. He was intelligent and confident, and his eyes lit up when he spoke. She couldn't take her eyes off him. He wasn't wearing a wedding ring. Jesus, he was ten years older than her, at least.

Just because a man didn't wear a ring didn't mean he wasn't married. She'd found that out in Chicago. She wouldn't be forgetting that lesson any time soon. She'd gone without romance in her life for a few years now. Most of the time, she felt better off without it. She had her friends, school, and her work at Gabriella's. No real emotional highs, but no real lows either. There'd be time for that later. It could wait until she passed the bar and was settled in a permanent job.

The meeting broke up and everyone went off in different directions. She hurried to get to her class at Suffolk. She tried to remember the cases she'd read for today's assignment but found that she couldn't put Richard and his lizard brain cross-examination out of her mind.

10

On Tuesday morning, Special Agents Mike Rizzo and Harry Smith enjoyed a cup of coffee in a diner near the FBI office in the JFK federal building. Rizzo licked his lips. The smooth, chocolaty flavor of the coffee in a mug was a lot better than a styrofoam cup of the bitter, stale brew upstairs in the squad room. Costa turning himself in was a relief. Now Rizzo was spared the trouble of chasing Costa down.

Rizzo was a career FBI man in his late forties. Like most agents, he wouldn't stand out in a crowd. Just under six feet tall, he had a receding hairline and carried a mere ten extra pounds. Smith was in his early fifties and his hair was all white. He kept himself in shape by playing handball and was proud of his trim physique. They'd been partners on the organized crime squad for five years.

Rizzo hated all the bureaucratic bullshit Washington required that got in their way. He finessed the rules when necessary. Smith had no problem with that. Protecting the so-called constitutional rights of criminals was less important than solving crimes.

"We got the okay to hold Brady in a safe house instead of the jail until the trial's over," Rizzo said. "We can move him later today. That'll make the asshole happy. He's been bitching about wanting to see his girlfriend alone."

"Great," Smith said. "Now we can keep better tabs on him. He doesn't need to be talking to anybody at the jail. Who knows what somebody might say to him—or do to him?"

Rizzo nodded. Exactly. They'd used the fact that Brady was in general population in the jail at Dedham to get him to become a cooperating witness. Now they needed him to be isolated. They'd been clever. They'd gone to see Brady after he got bagged on a gun charge by a local cop. It was his third felony and the D.A. was threatening to have him sentenced as a career criminal. They saw him in a private interview room. The tall and muscle-bound criminal was menacing, even in their presence. Rizzo went straight at him.

"Joe, we talked to the New Bedford cop and he's got you by the short hairs on this gun charge. You ran a red light, and when the cop asked you to get out of your car, the gun practically fell out of your pants."

"What's your point?" Brady asked.

"We've had ten unsolved homicides in Boston over the past five years where the victims were organized crime guys. No offense, but we're pretty sure you know something about them."

Brady gazed indifferently at Rizzo. "Like I said, what's your point?"

"You've got no chance at beating this charge, and you'll be in prison until you're eighty-something. You help us out, we help you out."

Brady shook his head. "I don't need any help from the FBI."

Rizzo stared hard at Brady. The man was a tough guy, but there was only one way out of the spot he was in. He had something Rizzo could use. The previous night he'd reviewed the files. His informants put Brady in one of the murders.

"That's bullshit, Joe, and you and I both know it. What about Francini? I know for a fact you were there."

"If you know so much about me, you know I'm not a rat. Even if I did know something, I wouldn't tell you assholes. And if I did, I'd never see eighty anyway."

"We can take care of that, you know," Smith said. "We can give you a new identity, relocate you to another part of the country, get you a job, money. You testify in some of these cases, and you get a pass on all the shit you've done."

"Says you," Brady replied. "I'm not interested in what you're selling."

Brady called for the guard and asked to be taken back to his cell.

Rizzo had desperately needed to make progress on these murders. Ten people were dead, and it felt like nobody gave a damn. He'd been chasing mobsters for ten years but never nailed any important ones. Romano and the people close to him were scum. They didn't play by the ordinary rules of society. They acted like the FBI couldn't touch them. The local cops weren't much help. He'd like to know how many of them were bought off. He'd started out with the Boston P.D., but gone over to the Bureau to try to make some progress against organized crime. He still ran into one roadblock after another.

A transfer to Florida is what Rizzo wanted. He was done with cold and snow. Mike Jr., his only kid, had graduated from B.C. and moved out to California to work in high tech. The divorce had finally gone through and he wanted to take off someplace with his girlfriend. Quit hiding like they were doing something wrong. Take her out in public and be proud of her. Kick back on the beach. Play golf all year round. But there was no chance of a transfer with ten unsolved homicides around his neck. And he couldn't break any of those cases without a witness.

Talking was in Brady's self-interest, but the code against ratting was strong. So strong that the Bureau had almost never developed a cooperating witness from the mob at this level anywhere in the country. He needed to find a way to flip this piece of shit.

Eddie Baker, a hood at the Dedham jail, was doing six months for his fourth conviction for driving under. Brady and Eddie were close, but Brady didn't know that Eddie and Willie, his older brother, were FBI informants. Eddie was a quick-tempered, violent guy. Short and wiry, he enjoyed hurting people. At fifteen he challenged a bigger kid, three years older, to a fight. Each had his left hand tied behind his back and held a brick in his right. Eddie ended up with eighteen stitches and still had a thin white scar running from the left side of his mouth to his ear. The other kid hadn't been so lucky. Died on the way to the hospital. Eddie was convicted of manslaughter and committed to the Department of Youth Services. Got released at twenty-one.

Willie was bigger, better looking, smoother and more intelligent than his kid brother. A very convincing liar. He was fanatically loyal to Eddie but possessed no moral compass whatsoever.

After that first meeting, Rizzo came up with the idea of letting it slip to Willie that the cop had stopped Brady on a tip from one of Romano's guys. No truth to that, but it was well known that Brady and Romano distrusted each other already. Rizzo figured Willie would repeat the story to Eddie, who'd pass it along to Brady. Smith liked it. The next time they saw Willie, they planted the seed.

The agents waited a couple of weeks and then went back to Dedham. Brady came into the interview room on fire.

"I heard it was Romano's fault I'm in here," Brady said. "One of his guys told that cop that I was carrying."

"Oh yeah?" Rizzo said.

"I hate that bastard."

"If any of his guys got convicted of murder, he'd take that pretty hard," Smith pointed out.

Brady grinned. "Hell, it was his guys who did Francini.

Suppose I did agree to talk. Are you sure you could get the D.A. to go along with me not doing any time?"

"These cases have been lying around for too long," Rizzo said. "The D.A. needs convictions, so he'll go along with anything we ask for if we come up with a solid witness."

"Look, I gotta tell you, I would never give you anything that would allow Eddie Baker to fry," Brady said.

Rizzo had been worried about what Brady was going to do about Eddie. Rizzo knew that Eddie did the Francini hit with Brady, but the informants who told him that weren't willing to testify. Besides, once Rizzo recruited Eddie as an informant, he didn't want him burned. Brady taking Eddie out of the story solved the problem. Of course, someone else would have to get tagged with Francini's murder.

"Are you insisting on that as a condition of any cooperation?" Rizzo asked.

"Absolutely," Brady said.

Rizzo and Smith looked at each other. Smith nodded. "We can live with that," Rizzo said. "Tell you what, Joe, why don't you tell us what you've got on who killed Francini. If we don't end up working anything out with you, we'll forget we ever heard it. We're not taping anything here."

Brady asked them for a tonic and spent the time while Smith was getting it apparently thinking things over. They sat there in silence. Rizzo was asking Brady to turn his back on everything in his life. There'd be no going back if he did. The guy didn't look happy. No surprise. Brady had no good choices. If he wanted to get out of prison while he had any life left, he needed to make a deal. That could get him released, but it might not keep him alive. Rizzo wasn't about to lose any sleep over it if Brady got bumped off after he testified. Rizzo sure as shit didn't feel sorry for him. Brady put himself in the position he was in. He was simply a pawn who could be sacrificed in pursuit of bigger game.

Smith came back with a Coke. Brady took a gulp. "Okay," he said, "I maybe could tell you about Francini. I'm still worried that if I admit I was there, even though I wasn't the shooter, it's hard to believe the D.A. would just let me walk."

Brady was smart enough to know that he wasn't getting out of jail right away. So, Rizzo told him the truth. "It's going to take time to get these cases tried. You'll have to be locked up somewhere during that time. Maybe not in a jail. What you'll get will be time served. That'll be enough for the D.A. We'll get rid of this recent gun charge by having the cop admit that it was an illegal search. And we'll set you up in witness protection like Smith said last time."

Brady leaned forward. "Like I said, it was Romano's man who asked for my help in whacking Francini. Romano thought the Aamccountant was stealing from him. I got Nicky Marino to shoot him. Then we dumped his body in front of his girlfriend's condo."

"Who's Nicky Marino?" Rizzo asked.

"He's an ironworker, does jobs for us sometimes."

"Who else was involved?"

"Who do you think?" Brady asked.

Rizzo looked at Smith and then back at Brady. The guy was asking if the agents had anybody they wanted taken down. The FBI had long wanted to bust Danny Costa but had nothing that connected him to murder.

"You know," Rizzo said, "Danny Costa is close to Romano and if he got sent away it would hurt Romano bad. And we'd sure like to know if he was involved in a homicide."

"Bingo! You got it. That's exactly who it was."

Brady agreed to cooperate. He would testify against Marino and Costa. Rizzo and Smith delivered a nice big package to their bosses and to the Suffolk D.A.

Rizzo was thrilled with how well things had gone. The agents finished their coffee and left to make the necessary calls to move Brady to a safehouse. They needed to make final arrangements for security at the new location with the Marshall's Office. Brady would spend the next several months until the trial at an isolated beach house north of Boston, where he'd have a private bedroom with its own widescreen TV and all the comforts of home, including overnight visits from his girlfriend. Marino and Costa would spend those months much less comfortably at the Plymouth House of Correction.

11

On Saturday, Susan went to the gym. She tried to go three times a week to do some stretching and work with weights. Usually, she had to force herself to make the effort, but today she was glad to be there and out of the office. She kept picturing Patty Marino, alone in her house with her kids. Patty had switched to working days with Nicky gone. Now she's stuck sitting around by herself at night after the kids go to bed. Maybe zoning out in front of the TV. Hopefully, she's not a drinker.

Susan wasn't sure how close she should get to Patty. Her professors said it was important to be empathic, but that it was a mistake to get so close to clients that you were unable to be objective. Susan worked for Nicky's lawyer. She wasn't Patty's friend or social worker. Still, the pull to help Patty was a strong one. Drawing appropriate boundaries was proving to be more difficult than Susan imagined. She'd invited Patty to call her if she needed something, so she'd left the initiative to her for now.

Susan changed in the locker room and got out onto the gym floor. The machines, freshly wiped down, shined in the late morning sunlight. A decent crowd of hard-charging fitness enthusiasts attacked the equipment. A handful of trainers assisted clients with enough money to afford their services.

On the other side of the gym, a woman with long black hair tied in a ponytail was bench-pressing dumbbells. Maybe in her late thirties. There was something familiar about her.

It was Rena Posso. Francini's girlfriend. Three years after the murder now. Was that enough time to get over having her boyfriend's dead and mutilated body dumped on her doorstep? Rena moved from one exercise to another with remarkable physical intensity, executing everything with perfect form, using free weights, ignoring the machines. Most of her exercises focused on strengthening the core. Her muscles were taut and she carried no unnecessary fat.

The papers said she was no longer acting. None of the reporters had been able to interview her since the arrests. She worked out alone, not talking with anybody, not even making eye contact with the people right around her. Her face was neither happy nor sad. Other than her attention to the physical requirements of her routine, her focus seemed to be somewhere else. Almost like she had a secret life and only her body was at the gym. Susan would love to know what was going on in her head.

Coughlin had told her to leave witness interviews up to him. He'd probably blow up if she talked to the victim's girlfriend. Still, he wasn't exactly pulling his weight on the case. Unlike Richard, he hadn't even hired an investigator. She could tell Coughlin that she met a woman at the gym who she only learned later was Rena Posso. He probably wouldn't buy that, but she wasn't going to pass up a chance like this.

Susan did a light workout on the TRX cables and kept watch on Rena out of the corner of her eye. Susan finished her third set of rowing exercises and caught sight of her quarry heading toward the locker room. Now or never, she thought. She hustled after her, showered, then stood next to Rena while they were blow-drying their hair.

"That's quite a routine, you have," Susan said. "I couldn't help noticing. It looks like you've worked with a professional trainer at some point."

"Oh, thanks," Rena said. "I did. I work as a model and I'm not getting any younger, so I have to work hard to keep the pounds off."

"Obviously it's effective. What kind of modeling do you do?"

"There are a few clothing lines that use me for magazine shoots. You're a pretty girl, you could probably get some work if you wanted it."

Susan shook her head. "I don't think I'd have the discipline to stay in the kind of shape that you're in. Do you enjoy it?"

"I do. It's good money and the posing and all, it can be fun. Although sometimes it can just be exhausting. I want there to be more. If you have a brain, you want to use it, and you want to be appreciated for it. I've done some acting too, although not lately."

"I'd like to hear more about it," Susan said. "I'm going to grab something to eat up the street at Silvertones. Would you like to join me?"

"Okay. My name's Rena."

"Susan."

They left the gym and walked to the restaurant, where they ordered white wine and mussels in a garlic sauce at the bar. The place felt like a cafeteria but served great food. It was a favorite for Suffolk professors and students for lunch, and at night it was a hangout for people who worked at other restaurants. This Saturday afternoon, there were only a few customers.

Rena took very small sips of wine and ate only a couple of the mussels. Susan gathered that she must be careful about food to stay slim. Rena had a killer figure. Yet she didn't give off the vibe that a lot of beautiful women projected of trading on their appearance. She wasn't wearing makeup and her clothes didn't look any different than those of most young women. The longer they talked without Rena knowing that Susan was working on the murder case, the more difficult it would become. She'd better just come right out with it.

"I need to tell you something, so you don't think I'm trying to hide anything," Susan said. "I recognized you at the gym. I'm working for a lawyer who represents one of the defendants charged with Tony Francini's murder."

Rena's eyes went cold. "What? Which lawyer?"

"Bobby Coughlin. His client is Nicky Marino."

"What are you playing at?" Rena asked loudly. "I don't like to talk about Tony. Much less with lawyers."

Susan looked down, unable to meet Rena's eyes. "Honestly, I wasn't trying to ambush you," she said. "That's why I told you who I am now. I'm just a law student. This is my first big case. and I'm pretty sure that Marino wasn't involved in Tony Francini's death. I'm desperate to learn more about the case however I can. But if you don't want to talk to me, I'll leave." She stood up and put some money on the bar. She turned toward the door.

"Wait," Rena said. "You don't have to go. If you were being sneaky, you wouldn't have said anything. I'm pretty defensive about this whole thing. You seem nice enough, and to tell you the truth, I don't have many female friends these days. It feels good to have a glass of wine with another girl."

Susan sat back down. "I can understand why you might not want to talk to somebody who's defending a man accused of killing your boyfriend. Well, I mean, everyone says he was your boyfriend. I guess I don't really know if he was. Maybe I shouldn't have called him that, I'm sorry."

"Tony was my boyfriend, all right. I haven't gotten over what happened to him. I don't know anything about that night. I do know that a lot of what you read in the papers is crap."

That took Susan by surprise. She'd read all the press reports, but she didn't know what Rena might be referring to.

"I loved Tony," Rena said softly. "Yeah, I knew he was

involved with the rackets. It wasn't like he was a violent guy or like he committed crimes. Maybe he got off a little on hanging out with tough guys. But he was basically an accountant."

"Can I ask how long you two were together?" Susan asked.

"A few years. He was sweet. He went to all the shows I was in and he read all the plays. He genuinely cared about what I was doing. If I read for a part and didn't get it, he knew how to cheer me up. What pisses me off is all this junk about him stealing money to take care of me. Sure, he gave me presents, like any boyfriend. He didn't give me money, though, and he didn't pay my expenses."

Rena's bitterness startled Susan. She realized she'd assumed that it was true that Francini was supporting her, just based on the newspaper stories. Most people probably did the same thing.

"I live in the North End," Susan said. "You have a condo in the Seaport, right?"

"Yeah, the famous condo where they left Tony. You know, what the papers say about Tony buying the condo for me isn't true. I bought it when my father passed away. I was an only child, and my mom died when I was a little girl. My dad was in real estate in New York. He died at sixty from a heart attack and left me a fair amount of money. The papers make me sound like some kind of kept woman. The fact is I had more money than Tony and didn't need or want any from him.

"Tony kept me away from the unsavory parts of his life. I went out with him a few times with some of the men he worked with, but that was rare. On the other hand, he was really interested in my work in the theater. I didn't know what kind of life we might have worked out if we'd lived together, and now I'll never know." Rena's eyes filled with tears.

Susan took some tissues from her pocketbook and passed them over to Rena. "I'm sorry. You've had it tough. I know about that—my mom died too and my dad raised me as an only child. I don't know what I'd do if I lost him. And then you lost Tony."

"There's been no one to talk to about this since Tony got

killed. Some of my old friends dropped me when I started going with someone from the wrong element, as they say. After he was murdered, no one called. I mean no one. I was terrified that the killers might come after me. Nobody has bothered me, but I've been pretty much of a hermit since this happened. You saying that you were working for one of the defense lawyers just shot through me like lightning."

Rena wiped her eyes with the tissues. "Why do you believe Marino is innocent?"

"We've got information that contradicts Brady's story," Susan said. "I really can't say any more. Besides that, what you just said about your condo undercuts the cops' theory that Tony was stealing from Romano because he was supporting you. Do they know you bought it yourself?"

Rena snorted. "No one from the police or the D.A.'s office has ever asked me anything about my finances or where the money came from for the condo. I think they just assume Tony bought it, or they don't really care."

Susan took a sip of her wine. "I hope you're going back to acting."

"I want to, at some point. I was really scared after Tony got killed. It must be a little scary for you just to be working on a murder case."

In a strange way, Susan felt protected by Frank Romano. He talked with her in such a confidential manner, and he knew her father. Still, he didn't owe her anything. It would be stupid not to see that this was a dangerous case. "Yeah, a little," she said.

"I wouldn't have expected to get along with someone working for one of the defense lawyers," Rena said. "I like you. Let's get together again." They left the bar, and Susan walked back to the North End.

Rena seemed like a nice person. Susan would like to make friends with her, but she'd have to be careful because of the case. She was struck by the agony of the women she'd met; first Patty, and now Rena. She'd only seen her from across the courtroom, but it was clear that Costa's wife was hurting as well. The bullet that killed Francini had passed through the hearts of many innocent women before it stopped.

12

Bobby couldn't bring himself to go out to talk with Marino. It was like listening to a broken record. "I'm innocent. I don't know anything. This is a big mistake." Bobby didn't need to hear it. He needed Marino to make a deal. He needed the client to agree to the outcome. That was the great thing about a plea. The defendant *agreed* to it. It wasn't the lawyer's fault.

Susan knocked on his door. There was a look on her face like she had another surprise for him as she stepped into the room. He didn't need that, either. Bobby enjoyed having this good-looking young woman available to do some of the work that he didn't want to be bothered with. Now she was getting to be a pain.

"Mr. Coughlin, I have some more information on Nicky's case. I know you told me not to talk to any witnesses, but I ran into someone by accident. I told her I worked for you, and she started telling me things."

"Who did you talk to this time?"

"Rena Posso."

Bobby held his head in his hands. No way. The head of the mob, then the victim's girlfriend. It would never have occurred to him to try to interview either one of them. Susan had some moxie. This was totally out of control.

"She goes to my gym. I ran into her, and we went out for a drink. I thought I'd better tell her right away about my connection to you, you know, so no one could say that I did anything underhanded. Anyway, she says that the police and the papers have it all wrong about Francini supporting her. That story that he bought a condo for her on the waterfront? That's not true. She inherited a lot of money from her father and bought it herself. Francini never gave her any money."

Bobby took it for granted that Francini was killed because he was stealing from Romano to support his girlfriend. Why else would the beautiful young actress be going with such a slob?

"You just assumed she was telling you the truth?"

"She's nice, and she's smart. I believed her. And where the money came from to buy the condo can totally be checked out and documented. There'll be bank records and the Probate Court files. Rena's still tormented by Francini's murder. She was in love with him. She's not the kind of woman who would've been looking for a sugar daddy."

Susan was right—the records would corroborate Rena Posso's claims. Unlike Romano, this woman was a credible witness. No one suggested that she was connected to organized crime, except by the fact that Francini was her boyfriend.

"Plus, get this," Susan said. "The cops and the D.A.'s office never talked with Rena about where she got the money to buy the condo, or whether Francini was supporting her. Apparently, they don't know yet that it was her money."

"The prosecutor will probably subpoena the real estate closing documents," Bobby said.

"Perhaps, but all that would show is that the money came from Rena's account. If he doesn't go back any further, and maybe he won't, he won't learn where she got the money. You might be able to surprise both him and the jury with the truth that the money for the condo came from Rena's father's estate."

This girl sounded like she was ready to impanel a jury and try the case right then. What Rena Posso said was interesting, but it wasn't that important. Even if Francini wasn't ripping off Romano, Marino might still be the shooter. Brady might have had some other problem with Francini, one he couldn't or didn't want to, tell the government about. Maybe Costa wasn't involved. That didn't mean that Marino was innocent.

"I suppose you want to see her again," he said.

"That depends on what you want me to do. I didn't mean to be going against what you said about contacting witnesses—this just sort of happened."

Bobby needed to get Susan under control. On the other hand, he might want more information from Rena Posso and Susan would probably be better at getting it than he would.

"You'd think it would bother her that you're working for the defense," Bobby said.

"Yeah, right? But she doesn't seem to trust the cops and doesn't necessarily assume that they've arrested the right people. Odd as it is, I think she likes me and trusts me."

"Okay. Stay in touch with her. Bring everything she tells you back to me. Don't start investigating anything yourself."

"Are you going to tell the other lawyers about this?"

"Not just yet. I don't want a lot of people trying to talk to her. It might scare her away." Besides, if the other defense lawyers already knew the story, Bobby couldn't threaten the prosecutor with revealing Rena Posso's information to them. As long as those lawyers didn't know about it, Bobby would have some leverage to negotiate a better deal for Marino. Bobby wouldn't share that idea with Susan. She wasn't cynical enough to appreciate the necessity of such tactics. He'd let her continue to work on the theory that Nicky was innocent.

Bobby checked his watch. "I'm late for court. I've got a drunk driving on this morning. Guy blew a one point two on the

Breathalyzer, but on the video from the camera at the booking desk he looks as sober as he could be. His speech is clear and his handwriting where he signed the property inventory is very readable."

"Doesn't the prosecution have to show impairment to prove drunk driving? Your guy sounds okay. Was there an accident?"

"No. The only reason he was stopped in the first place was a defective muffler." Bobby had been planning on copping the guy out to probation conditioned on participation in the drunk driving school. He suddenly decided to try the case. The guy had a shot, and it would only be his first offense if he were found guilty so he wouldn't get hurt too bad. It was a lot easier to contemplate trying the drunk driving than the goddam murder case.

13

The prosecutor Tom Flanagan was in his office at night putting together the materials he'd have to furnish to the defense in Francini's case. Usually, he liked staying late. The phone didn't ring, the judges weren't around to summon him into court, and it was much easier to concentrate without all the people who were constantly in and out of his office during the day. From nine to five, he was always in a hurry. Now he could take his time. Unfortunately, Flanagan hated this case.

He'd just finished rereading Brady's grand jury testimony. Listening to him in the grand jury room had been sickening. Brady described the murders he'd committed without remorse or any emotion. Worse, he seemed to have no sense that there was anything unusual about his criminal career. Occasionally a brief smile would cross his face as he spoke. Flanagan thought if it meant anything, it was merely a sign of Brady's appreciation of his technique. Killing people is what he did. He didn't give any more thought to his victims than a butcher did to the hogs he slaughtered for pork chops.

Despite that, Brady would make a strong witness. Flanagan questioned the man in painstaking detail three times, in addition to the formal testimony at the grand jury. There were no inconsistencies in Brady's account, and the corroboration for his involvement was overwhelming. Brady knew that the killers cut off the victim's fingers *after* he was shot. Because the M.E.'s conclusion that blood stopped flowing through Francini's body before the amputation wasn't public, that was significant. The examination of Brady's SUV with luminol disclosed bloodstains. The DNA extracted from the blood matched Francini's. Vacuuming the floor of the vehicle yielded hairs that were consistent with those that were taken from Francini's head during the autopsy. Fibers found on the victim's suit matched the carpet in Brady's vehicle. There was no doubt that the SUV was used to transport Francini's body.

Brady told the investigators that he'd met with Danny Costa to discuss the hit at Lucca—the restaurant—precisely one week before the murder. The response to a grand jury subpoena for Costa's credit card records documented that he used his MasterCard at that North End restaurant on that very day. Flanagan went through all the forensic reports several times and didn't find anything that the defense could use to its advantage.

Flanagan organized the grand jury testimony and the scientific evidence in individual files, prepared a cover letter to defense counsel identifying everything he was turning over, printed out a copy for each lawyer, stacked everything neatly on a table, and penned a note to his assistant to have the stuff hand-delivered by a messenger. Nice and tidy. And it stunk.

Flanagan flicked off the overhead fluorescent lights. He'd needed them for going through the papers, but their harsh glare was no good for meditative thinking. Now there was only a small pool of light from the green library lamp on his desk. He leaned back in his chair and contemplated the piles of material in the shadows on his worktable. Flanagan had requested the court to give Brady immunity for his testimony at the grand jury. Giving a witness immunity meant that the Commonwealth couldn't use his testimony, or any leads that were developed from it, to prosecute him for any crimes. Once the judge issued the immunity order, Brady exploited it by admitting his involvement in nine murders, in addition to Francini's murder. He was eager to talk about as many crimes as he remembered. Technically, it would be legal to prosecute him if new evidence independent from his testimony surfaced. But as a practical matter, it would be too hard to prove that such evidence wasn't connected to what the Commonwealth learned from Brady.

Some of Brady's victims were rival hoodlums that he'd eliminated to further his own criminal interests; others seemed to have been spur of the moment killings triggered by his vile temper. Brady cut off one victim's head on Halloween and left it on the front steps of the victim's apartment building, among some carved pumpkins. Some early trick-or-treaters discovered this grotesque adornment. Those second graders might never go out on Halloween again.

As a practical matter, they'd given Brady a bath in immunity that washed away responsibility for all his murders. The FBI made the deal and Flanagan was stuck with it. The D.A. agreed to do the FBI's bidding and Flanagan took his orders from the D.A. The deal wasn't worth it. Brady claimed all the murders were solo jobs, except for Francini. As a result, they could only prosecute this one case. Brady would walk away, and all the Commonwealth would get were the Francini co-defendants. They were just whipped cream on shit. Brady was clearly the worst of the bunch.

The FBI maintained its own agenda when it came to organized crime. Flanagan knew of two other cases where they'd made deals with guys who'd committed multiple murders. Brady might've put more on the table for the government than his testimony against Costa and Marino, but Flanagan had no idea what that might be. Nor were the agents going to tell him.

Flanagan had made deals with bad guys before. It was

necessary. Brady, though, was the most repulsive killer Flanagan had encountered. It was torture to be in the same room with him. Rizzo and Smith would sit joking with Brady as though they were friends. Flanagan knew street cops who had more in common with the people they arrested than with law-abiding citizens. These FBI agents seemed no different.

Flanagan didn't have any choice—he was forced to prosecute this case. He'd play to win. Getting convictions on a mob murder would be good for the D.A.'s office, and it'd be great for Flanagan's career. For sure, it'd be nice to have more evidence linking Costa and Marino to the crime. There might be an innocent explanation for the credit card evidence. But Brady's testimony would be enough if that's all he had.

Flanagan would feel better about it if he knew a little more about these men before sending them to prison for the rest of their lives. The vice cops told him that Costa was part of Romano's gambling operations. That didn't make him a murderer. Nobody knew anything about Marino. Maybe Flanagan's detectives would dig up something before the trial.

Eventually, he'd be able to put the stink of the Brady deal behind him. Even so, Flanagan didn't want to keep prosecuting homicides much longer. He spent way too much of his time in the company of scumbags. He'd like to know what normal people thought about during the course of a day's work. The incumbent in the local congressional district was talking about retiring. Some of the money people in the party had already asked him if he'd be interested in running for the seat. He was giving it serious thought. He held no great respect for politicians, but he presumed they were somewhat more moral than killers.

14

Rizzo balanced four glasses of beer on a tray and made his way to a dark corner of Magoun's, at the base of Winter Hill. He preferred the working-class feel of Somerville to the privileged academic vibe of Cambridge. A crowd of softball players was loudly reliving the high points of their game at the long bar that ran down one side of the room. The tables scattered across the floor were mostly empty. Here Rizzo and Smith were able to talk to Eddie and Willie Baker, the informants who'd helped them recruit Brady, without being overheard.

Eddie had just wrapped up his drunk driving sentence. Rizzo wanted to meet with Eddie as soon as he got out of jail to pump him for whatever he'd learned on the inside. Inmates were stupid about spilling their guts to each other.

Rizzo sat down sat the table and passed out the beers. "How you doing, Eddie?"

"Now you want to know," Eddie said. "If you're so concerned about me, why'd you let me rot in Dedham for six months?"

"The FBI doesn't have any jurisdiction over drunk driving,"

Rizzo said.

"You coulda done something. Talked to the prosecutor on my behalf. Shit. You're supposed to be protecting me. Instead, you just looked the other way."

Rizzo wagged his finger at Eddie. "Getting drunk and smashing up your car isn't what our deal is about."

Eddie was steaming. His face was red, which made the scar from his mouth to his ear all the whiter. He laid his palms flat on the table and was starting to rise like he was about to push himself up and walk out of the place.

"Calm down," Willie said. "You didn't really want an FBI agent showing up in Dedham District Court on a chicken shit driving under to get the prosecutor to drop it. You may as well put on one of those jackets that says FBI on the back. That wouldn't go over too great in the joint."

"Easy for you to say," Eddie said. "You weren't doing the time."

"Rizzo's kept you out of a lot of trouble, and you know it," Willie said. "You'd still be serving time for that little business at the 7-11 if he hadn't stepped in."

Two years before, Eddie lost it when the kid working the register told Eddie to fuck himself when he demanded the money in the till. Eddie hadn't taken his gun out yet and the kid didn't think he was serious. Eddie went over the counter and beat the guy half to death, like he'd enjoyed having the excuse to do it. The victim was so badly messed up that his ID of Eddie was shaky, at best. Rizzo found someone to put Eddie at a poker game miles away at the time of the robbery and vouched for the alibi witness's credibility with the prosecutor. The charges were dismissed. Rizzo didn't like the fact that his fingerprints were on the deal.

Now Rizzo said nothing. They all drank their beers in silence. Rizzo went to the bar and got another round.

"I may have something for you," Eddie said to Rizzo when he got back. "But in the future, you gotta take better care of me."

"Let's hear it," Rizzo said.

"You remember them guys that walked into the jewelry store on the second floor of the Jewelers' Building on Washington Street in Boston in broad daylight and walked out with about a hundred grand worth of diamonds?" Eddie asked. "About a year ago?"

Rizzo took a sip of his beer. "The insurance company didn't want to pay because the video camera wasn't working." He remembered the heist. Nobody had been arrested for it. "Everyone figured it was an inside job."

"No way," Eddie said. "It was Tommy O'Neill and a couple of his Charlestown guys. Tommy's brother was doing a stretch at Dedham and he told me all about it. They got special locks on all them places so you can't just walk in there. The three guys put on their best suits and got cleaned up real nice, so they'd be buzzed through. They wait until no one else was in the place, then in they go."

"Who are the other guys?"

"You got me. You bust Tommy and you'll find out. Anyway, there's only two people working there, an old man and a young guy standing behind a case full of necklaces. Tommy and his crew go through the door, and immediately jerk out their guns and tell them to keep their hands on the counter. They don't want them pulling alarms. Then Tommy's buddy puts his piece right under the young guy's nose and he says to the old man—he figures he's in charge—'My partner here is gonna give you a bag and if you don't want to see your friend's brains plastered all over the wall, you fill it with diamonds. And don't trigger any alarms, or you'll both get it.' Tommy hands the old man the bag and he gets right to work."

Rizzo scratched his head. "What were they going to do if some other customers came along?"

"Maybe shoot them. These are the kind of guys who don't give a shit, you know what I mean? Anyway, no one did. They was only in there about two minutes. The old guy fills the bag, they put their guns away, and they just walk out of the building. They tell him they have someone watching to make sure he don't pull any alarms for at least five minutes. This is complete bullshit, but the old guy's already so scared he's pissing his pants, and so he waits."

"It doesn't sound like we can make a case," Smith said. "We can't put you on the stand and you've only got hearsay from the brother anyway."

Eddie smiled. "They didn't wear any masks. And Tommy O'Neill is easy to identify. He got whacked with a hockey stick when he was a kid and it left a long scar on his forehead. Worse than mine. You put him in front of the clerks from the jewelry store and they'll pick him out."

Rizzo's eyes narrowed. "The cops must have shown them mug books."

"He's never been busted. They don't have his picture."

Smith turned to Rizzo. "This isn't worth it. If it ever comes back to Eddie, he gets blown and all we get is some punk with no previous record."

"Harry, it's not about O'Neill," Willie said. "I know this kid. He's tough, but he doesn't want to go to prison. He'll make a deal with you and give you somebody you want."

"I don't care about the punks he did this with. I mean it's a decent heist, but they're still small-time," Smith said.

Willie took a long pull on his beer. "He's gotta sell the diamonds to somebody, doesn't he? What would you say if I told you it was Frank Romano?"

This was getting better. All roads lead to Romano. Rizzo leaned in, closer to Willie. "Was it?"

"It could be," Willie said.

Rizzo held up his hand like a stop sign. "Romano doesn't deal directly with guys like O'Neill. He'd never even take a meeting with him."

Willie thought for a minute. "No, but what if he sold them to Romano's friend Danny Costa?"

"You're saying if we bust O'Neill, he'll tell us he sold the diamonds to Costa?" Rizzo asked.

"I'm saying if you bust O'Neill, he'll tell you whatever you want."

Rizzo's pulse quickened. He'd been working to get something on Romano for years. Nailing him would be like winning a World Series ring. At times, Rizzo'd seemed to be getting close, but the bastard was clever and eluded him. Rizzo had thought he might get to Romano through the Francini murder. The plan was to flip Danny Costa. Costa's lawyer made it clear that wasn't going to happen. And Brady never talked to Romano about any of the people he killed. Rizzo needed something new. If O'Neill sold a hundred grand in diamonds to Costa, it would make sense that he was buying them for Romano. They'd tell O'Neill to say that Costa happened to mention that.

It would be even better to show that Romano set up the deal in the first place. O'Neill would never have risked stealing the diamonds unless he already had a buyer. He'd have known that Costa didn't have that kind of money. O'Neill would have asked Costa where the dough was coming from. Costa would have told O'Neill it was Romano's plan. With Romano in on it from the beginning, he goes down for armed robbery—a life sentence.

It would work.

Rizzo had no problem plotting out the factual details. And if the Bakers were right, O'Neill would go along with whatever script Rizzo came up with. He wasn't that confident about the legal technicalities, however. That was Smith's job. He got Smith to go along with him on his schemes. They usually got results. Smith was lazy, but he was a smart guy and he knew something about the rules of evidence.

"Is what O'Neill says Costa told him admissible in a trial against Romano?" Rizzo asked Smith.

"We'd have to ask someone in the U.S. Attorney's Office. It might be hearsay. But if they bring a conspiracy case, Costa and Romano would be co-conspirators and I think they could use whatever Costa says against Romano," Smith said.

Rizzo reached in his pocket and took out five C-notes, folded them over once and passed them discretely across the table to Eddie. "Okay, thanks. We have to think about what we're going to do with this. We'll get back to you. In the meantime, stay out of trouble."

"I stay out of trouble, I'm not much use to you, am I?" Eddie asked.

"Just don't get caught doing anything stupid," Rizzo said.

Smith left some money on the table for the beer and they walked out of the bar. They headed down Broadway toward Boston with Rizzo driving. He lit a cigarette and turned to Smith. "Think this could work?"

"Well, if O'Neill's going to be our witness, we'll have to see what kind of a poker face he has."

The play was risky. Rizzo didn't know O'Neill like he knew the Bakers. Brady was protecting Eddie on the Francini murder and the Bakers had probably figured out that the agents were going along with it. In any event, the Bakers needed Rizzo and Smith as much as the agents needed them. And Brady was going to perjure himself in a first-degree murder case. The penalty for that was life without parole if it ever came out. So, Rizzo didn't worry about those three. He didn't know if he should trust O'Neill to the same extent. Rizzo would have to meet O'Neill and feel him out. If this deal with O'Neill worked and Rizzo got Romano—yeah, that would be something. No question, the judge would give Romano the maximum for armed robbery. He'd never see sunshine again. Unlike Rizzo, who already saw himself on the beach in Florida.

15

Susan was reading the discovery material with Coughlin. They passed the documents back and forth. Flanagan had responded to the defense motions with a letter, enclosing copies of the scientific evidence reports. He gave formal notice that Joseph Brady would be a witness for the state and that the government would consider his cooperation at the time of his sentencing. Flanagan disclosed that Brady would be going into the witness protection program. Given his lengthy rap sheet, Brady was getting one hell of a deal. The prosecutor's letter said that no evidence would be offered from the searches of the defendants' homes and that none of them had made any statements that would be introduced at trial.

The reports reminded Susan of the time her Scientific Evidence professor arranged with the Medical Examiner's office for one student to attend an autopsy. Her professor picked Susan, and she reported to the class afterward. It was the highlight of the semester.

The M.E. performed an autopsy on a man who'd been

found hanging from a tree in the woods with a heavy electrical extension cord around his neck. The police presumed it was a suicide, and the pathologist examined the dead man to determine whether there was any evidence of homicide. He carefully probed every inch of skin, looking for wounds. Then he hovered over the body and made a Y-shaped incision with a scalpel, pulled back the flesh, and opened the deceased's chest. Noxious smells flooded the room. Susan became light-headed and choked down the bile in her throat. The doctor removed the internal organs one at a time, weighed them on a little scale, and bagged them for submission to the lab. He rinsed the inside of the body with a hose. Susan stepped forward and peered down into the hollow cavity inside the rib cage, where the front of the spinal column was exposed. "This is unbelievable," she said softly. "Unbelievable."

The pathologist began cutting into the skull with a circular saw. Susan jumped back at the grinding noise and turned away. The doctor reached into the skull and removed the man's brain, dropped it on a slab and cut it into sections, like carving slices off a loaf of bread. They lay there inertly. He completed his exam. "No evidence of foul play," he said.

The autopsy took about an hour and Susan managed to keep from puking. Later, sitting on her couch at home, she found herself trembling. The experience was surprisingly spiritual. She searched for what constituted the essence of a person. The brain? Where did all the information stored there go, once it stopped working? A soul? She'd wanted the pathologist to put everything back together and make the man work again. The disassembled body showed her that the whole was more than the sum of its parts. But she couldn't wrap her mind around what else there was.

Now, she held reports from an actual case in her hands. She knew enough not to expect the magic that television gives to CSI. The computer whirs and out pops the name of the perp. Not in real life.

Crime scene technicians examined Brady's van and found old bloodstains. They extracted DNA from that blood and compared it with Francini's DNA. No doubt that it was his blood in the van. The technicians vacuumed the vehicle and collected twelve human hairs, which they compared with hair taken from Francini's head at the autopsy. The report said that the hair from the van and Francini's hair were "similar in all respects that could be observed microscopically."

Coughlin held one of the reports in his hands. "Look, the lab report says the hair found in the trunk was a match with Francini's," he said.

Good god, he really didn't know anything about scientific evidence.

"They can't really claim it's a *match*," Susan said. "All the expert is qualified to say is that the hair in the trunk *could have come* from Francini. The expert can't *identify* the hair in the trunk as coming from Francini. There's no database indicating how common the various characteristics of hair are, or how many people have hair with the same set of characteristics. The lab tech couldn't even tell us how many people there are in Massachusetts who might also have been the source of this hair."

Susan showed Coughlin the report on the fibers that the police had collected from Francini's clothing. It said, "In every observable respect the fibers found on Francini are similar to the carpet in the van."

"All that means is that they were nylon, the same color, the same length, and so on," Susan said. "An expert wouldn't have a sufficient basis to say they definitely came from the van. They might have come from any car of that make and model from the same year, and perhaps from a large number of other vehicles that used the same carpet."

"Judges tell jurors to use their common sense," Coughlin said. "The average juror will buy the combination of the hair and fiber evidence. And it's a moot point, given the DNA evidence.

The jury is going to conclude that Brady is telling the truth about killing Francini and transporting his body in his van."

Susan couldn't quarrel with that. Her conclusions about the limitations of the hair and fiber evidence were only of academic interest. If the experts exaggerated the significance of their findings, they'd be able to call them on it, but it wouldn't make any difference. Too bad. She'd been looking forward to using what she'd learned about trace evidence in a real case. She read through the reports again, this time looking not for what they said, but what they didn't say. Coughlin, meanwhile, lost interest and was looking at other papers on his desk. He gave up so quickly. Disgusting. She'd hoped that their meeting would be like a little seminar, in which she could learn something from an experienced lawyer. She should have known that wasn't going to happen.

Susan finished going through the papers and put them down. No forensic evidence tied Marino or Costa to the crime. "There's nothing about Marino in here," she said. "The whole case against our client rises or falls on Brady's credibility."

"Flanagan will use this evidence to bolster his credibility," Coughlin said. "It proves that the basic physical facts of his story are beyond dispute. Other than our client's claim that he's innocent, the only attack we can make on any part of Brady's story is to question the motive for the killing. We can put Rena Posso on the stand to say that Francini wasn't supporting her and didn't buy her condo. We'll be able to prove that. Her testimony, however, doesn't prove that Francini wasn't stealing from Romano. It just shows he wasn't spending the money on her. You know what? Even if Francini wasn't supporting Rena, Romano might've thought he was. Let's face it, most people would find it hard to believe that a beautiful, talented woman like Rena was attracted to Francini, much less in love with him. It makes more sense to think he was her sugar daddy."

Susan wondered what attracted Rena to Francini. The argument that Romano might have incorrectly assumed that the attraction was based on money hadn't occurred to her. Coughlin owned a brain after all. At least when it came to thinking up arguments for the prosecution.

This was depressing. She sifted through the reports and looked at Flanagan's letter again. If only she had a brilliant insight that would allow them to use this material to their advantage, but there was just nothing there. All they had at this point to challenge Brady's story was Rena and the fact that someone getting Brady's deal might say anything the government wanted him to. Coughlin was right. That wasn't much.

In law school, she'd fantasized about working on a murder case. The excitement, the drama. She'd pictured herself assisting a lawyer who'd stop at nothing to unearth evidence of his client's innocence. Someone who had the skill to somehow turn bad facts around and use them to the defendant's advantage. Someone who'd hammer away at witnesses until they gave up the truth. Maybe she'd seen too many old Perry Mason TV shows. There was nothing like that here. Coughlin was just going through the motions. She needed to get him to start working this case.

16

"Patty Marino is on the phone," Coughlin's secretary said. "Bobby won't be back from court until late."

"I'll get it," Susan said. She picked up the extension on her desk.

"Hey, Patty," she said.

"Listen, Nicky and I talked about the case," Patty said. "I remembered that we'd run into Brady once. I don't know why neither of us thought about it before. Maybe we were so frightened that we blocked it out."

"Oh, really?" Susan said. "Tell me about it."

"One night, a little over a year ago we went to Magoun's to watch the Sox and have a couple of beers. Nicky was in the john and I was alone at the bar. This guy comes over and offers to buy me a drink. He was creepy. He put his hand on my shoulder and was—like leering at me, you know what I mean? He was drunk. I told him, 'Hey, I'm here with my husband.' He goes, 'I don't see any husband,' and calls over to the bartender to give me another beer. I tell the bartender thanks, but no thanks. This guy was leaning on me at this point, so I sort of pushed him away. He gets pissed off and says to me, 'You're pushing me? Who the fuck do you think you are?' I started to get scared."

Susan scribbled notes on a pad. "I don't blame you."

"Just then Nicky gets back, in time to hear the guy swearing at me. He says, 'She's my wife, take your hands off her.' The guy turns to face him, and Nicky realizes it's Brady. He'd heard about him—that he was a tough guy. Nicky says, 'There's no problem, we don't want any trouble, we're leaving.' Brady says, 'Your wife is a fucking bitch.' Then Nicky loses it. It was so fast. I didn't even see it coming. Nicky pastes the guy right in the face. Brady goes down and just sits there on the floor. Doesn't even try to get up. Nicky drops a twenty on the bar to cover our beers and we beat it."

Susan pounded her desk with her hand. This was huge. Nicky had knocked Brady on his butt. This was something that would explain why Brady would accuse an innocent man of murder. It was exactly the kind of thing they needed.

"Patty, this is great."

"Yeah, well, we get in the car and I say, 'Nicky you're my hero, but what happens now?' He tells me who the guy was. I'm scared to death. Nicky says, 'Maybe he's too drunk to remember what happened.' We go home."

Susan wondered how she'd feel if she'd been in a bar and her date got into a fight with a real gangster. The whole scene was foreign to her experience. Wiseguys didn't come into Gabriella's. Well, except for Frank Romano. He probably didn't get into fistfights. He must have a couple of men whose job that was. Some of the guys at law school were on the macho end, but they probably weren't really tough. They wouldn't take a swing at Brady. If she'd been Patty, she would've pissed in her pants.

"I assumed Brady might've figured he deserved it and just dropped it," Patty said. "I forgot about it. Now I think this case is payback."

"You bet. I'm going to tell Mr. Coughlin about this right

away. You know, you might have to testify at the trial."

She didn't have to check with Coughlin to know that Patty was going to be an important witness. This was the first concrete thing they had to undermine Brady's credibility. Maybe it would finally motivate Coughlin to get his ass in gear.

"Oh, my god, I'd be so nervous I'd die. But you know I'd do anything for Nicky."

Susan nodded. Unfortunately, that's exactly what the prosecutor will say.

"Patty, did anyone else you know see this happen?"

"No, and it was the only time we've ever been in that place. We heard it was a good bar and wanted to try it, but we never went back."

"What about the bartender?"

"There were two bartenders, a guy, and a girl. They were young and they were white. That's really all I can say about them."

"Patty, please do something for me. Just close your eyes and try to see yourself back in Magoun's. Can you do that? Are you there?"

"Sort of."

Susan stood up and paced back and forth behind her desk. "Push whatever else you're thinking about out of your mind. Think about what you and Nicky were wearing that night. Get a mental picture of the bar. Look at what's behind the bar. Look at the rest of the room, the tables, any people who might be around. Look at your glass of beer. Now, look at the male bartender. Watch him moving around. Pouring drinks. Look at his face. Tell me what you see."

"Like I said, he's a young white guy."

"Tell me every detail you see, whether you think it's important or not."

"He's just a guy. Wait. He has a ponytail. He has long hair tied back in a ponytail."

Well, that was something. Susan wasn't sure, though,

whether she'd evoked a real memory, or whether Patty was stretching to come up with some particulars just to please her.

"Look for the female bartender," Susan said. "Watch her pouring drinks. Look at her for a minute and tell me what you see."

"She's got dark hair. That's all I remember."

"What do you think Nicky saw when he looked at her?"

"I don't know."

"Try to put yourself in his head. What did he see?"

"You know what? She's wearing a Red Sox jersey with Varitek's name on the back."

Susan was pleased with that. Patty seemed confident about this detail. Susan had used three of the methods from the cognitive interviewing technique she'd read about—the mental picture, asking for details, and asking the witness to look at the scene from another's person's perspective. She had enough to start looking for these folks.

"That's good. If you or Nicky remember anything else, let me know. Don't mention this to anybody, and tell Nicky not to talk about it at the jail."

"We never talk about the case with anyone except each other."

"Good. You never know how someone else might twist your words."

"Are you going to try to find the bartenders?" Patty asked.

"You bet."

"Thanks," Patty said. "And you know what? I talked to the kids about what's happening. And I made Nicky let me bring them to the jail. They were scared when we first got there, but they were so happy to see their dad they didn't care where they were. He was pleased I brought them and now we're going to see him every week."

"I'm glad to hear that. Call me whenever you want to talk or if you have any questions. Hang in there."

Susan hung up. This new information answered the

question of why Brady would accuse an innocent Nicky Marino of murder. Admittedly, taking a punch wouldn't be enough for most people to send an innocent person to prison for life. Brady was apparently a vicious sociopath. He probably didn't need much of a reason.

The problem was that jurors would expect Patty to go to bat for her husband. Brady would deny the whole thing. To prove it, Susan would have to find one of the bartenders or someone else who was in Magoun's that night. It was over a year ago, which didn't bode well for an investigation just getting started now.

She headed over to the courthouse. Coughlin was sitting on a bench outside the courtroom where his case was tried. The corridor was dirty and littered with paper—scribbled notes, gum wrappers, pages from *The Herald*. The first time she'd come to the Boston Municipal Court, she'd possessed an idealized notion of what a courthouse would look like. Orderly, clean, people speaking quietly in respectful voices. Instead, the reality was that by four in the afternoon the house of justice looked like a deserted bus station.

Her boss was slumped against the back of the bench. His tie was pulled to the side and the top button of his shirt was open. The lids of his eyes drooped.

"The client got convicted," he said. "I'd won the case for the guy who looked so good on the booking video. So, I decided to try this one too. There was a good chance of getting the Breathalyzer thrown out. The only other evidence of intoxication was the cop's testimony about the field sobriety test. I thought I could beat the case."

"Didn't the judge keep the Breathalyzer out?"

"He did. And the cross of the cop went great. He said the defendant failed the straight-line test. I asked him whether the straight line was the centerline on the road, the white line on the side, or whether he had drawn a line with chalk. Get this—he said it was an imaginary line. We had the case won. I mean, are you kidding? The guy's supposed to satisfy the cop he's walking straight on an *imaginary* line? Then the client wanted to testify, and I let him take the stand. That was a mistake. I should've left well enough alone. On cross, the prosecutor asked him how he did on the straight-line test. He says, 'I was doing okay for most of it, but I really fell off it near the end.'"

She laughed out loud. "I'm sorry, Mr. Coughlin, but that's not your fault. Maybe on some subconscious level, your client wanted to be found guilty."

"At least the judge wasn't bad. He gave him a five hundred dollar fine and no jail time. He didn't lose much by going to trial. Still, it should've been a not guilty."

"Maybe I can cheer you up. Patty Marino called. She says that a year ago Brady made a pass at her at Magoun's Bar in Somerville and Nicky slugged him. That gives him the motive to drag Nicky into the Francini murder, even if he didn't do it. The only witnesses she knew of were the bartenders, and she gave me their description. Can we make a motion for funds for an investigator?"

"They're just now coming up with this? Marino slugged Brady? You think maybe they made this up?"

"I don't think Patty's the kind of person who would lie. Even to help Nicky."

"We'll have to check it out. It won't mean much without corroboration. The judges usually don't give you a lot of money for an investigator. You can't buy very much of his time. Pretty soon you have to go back for more funds and the whole thing drags out."

"What about Richard's investigator? If we can undermine Brady's testimony about Nicky, that would also impeach Brady's testimony about Costa."

"We can ask him. By the way, how come you call him Richard, but you always call me Mr. Coughlin? Why don't you just call me Bobby?"

"My father told me always to call an older man 'Mister' unless he asked me to call him by his first name. Richard asked me to use his first name, but you never did."

Coughlin winced when Susan called him an older man. That was just as well. She was afraid he had a little crush on her, and she'd like to nip that in the bud. She was having enough trouble getting him to take her seriously. If he was thinking of her in sexual terms, there'd be that whole dimension in which she might disappoint him. She had no interest in that. She did have her eye on Richard Charles, though. He had a way about him, and he exuded confidence. He got things done once he set his mind to them. It might be a bad idea to entertain such thoughts, but she didn't work for Richard. Besides, nothing was going on. Not yet.

Her boss stood up and picked up his briefcase. "Tell you what, if you have time, let's go back to the office and call Richard and see if he wants to work with us on this."

She smiled. "Okay, Bobby."

17

Bobby should have been more excited than he was regarding the lead that Patty had supplied as he sat at Richard Charles's conference table for a meeting with the investigator. Still, the new evidence was good though not strong enough to guarantee an acquittal. And Marino would get his hopes up about beating the case. It would be harder to bring up the idea of taking a plea. Bobby was having trouble sleeping, and food didn't taste the same anymore. He'd taken Marie out to dinner at Legal Sea Foods and he'd left half his lobster on his plate. He never did that.

Richard finished introducing his investigator, Paul Finn. He was a gregarious Irishman in his mid-fifties, a good-looking guy with a wide smile and quick wit. He dealt with his receding hairline by wearing his hair short. Bobby had seen him a few times at the gym where he worked out, beating out a steady rhythm on the speed bag. Finn had been a homicide detective for the Boston Police and took retirement after twenty-five years on the job. He probably enjoyed both his pension from the City and his income as a private investigator. You could live well that way. Richard said he'd used him in several cases.

"Susan got a lot of information from Patty," Finn said. He turned to Susan. "From what I've heard about what you've been doing, you seem to be a natural at investigation."

"I just hope the bartenders will still be working at Magoun's," she said.

"The problem isn't finding the bartenders," Finn said. "Even if they've moved on, we'll track them down. The problem is persuading them to testify. They'll be scared to death of Brady and his friends."

"What kind of a reputation does Brady have?" Richard asked.

"The word on the street is he's a mean bastard and a cold-blooded killer. They say he's killed at least a half dozen, and maybe a dozen people. Murder means so little to him he might not even remember himself exactly how many people he's killed."

Bobby winced. He'd known that Brady had a heavy reputation, but the way Finn put it, and the way he'd dropped his voice, made the gangster sound even more formidable.

"What do we do?" Richard asked.

"It's tough. You know how hard it is to get witnesses to come forward in a criminal case. People are afraid to get involved. With someone like Brady in the picture, it's going to be that much harder. When I was working for the Department, we'd tell people we would try to protect them. Although anyone with any street smarts knew we didn't really have the resources to do that. And here we don't even have that. We'll just have to see what these people are like and try to find some way to motivate them," Finn said.

Bobby twisted his wedding ring on his finger. What if they couldn't protect their witnesses? They were required to disclose their witness list to the prosecution. Brady might have them wiped out. These people were just a couple of bartenders who happened to be in the wrong place at the wrong time, from their point of view. They didn't deserve to get killed.

"It might help if you come with me while I talk to people," Finn said to Susan. "Just the fact that there is a young woman on the case might reduce the fear factor."

This was getting worse. Finn wanted to put Susan on the firing line. She was Bobby's intern. He was responsible for her safety. Asking bartenders questions about Brady was a lot heavier than talking with Rena. Finn was about six-two, fit, and carried a gun, but he'd just admitted he couldn't protect people.

"I think you're right. I'd like to go," Susan piped up.

"I like your moxie," Richard said. "Stick with Finn. Don't do any nosing around on your own about Brady."

It wouldn't do any good for Bobby to raise the issue now. Richard wasn't bothered by the plan. He'd speak to Susan when they were alone.

"Let's go to Magoun's on Monday," Finn said. "It won't be that crowded."

The group broke up. Bobby and Susan left together.

"How did you get to be so tough?" he asked her, as they walked down the street. "You don't seem to be afraid of anything."

"I'm not really tough, Bobby. To tell you the truth, I'm frightened about doing this work with Finn."

"So why did you agree to it? I don't think it's a good idea. Finn could have found a licensed female investigator to go with him."

"I'm not sure I know myself. It sounds exciting. It's like talking to Romano. It gets my heart pumping. There's a lot more action on the street than in the courtroom. Getting close to that feels worth some risk. And the risk itself is somehow appealing, as long as it's not out of control. I'll be all right if I stick close to Finn. I mean we're just going to talk to witnesses."

He had no answer to that. He was afraid to challenge Susan any further on this. She might think he was a coward. He was supposed to be her supervisor, but somehow, she'd taken control of what she was doing.

Bobby walked into his office, closed the door, and sat down at his desk. Susan went back to Suffolk. There was a stack of pink telephone call slips in front of him. He pushed them aside and took the files out of his briefcase, dumping them on his desk. He leaned back in his chair and sat quietly, thinking about what Susan had done. For the first time in a long time, he began to wonder whether he could have become a better lawyer and a better man than he was.

18

Susan spotted Finn's dark blue Lexis as it pulled up in front of the law school on Tremont Street. She slid onto the passenger seat. Going for a ride with a private eye was exciting. Like riding off with Philip Marlowe in search of the Maltese Falcon.

"I have some ideas about how we should approach this tonight," Finn said. "Is it okay with you if I do most of the talking?"

"Let's give me a couple of lines, just so I get mentioned in the credits as having a talking part."

Finn colored. "I didn't mean any offense."

"Relax, Paul. I'm fine with you taking the lead. I've never done any investigation before. I'm looking forward to seeing how you work."

In fact, she had mixed feelings about this assignment. She was being used. Playing the role of a pretty girl to distract the bartenders from the fact that they were being interrogated. On the other hand, Susan agreed to go along, knowing full well what the deal was. She possessed some agency. She'd learn something by watching Finn work. And it was a relief to be with a professional who was comfortable taking charge.

"If we find the bartenders, I don't want to let them know right away that we're on the Francini case," Finn said. "That could spook them, and we might not get much out of them. Let's just get something to eat and chat for a while before I try to steer the conversation around to Brady."

"Sounds good to me."

Finn worked his way around the Boston Common to Storrow Drive, took the bridge over the Charles River, passed the Museum of Science, and headed out McGrath Highway to Somerville. He talked about the difficulties of getting witnesses to come forward in criminal cases. He'd butted his head against this problem both as a cop and as a private investigator.

"I don't know which I think is worse, people who won't come forward to help the cops put a guilty person away, or those who won't step up to help defend someone they know is innocent. I can't tell you how many people I've interviewed who *can't remember* something it wasn't possible to forget."

"What are they afraid of?"

"Who knows?" Finn said. "Most of the time they couldn't tell you themselves. Sometimes they're legitimately afraid of the defendant or his friends. But a lot of times they just don't want to get anywhere near a criminal case. Or maybe it's just public involvement in general. I mean look at how many individuals don't vote. And they come up with all kinds of bullshit reasons not to do jury service. We live in one of the freest countries in the world, and yet a lot of people are too afraid or too busy to enjoy their democratic privileges."

Susan hadn't expected philosophy from Finn. She thought about the people she knew in the North End, the people who worked in the restaurants and the little shops, and the people who were out of work. A lot of them didn't bother to vote. What if everyone at the bottom of the economic pyramid suddenly showed up at the polls? It wouldn't change anything unless they voted in favor of their own self-interest. People didn't understand where they stood on the food chain. They were brainwashed by the American dream. They believed they were going to get rich and benefit from things like tax cuts. For most people, there was no chance of that happening. The rich got richer. The poor stayed poor.

Only a handful of customers were scattered around Magoun's when Susan and Finn walked in. A young white guy with his hair pulled back into a ponytail was wiping down the bar. Susan caught Finn's eye and they nodded at each other. They sat down and asked him for menus. The Celtics-Knicks game was on three televisions along the length of the bar and a huge screen at the end of the room. The bartender came over to see what they wanted. "Are they up?" Finn asked.

"No, they're down—it was six points last time I looked."

"What's your name?"

"Jerry."

"I'm Paul," he said. "This is Susan."

"Nice to meet you." Jerry smiled. "The steak tips are good tonight."

Finn gestured toward Susan and she ordered the steak tips and a Sam Adams on tap.

"I'll have the same thing, only with a club soda with lime instead of the beer."

Jerry went to take care of the order. "Was it a mistake to order a beer?" Susan asked.

"No, that's perfect—very natural. I presume one or two beers isn't going make you tipsy."

They watched the basketball game. Susan had played intramural basketball at Smith, but she wasn't big enough to go out for the varsity squad. Now she missed playing team sports with other women. She'd loved going to a women's college. No male egos to put up with. In a way, she was on a team now for the Francini case, but she was the only woman, and Bobby wasn't exactly a team player.

Jerry brought their drinks.

"I've never been in here before," Finn said. "Seems like a nice place."

"Yeah, Monday night is always slow, but on Tuesdays, the trivia guy comes in and later in the week we set up buffets for the softball teams that play at Trum Field around the corner."

"You worked here long?"

"A few years. I'm getting my Ph.D. in history at Tufts, so this is pretty convenient."

"How much longer will that take you?"

Jerry wiped down the next section of the bar. "Another year probably. Where're you guys from?"

"I live in Southie," Finn said, "and Susan lives in the North End."

Jerry moved off to handle some drink orders from the waitress. They turned their attention back to the game. Boston tied the score.

One of the Celtics was at the line shooting a free throw. Jerry came back with their food. Susan said, "This is going in."

Jerry turned around to look. The ball fell cleanly through the net. He turned back and smiled at her.

"You called it. Another beer?"

"Sure," she said.

"What about you?" Jerry asked Finn.

"I'll just have another club soda, thanks."

Jerry pulled the beer and refilled Finn's drink, giving him a new slice of lime on a napkin.

"Steak tips okay?"

"They're great," Finn said. "Thanks for the tip, no pun intended. I'll buy you a beer if they let you drink one while you're working."

"Thanks, but I'll have to pass."

Jerry leaned comfortably against his side of the bar. "You must get some characters in here," Finn said.

"Oh, yeah, mostly locals, but every now and then somebody

recognizable comes in. Jason Varitek and some of the Sox were here one night. Someone's kid they knew was playing softball. The guy who does the weather on Channel Five came in, but everyone gave him so much shit, he hasn't been back."

"I love Varitek. He's a clutch player," Susan said.

"We used to have a girl tending bar who was over the moon for him, but she left," Jerry said. "If you want a real clutch player, Big Papi's your man."

Susan knew Finn wouldn't ask any more questions about the bartender who liked Varitek. It would be too obvious. They'd follow up on that later.

"My friend who told me about this place said that guy who supposedly shot that mob bookkeeper used to hang out in here— what's his name, Brady?" Finn asked.

"He used to come in. I guess he's in jail now," Jerry said.

"He's got quite a reputation. He ever cause you any trouble?"

"Not really. He did sort of get his ass kicked in here one night, though, quite a while ago. He was making a play for some woman. She didn't go for it and he called her a name. Her husband had come up while they were talking and, you know, he didn't like that, so he laid Brady out with one punch. Guy packed quite a wallop."

"You saw this?"

Jerry nodded. "Yeah. I was freaked out. Everyone said Brady was so tough. I was afraid he would do something, but he didn't. He just let the other guy walk out."

Susan was thrilled but didn't show it. A distraction was called for. She put a little nervousness into her voice. "You have fights in here very often?"

Jerry laughed. "No, don't worry. This place is safe, although the softball players can be pretty noisy."

Jerry went down the bar to pour drinks for the waitress again.

She lowered her voice. "We're not going to tell him who we are, are we?"

"No need to yet," Finn replied softly. "We've located our witness and he confirms what Patty said. Let's just finish our meal and head out."

When they were done, Finn asked for the check and left a generous tip on the bar. He waited until Jerry was looking his way before he got up.

"Take it easy, Jerry. Food was great—we'll be back."

Jerry waved. "Have a nice night."

Susan and Finn left the restaurant. She let out a huge breath. They had someone to back up Patty's story. They'd been lucky. It'd been easy so far, but they might have trouble convincing Jerry to testify. He'd been friendly, but as she well knew, that was his job. The fact that he was a Ph.D. student in history was encouraging. An intellectual was more likely to be motivated by principle. That's if he wasn't too frightened by Brady's reputation. Someone like Brady might go pretty far to intimidate or eliminate a witness. Killing didn't seem to bother him. Good thing Brady had no way of knowing that she'd developed the only two witnesses that the defense had so far.

—

Mike Rizzo sat alone at a table about fifteen feet from the bar, got up, and crossed to the window. It was a coincidence that he'd chosen to have his dinner at Magoun's that night. As soon as Susan came through the door, he realized who she was. She'd been with Coughlin at the defense table when Costa was arraigned. Rizzo's ears perked up when they started asking about Brady. He carefully followed the rest of their conversation with the bartender, but he couldn't hear the guy or Susan when they spoke softly between themselves.

Rizzo peered through the glass. Susan and the guy got into a Lexus and it pulled away. Rizzo jotted down the license number. He'd find out who the registered owner was as soon as he got back to his computer at the FBI. It was obviously no coincidence that someone from the defense team was asking about Brady.

The guy who the bartender said slugged Brady must be Nicky Marino. Brady wouldn't have been interested in Danny Costa's wife and wouldn't have dared to fuck with her. Costa was too close to Romano, and Brady wasn't that reckless. Susan was working for Marino's lawyer. The guy with her must be a private investigator.

What a stupid shit Brady was. He hadn't told Rizzo that he had a beef with Marino. Brady was probably too embarrassed to admit that Marino had decked him. Rizzo should have guessed there was something like this. Nicky Marino was a nobody. There had to be some reason why Brady would drag him into the story.

Up until this moment, Rizzo had thought just maybe Brady was telling the truth about Nicky Marino. Clearly, the part about Costa was pure fiction. Marino could've been there, however. God knows it might've taken three guys to lug Francini's body up to Rena's condo. Now it was clear Brady was lying about Marino. Brady wouldn't have gone on a hit with someone who'd knocked him on his ass in public. Rizzo and Smith had been careless. They should've asked Brady more questions about Marino. Now they'd have to do some damage control.

19

Susan's phone rang. She stumbled out of bed and picked it up. "Yeah," she said.

"Hi," Rena said. "Did I wake you?" Her voice was playful. "Can you come to dinner tonight? I'm auditioning for a part in a new play and want to read my lines to someone."

"I'd love to," Susan said. They chatted for a few minutes and then hung up.

It'd be fun to see Rena again, but developing a friendship with her was tricky. Nicky was probably innocent, but Susan couldn't rule out a slim chance that he'd shot Francini. Defending a guilty man didn't bother her. Most of her clients as a criminal lawyer would be guilty of something. Manipulating a friendship with the victim's girlfriend to get her job done was a different story. It would suck if being a lawyer required mucking up her personal life so she could do a good job in her professional life. It'd be helpful to have someone to talk to about this, but Bobby wouldn't provide much guidance. He didn't seem to have many existential moments.

That evening Susan stopped in the North End to pick up some supplies and headed over to Rena's condo. Rena answered the door with a wide smile. She was wearing jeans and a white t-shirt with a reproduction of a simple Picasso line drawing of a woman's face. The actress was as cool as Susan thought when they'd first met. She'd want to be friends with this woman even if Rena had nothing to do with the case. Trouble was, Rena had a lot to do with the case. Susan gave her a big hug.

Susan opened the paper bag she was carrying. "Here's some bruschetta from my father's restaurant. You should run them under the broiler for a minute or two just to heat them up. And here are some lemons."

"How perfect!" Rena said. "I picked up some fresh penne and made some arrabiata sauce. I've got some ice cream, so we'll have a little feast. What are the lemons for?"

"You know what they say—when God gives you lemons . . ."

"Make lemonade?"

"No. Make lemon drop martinis! You do have a martini shaker and glasses, don't you?"

They moved into the kitchen. The aroma of onions, garlic, and hot peppers fanned Susan's appetite, as a red sauce simmered slowly on the stove.

"Put some martini glasses in the freezer," Susan said. She pulled a bottle of citron vodka out of her bag and dumped the lemons on the counter. She expertly peeled them and sliced the fruit into sections that she tossed into the shaker with sugar. She mashed them together with a wooden spoon, added ice cubes and vodka, put the top on and shook it up. She spilled sugar into a dish and got the frosted glasses from the freezer and dipped them in the sugar to put a little around the rim.

Whenever she prepared food or made drinks for her friends, she was glad she'd grown up with a chef for a father. She almost never needed to consult recipes—she could just open the refrigerator, check the pantry, see what was on hand, and whip up something. That gave her a feeling of competence and independence that she treasured. She poured the drinks and they raised their glasses.

"To new friends," said Rena, "and my new bartender." The women sipped their martinis.

"There's a new play about a woman who cheated on her husband by having an affair with a United States Senator," Rena said. "I'm going to try out for the lead."

"Do you think it will be hard to play someone who's so duplicitous?" Susan asked.

"Playing any role is already duplicity," Rena said. "You set your real self aside and become someone else on the stage."

Susan wondered if that skill spilled over into Rena's personal life. It would complicate things if you were often tempted to act like someone other than who you really were. Everyone probably did some of that. Susan was more genuinely herself with her father than she was at the law office. With Bobby, she was required to act the part of the respectful law student, even though her feelings about him were more complicated. It seemed that he might've been damaged somehow, but it pissed her off that he didn't have much to teach her.

"Are you ready to get back in front of the public?" Susan asked.

"I'm not sure. I'm getting bored with just modeling, and I love working in the theater. But I'm anxious about it."

"I think you should give it a try," Susan said. "If you have a panic attack at the audition, you can always decide to wait a while longer. I bet you won't, and you may get the part. I'll back you up either way."

"You remind me of my best friends in drama school. It was a cutthroat environment, but there were a few of us who stuck together."

They moved to the living room. Overstuffed couches and chairs invited Susan to relax. The deep hues of a handmade Persian rug complemented the soft pastels of the upholstery. A picture window overlooked the Boston Harbor. Planes were taking off and landing across the water at Logan Airport. They stood for a while admiring the view from the fifteenth floor and then flopped down onto the couches.

Susan would probably never have an apartment this nice. She lived in a tiny one-bedroom in the North End, furnished with hand-me-downs and bargains from flea markets. She didn't even have anything from Ikea.

A stack of photographs lay on the table. The one on top was of Rena and Francini in front of Fenway Park. "Hey, this is a nice picture of you guys," Susan said.

"Oh, I forgot to put those away. I was just going through some old photos of Tony and some of his, ah, associates. I never got around to putting them in albums."

Susan picked up the top picture. She was dying to go through the others. She'd like to see who Francini's associates were and how he related to them. If Marino didn't kill him, she needed to find out who else had a motive to do so. That wasn't likely to be apparent from a snapshot, but she might see something that could point her in the right direction. And she might understand the case better if she saw what Francini looked like in life. It was macabre to think about him merely as a corpse who'd had his fingers cut off. On the other hand, going through these pictures wouldn't make the evening any easier.

"You can look at them if you want," Rena said. "That pile is from a Red Sox game."

Susan flipped through the pictures. Suddenly there was a picture of Francini standing with Joseph Brady and another man. Awkward smiles were plastered on all three faces. She picked up the photo. Unbelievable. Francini, with one of the guys who murdered him.

"Rena," she said, "The man on Tony's right in this picture is the guy who admitted killing him. Do you know Joseph Brady?"

Rena came over to the couch. "Let's see." She and Susan stared at the picture. Brady's dark eyes were foreboding. "No, I didn't realize that's who this was. We didn't go out that often with the men Tony worked with. Someone gave Tony a bunch of tickets to the game and so we went and some of these guys came along." Rena started to shake and sat down. Her eyes filled with tears.

As Rena's friend, Susan should drop this. The poor woman was already crying. She didn't know how upset Rena might get. The murder was three years ago, but Rena's emotions were still raw. Still, for Nicky's sake, Susan should find out as much as possible about these guys. "I'm sorry, this must be so painful. I have to ask, though, do you know who the third man in this picture is?"

"No. I took this before we went into the park. These two guys didn't talk much. If Tony said his name, I don't remember it. I only saw them once more. A couple of months later, Tony and I went to the European Restaurant in the North End. These guys were leaving as we arrived. They barely greeted each other. I asked Tony if they weren't his friends we saw at the ball game. Tony said, 'They're no friends of mine.' He used a tone of voice that made me think it would be a mistake to ask him any questions about it, so I dropped it."

"How long was that before Tony was killed?"

Rena thought for a minute. "Just a few weeks. We went to the ball game in the spring and then we ran into these guys in June and then Tony was killed in July."

"They look sort of friendly with each other in this picture," Susan said.

"Tony was never really that close with any of these guys—it was a job. Sometimes he needed to seem friendly with them, but mostly it was just an act."

Rena got up, walked quickly into the kitchen, and returned with a brown grocery bag. She was crying. She swept the pictures off the table into the bag. "I'm sorry," she said. "I never really knew any of these men. I don't need to save these. I'm going to throw them out." She took the bag back into the kitchen, and then dashed through the living room toward the bathroom, with tears running down her cheeks.

The picture with Brady and the third man was still on the table. It'd been under Susan's hand when Rena cleared the others away. She didn't seem to have noticed. Susan needed to find out who this man was. She picked up the photo and slipped it into her pocketbook.

She would never have done anything like this before she had someone else's life in her hands. Rena clearly wanted to toss these pictures and Susan took one without asking her. If she'd asked, Rena might've said no. Susan hadn't wanted to run that risk. She needed this picture. She just knew this guy was important, particularly since Francini had said both the mystery man and Brady were not his friends. Still, it was a betrayal of Rena to take it. There could be no good explanation for how it ended up in her purse. Susan's skin crawled.

Rena returned. She'd washed her face and was no longer crying. "Sorry about that," she said.

"No, I'm sorry." Susan was sorry her questions made Rena cry. Susan's whole body tensed up while she waited to see if Rena said anything about the picture.

Rena broke off a piece from one of the bruschettas and took a bite. She looked at Susan. "It's hard for you not to be preoccupied with the case, isn't it?"

Susan nodded, trying to remain outwardly calm. Then Rena took a large sip of her martini. She was still staring. "Let's talk about something else," Rena said.

Susan flopped back on the couch. Thank god Rena couldn't read her mind. Susan forced herself to act normally. "If you like the bruschetta," she said, "you have to come to Gabriella's some night. You'll be my guest."

They finished the martinis, opened a bottle of Chianti and got dinner together. The arrabiata sauce was almost good enough to be served in her dad's restaurant. She told Rena she loved it. Now that they were no longer talking about Tony, Rena became animated. She got out the script for the new play. She did a short scene, jumping back and forth to play all the roles. Susan was in stitches. Then Rena got Susan to read different parts, so she could respond to them. First, Susan read the part of a newspaper reporter interviewing Rena's character about her relationship with the Senator. She tried her best to imitate Barbara Walters's voice. Then Susan played the Senator in a tryst with Rena's character at the bar at the Hay-Adams. At first, she was a little creeped out by how seductively Rena came on to her, but then she got into being the Senator and it was fun. Susan almost forgot about the picture, but not completely. Around eleven o'clock, she realized she'd better go home and get some sleep.

As she made her way home to the North End, she thought about the ethics of what she'd done. To know whether taking the picture was worth it, she needed to find out who the third man was. The quickest way to do that would be to arrange another conversation with Frank Romano.

20

Susan sat at her kitchen table with a cup of coffee. She grabbed her cell and pressed the speed dial for her father. They chatted for a few minutes about the restaurant, then she got to the point.

"I need to get in touch with Frank Romano," she said. "Do you know how I can reach him?"

"What do you need Romano for?"

"I need to ask him something to follow up on what he came to talk to me about."

"I don't know, honey."

Susan glanced at her watch. "You don't know how to get in touch with him, or you don't know if you want me to?"

"It's one thing for him to come here, to the restaurant. I mean, I'm here, the whole staff is here, nothing can happen. For you to go looking for him is maybe a different story."

"Daddy, nothing will happen. He wants to help me, not see me get hurt. I just need a little more information."

"There's no one else you can ask?"

She hadn't considered that. Probably there was. Bobby wouldn't recognize the man in the photo, but Richard or Finn might. For that matter, Nicky or Patty might know him. Perhaps Susan was just using this picture as an excuse to see Romano again. She liked having access to him. It made her feel—she wasn't sure exactly how it made her feel. Maybe like an insider. It sure wasn't anything any of her classmates at law school was doing. Most of her teachers would disapprove. Maybe all of them. There was something about the way he spoke to her the last time. Like she could be trusted. Maybe the fascination had something to do with the fact that her father wouldn't tell her how he knew Romano. Susan would like to get to the bottom of that, but she wasn't about to ask Romano and didn't think he would tell her. She wasn't sure what drew her to this man that everything else in her life told her she should avoid. She'd better figure it out.

Talking to Romano was dangerous. Actually, that was one of the reasons Susan wanted to do it. Like riding a motorcycle at high speed, leaning into a curve. She'd never had the nerve to do that. She'd never been on a motorcycle at all. Her life was conventional when you got down to it. Seeking out a mob boss was spectacularly unconventional. She'd go with her gut. Besides, it was probably the fastest way to find out who the third man was.

"I don't think there's anybody else," she said. "I understand why you're worried, but it's important to the case, and I promise I'll only see him in a public place."

"I still don't like it."

"This is my job. You know I'm not going to call you every time I need to interview a witness. And a lot of them may be criminals."

"Romano isn't just any criminal. He's the boss and he's ruthless. And so are the men who work for him."

"I know that. I'll be careful. I just need to ask him a quick question. There's nothing to worry about. Just tell me if you know how I can contact him."

"No."

She checked her watch again. "You'd rather I just wandered around the North End, asking random people if they know where Frank Romano hangs out?"

"You're not going to do that."

They went back and forth. He held out for much longer than she'd expected he would. Finally, he relented. She assumed it was partly out of exhaustion and hoped it was partly because he wanted her to win.

"Oh, all right," he said. "I guess you're past me telling you what to do. I don't want you to think I don't trust your judgment. I've heard he usually has lunch at noon at Via Appia on Hanover. You can probably find him there."

"Thanks. I'll call you later this afternoon."

Susan was investigating a case. Still, it felt like she was doing something wrong. Something that a woman like her wasn't supposed to do. It reminded her of Mrs. Gianelli's class in high school. Susan went to see the teacher to discuss a topic for a paper. They'd only been talking a few minutes. An aide stuck her head in and said the principal needed to see the teacher in his office. Mrs. Gianelli asked Susan to wait and left the room. She wandered around, looking at pictures on the walls. She passed by Mrs. Gianelli's desk. The mid-term exam was sitting there. Susan turned over the cover sheet and read the first essay question. Then footsteps in the hall sent her dashing back to where she'd been sitting.

That night she prepared an answer to the question in advance of the exam. She got an A. She probably would have gotten an A anyway—she usually did. But she'd cheated. She never told anyone about it. All these years later it still bothered her. Susan believed she was a good person, but she couldn't forget about this. What she'd done wasn't all that bad. Probably everyone cheated at least once. Maybe not, though.

Susan thought about whether she'd always feel guilty about

taking that photo at Rena's last night. She had more justification for that, but it would probably haunt her just the same. She felt guilty about a lot of things. Some of the time it seemed silly. Like if she was reading the cases in the assignment for her criminal procedure class, she might feel guilty that she wasn't studying the materials for her tax class. She needed to get them both done, and it didn't make any difference which she did first. Criminal procedure was interesting, and tax was boring. If she put off studying tax, she felt like she was avoiding her responsibilities, even though she knew she'd get to it eventually. The result was that she undermined her enjoyment of criminal procedure by worrying about tax. Just like she undermined her enjoyment of her success in school by dwelling on that one history test question. Now it seemed like she was about to spoil the thrill of making progress on Nicky's case by sweating about how she got her hands on that photo. Screw that. She needed to keep things in perspective.

If Susan was being honest, she knew one reason why she'd taken the photo without asking Rena for it. She was attracted to the idea of doing something bad. Was that perverse? She didn't think so. Doing stuff you weren't supposed to do wasn't necessarily *evil*, or even perverse. She didn't want to be that predictable, good girl all the time. No doubt that was part of the attraction to Romano. She was a good person, went to school, studied hard, was going to be a lawyer. Somebody like her didn't hang out with mobsters. Not that she was exactly hanging out with Romano. She sort of wanted to, though. She wanted him to find her interesting. And a picture of a dead man standing next to his killer was pretty fucking interesting.

A few minutes before noon, Susan sat down at the bar at Via Appia and ordered an espresso. She almost asked for a whiskey. She was more nervous about seeking out Romano than she'd let on.

Romano came through the front door. He found her at the bar and walked straight to her, smiling.

"Susan, what a pleasure. How's your father?"

"He's fine. How are you, Mr. Romano?"

"I'm well." Romano had a little twinkle in his eye. "Do you just happen to be having espresso at my favorite spot for lunch, or may I assume that you dropped by to have a word with me?"

"I'd like to show you something and ask you a question about it if that's okay."

"If I can help you, I will. If it's something I can't talk about, I'll say so. This isn't the best place to have a private conversation, though. Let's take a little walk."

Apparently, Romano was afraid that the restaurant was bugged, given that he ate there on a regular basis. Susan was taking a stroll with the head of the Mafia to make sure the FBI didn't overhear what she was asking him about. That should satisfy the naughty cravings for today. To be sure, she didn't want the government to know how her investigation of the Francini murder was progressing. The idea of being subject to surveillance wasn't surprising, however. She'd read about the FBI's COINTELPRO surveillance of people in the civil rights movement in the sixties and seventies. She'd always assumed that if she became the kind of lawyer she wanted to be, she'd run afoul of the government at some point.

Romano took her elbow and they walked out to Hanover Street. The North End was his domain. It was like walking through medieval Florence with one of the Medici. Romano was a prince of this city, a modern student of Machiavelli. All the familiar coffee shops and neighborhood restaurants looked different with him at her side—smaller, less independent. The narrow streets of the neighborhood seemed to close in even further. The old men on lawn chairs in front of the social clubs looked down at the ground as they went by. A trace of fear infected the otherwise carefree European street life atmosphere. Susan chided herself. Romano didn't run everything. He didn't run Gabriella's. Still, she was glad they hadn't encountered anyone she knew. At least, she didn't think they had. Everything except Romano himself was sort of a blur.

"What would you like to show me?" he asked.

Susan fumbled in her purse, found the picture, and passed it over. Her hand was shaking.

Romano looked at it briefly and then handed it back. "What would you like to know?"

"I want to know who the other man is with Brady and Francini."

"What's your interest in him?"

"Rena Posso took this picture at a Sox game with some of Francini's associates. Later they ran into these men outside a restaurant. They barely acknowledged each other. Rena asked Francini why he didn't talk with his friends, and he said they were no friends of his."

Romano walked silently for a moment. Susan didn't interrupt his thoughts. They passed The Daily Catch, one of her favorite restaurants for lunch. Sicilian food. The whole place was about the size of her living room. The kitchen took up one corner and half a dozen tables for customers were crammed into the rest of the place. You could watch them prepare your meal. The puttanesca sauce on the homemade black pasta was to die for. She loved the fact that the color came from the ink they squeezed out of the squid.

Romano turned to her. "That's Eddie Baker, Brady's best friend. He and his older brother Willie are thieves, among other things. Eddie's a dangerous and violent man. The police suspect he's been involved in several homicides. Strangely, he's never been arrested for murder. Until you just told me, I didn't know Tony had any problems with him."

She was surprised that Romano knew what the police suspected and wondered what sources he possessed within the Department. She didn't know how much she could rely on what she'd seen in movies, but she assumed there were cops who took bribes from Romano. She had no idea what they might do for him and, obviously, couldn't ask.

"Mr. Romano, do you think this Eddie Baker might have been involved in some way in Francini's murder?"

"I couldn't say. Eddie Baker is capable of murder. If you and Coughlin decide to investigate this further, you shouldn't go anywhere near Eddie or Willie yourself. That's really all I can tell you."

The conversation was over. She shook hands with Romano and struck out for Bobby's office. It was past time to check in with her boss. He'd be pissed off about her meeting again with Romano. And Bobby seemed to freak out the more evidence she found suggesting that Nicky might be innocent. If Bobby ever became convinced that Nicky was innocent of Francini's murder, he'd have to try the case. Susan had seen enough to know the very idea terrified her boss. She'd have to handle him just right to keep things moving forward. Bobby hadn't told the other lawyers about anything that she'd turned up, except for Patty's story about Brady. Susan needed to get everything in Richard's hands. Good thing that men were predictable and easy to manipulate.

21

People Bobby met socially always asked him how he could stand the idea of representing someone who was guilty and getting him off. In reality, that prospect didn't trouble him, or other defense lawyers that he knew. In his practice, it didn't come up that much. Most of his clients confessed to what they'd done and pleaded guilty. On rare occasions, he'd gotten the charges thrown out for someone he thought was guilty, and figured he was just doing his job. That's how the system worked. It guaranteed that even someone who might be guilty could get a fair trial. But the risk that an innocent client would get convicted and go to prison was something else. For some reason, people never asked him about that at cocktail parties.

Susan came through the door of his private office. It startled him. He'd succeeded in largely putting Marino out of his mind for the past few days, and now all his anxieties about trying the case came rushing back. To make things worse, Susan looked like she had something up her sleeve again.

"I know you got a written report from Finn, but did you

want to talk about how things went at the bar?" she asked as she approached the desk.

Bobby shrugged.

"The bartender tells the same story Patty did," Susan said. "Brady had a reason to be angry at Nicky, although he brought it on himself. I don't know if the bartender will testify voluntarily. But if we subpoena him, he's not the kind of guy who'd lie about what he saw. He doesn't have an ax to grind, so once you get him on the stand, he'll make a good witness. We haven't told him yet that we're working on the case. The guy's a history Ph.D. student at Tufts, so he's not going anywhere."

"We can prove that Brady was upset with Nicky," Bobby said. "But is getting slugged while you're making a pass at somebody's wife enough to make you falsely accuse him of murder?"

"It would be if you're a guy with Brady's morals. He's a scumbag. He could care less about sending an innocent man to prison if he gets something out of it for himself," Susan said.

Bobby shook his head. "What does he get out of accusing an innocent man? He'll get a good deal for becoming a witness for the prosecution, but if Nicky's innocent, why doesn't Brady just rat out the guys he really did it with?"

"Yes!" she said. "That's the precise question we've got to answer. Who is it that Brady can't turn on and why can't he rat them out? Once we figure that out, we'll know who did the murder and we can show that our guy is innocent."

"Oh, no problem," Bobby said. "All we have to do is solve the murder ourselves, then figure out how to prove it, and Marino can skip home to his wife. Then after lunch, we can move on to the next case."

As soon as the words were out of his mouth, he felt bad. Susan was trying to be helpful, but it was one thing to come up with a lot of smart ideas and another to walk into a courtroom with them. The jury couldn't read Brady's mind and figure out if he was protecting someone. Brady sure as hell wasn't going to admit it on cross-examination.

"Look, I appreciate the point you're making," he said. "But winning a case by raising a reasonable doubt about whether the state's case holds together is hard enough. Taking on the job of proving that someone else is the real guilty party is almost impossible—that's the kind of thing that only happens in movies, not the Suffolk Superior Court."

Susan took a photo out of her bag and passed it across the desk. "Here's something else."

Bobby examined it. "That's Francini and Brady. Who's the other guy and what does this have to do with the case?"

Susan took a deep breath. "That's Eddie Baker, Brady's best friend. Evidently, there was some bad blood between Tony and Brady and Baker."

Bobby's head was swimming. "How did you get all this?"

"It was just luck. I was at Rena's for dinner and happened to see this picture when I was going through some photos on her coffee table. She didn't even know that it was Brady and Eddie Baker, although later she's the one who told me that Tony said they weren't friends."

"How did you explain that you wanted this?"

Susan hesitated. "Well, I didn't exactly ask."

"You just took it? You stole it?"

"She was throwing them out. I slipped this one into my purse."

Bobby threw his hands into the air. "Jesus Christ, Susan. This is a witness we need for the trial. She could get pissed off about this picture and refuse to cooperate."

Susan lowered her gaze. "She doesn't know I have it. She never said anything about it. She thinks she trashed it."

"I can't believe you did this. How did you find out who Baker was?"

"You won't like this either, Bobby."

"Maybe not, but I need to know who you're talking to."

Susan stuck out her chin. "Romano told me. He said that Eddie and his brother Willie are dangerous."

"You're talking with Romano again? And this time you sought him out? You're crazy! The D.A.'s office thinks that Romano is behind this murder."

"Yes, they do, but that's not what we think, is it Bobby? Aren't we working on the theory that someone is trying to pin this on Romano and his people? Isn't that where everything we've learned so far goes?" Susan clutched her hands together.

"It's far from convincing. If Romano really was behind it, he could be planting all sorts of ideas in your head," Bobby said. He picked up the photo, looked at it briefly and then threw it down on the desk. "This picture doesn't prove anything."

"By itself, it doesn't. But it gives us at least one idea of who we should be looking at, particularly given what Romano says about Baker." Susan looked Bobby right in the eyes. "I'm sorry I went to talk to Romano without talking with you. But this is good information. I was looking forward to hearing what you thought we should do next. I'd still like to know what our next move is."

Like it was up to her to set their agenda. Bobby should have seen this coming when she waltzed in that first time to say that Romano had paid her a visit. Bobby told her not to interview witnesses and she ends up dining with Rena. You'd think she was the fucking queen of the North End.

"Susan, you never should have taken the picture from Rena's house and you shouldn't have gone to see Romano, not without talking to me first," Bobby said.

"Well, I did. It's done. It's over and now we have this information. And it's something we can use."

Susan was jumping to conclusions. This picture wouldn't even be admissible in evidence. It had no apparent relevance. Francini could have had his picture taken with hundreds of people. But there might be something to the idea that Brady was protecting someone else by falsely accusing Nicky. He didn't know what to do with that. He needed some help.

"I think it's time to tell Richard what we know," Bobby said.

Susan nodded.

"We have to appear in front of Judge Morgan this coming Tuesday for a status conference," he said. "Let's see if we can get together on Monday."

This girl was so confident. No boundaries. Acting like she'd never been hurt. Well, he had been. He knew what happened when you went riding too high: things came crashing down. Maybe Richard could talk some sense into Susan.

22

Rizzo and Smith stared at a computer screen at the FBI office. The subject line of an email with a video attachment from the agent at the Via Appia suggested a romantic assignation: "Female Unsub and Romano." They played the video and there was Susan Sorella walking down Hanover Street with the crime boss. Rizzo rubbed his chin. "What the fuck?"

How could this girl possibly know Romano? Maybe her father was connected to the rackets somehow. Maybe through the restaurant. Rizzo had never seen Lorenzo Sorella's name on any reports. The idea seemed far-fetched. If Lorenzo were involved in any criminal activity, Rizzo should know about it by now. He'd been studying Romano's operation for ten years.

Rizzo pointed to Susan. "I can't believe her. On Monday night, she was in Somerville with a private investigator, Paul Finn, asking questions about Brady at Magoun's, where he apparently got knocked on his ass a while back by Marino. Then today, she meets Romano and takes a stroll with him."

"What?" Smith barked. "Brady had a fight with Marino?"

"Wasn't much of one. Brady was hitting on Marino's wife. The kid slugged him, and Brady went down. The asshole didn't bother to mention it to us, and now the defense team knows about it. I just happened to be sitting close enough to hear the bartender talking to them. We'll have to tell Flanagan about it so he can figure out how to deal with it."

"Shit," Smith said. "This girl is supposed to be just a law student working with that bum Coughlin. We figured he'd cop Marino out. Don't tell me he's actually working the case."

"I don't know what Coughlin's up to. But this student—Susan Sorella's her name. Her father owns Gabriella's on Hanover Street. She's coming up with stuff on Brady that even we didn't know about. I don't know how she knows Romano, or what they might have been talking about."

Smith brought his face closer to the computer screen. "Maybe Romano's cooperating with the defense."

"He probably knows it wasn't Francini stealing from him, but I doubt if he knows who it was. If he did, and he knew who killed Francini, he'd have had them snuffed by now. I wouldn't think he has much to offer the defense lawyers. He's talking to this law student about something, though."

———

The agents drove to the Sail Loft on Atlantic Avenue in the North End for lunch. They took a table at the end of the room overlooking the water, where they would have some privacy. Smith contented himself with a salad, but Rizzo splurged on the fried clam plate. His eyes feasted on the heaping mound of clams, french-fries, and fresh-cut lemons.

"You know what?" Rizzo asked. "This place smells of the sea like we were on Cape Cod. I'm going to miss this food in Florida."

"You'll find something to eat. They've got an ocean there you know. Maybe you'll find a friend with a boat, and you can catch your own fish. You like to fish. Or maybe you can stay with the

Bureau and work narcotics. Float around in the bay looking for bales of marijuana. 'Square grouper,' they call it."

Rizzo wasn't interested in going back to work. He was ready to take it easy. Dress in resort clothes and hang out at the beach and the golf course. Have a nice tan all year round. Maybe get a boat and go island hopping around the Caribbean. No more chasing bad guys. Last year he'd gone down to Clearwater beach with his girlfriend for a long weekend. They'd driven south to Treasure Island to see the sand sculpture competition. It was amazing—the figures these guys could make out of sand.

"How do you think your son will take you moving to Florida?" Smith asked.

Rizzo worried constantly about his sixteen-year-old boy. There'd been no question that his mother would get custody of him in the divorce. Rizzo's job took so much of his time that he'd never have been able to take care of his kid. He saw the boy as much as he could and when Rizzo could get a free weekend, they'd go down the Cape and go fishing. His son liked the fishing, but the two of them never seemed to have much to say to each other. The boy didn't seem to be very interested in much of anything, and Rizzo couldn't figure out what his son thought was important. When he asked the kid about school, all he got was, "It's okay." His son never asked him about his job, and Rizzo couldn't have said much about what he did anyway. Ever since Rizzo had moved out, he'd felt like a stranger to the kid, instead of his father. The boy's grades were slipping, and Rizzo suspected he might be smoking dope. He asked his ex about it, and she said, "Why, you want to bust your own son?" Rizzo didn't know how to make things better.

Rizzo didn't have anyone to talk to. Smith didn't have kids, and neither did Rizzo's girlfriend. He didn't think his son knew about her. He'd never brought her around when the boy was with him. The kid had enough trouble coping with the divorce without introducing her into the picture.

"I don't know," he said. "By the time that comes up, he'll

probably be finished with high school. Maybe I can get him interested in a college in Florida. You know what, maybe school vacation week in February, I'll take him down there and we can visit some schools."

"We've got some work to do before you can put in for that transfer," Smith said.

"Speaking of that," Rizzo said, "I had a little chat with Tommy O'Neill yesterday while you were in court. I'd gone to the jewelry store with a photo spread and the old guy picked Tommy out, just like Eddie said he would. Then I stopped by the bar where Eddie told me O'Neill usually has lunch and had a chat with him. I think we can get him to go along with us."

In fact, Rizzo was worried about the scheme with O'Neill but didn't want to share that with Smith. Smith might nip the whole idea in the bud before Rizzo had a chance to see how far he could push their witness. It'd been easy enough to get O'Neill to acknowledge his part in the robbery. It got more complicated when Rizzo suggested that there was someone else he wanted O'Neill to finger. At the mention of Romano's name, O'Neill's face turned white. Rizzo said he'd be back to talk to O'Neill later, instructing him to keep their conversation to himself. If the guy stewed for a while about the fact that he could go to prison if he didn't help the FBI, he'd probably be cooperative.

Rizzo and Smith finished lunch and headed back to the office. Rizzo wanted to ramp up their efforts to get information on Susan Sorella. They couldn't afford to let her derail the Francini case. He'd ask one of the newer agents to nose around Gabriella's to see if there was anything funny about the place. He'd check in with INS to see if Lorenzo, Susan's father, was a citizen. Rizzo was willing to pull out all the stops to get convictions in Francini. Meanwhile, he'd better see if there were any more surprises that Brady hadn't told them about. He didn't know what that might be, but they didn't want to learn about anything else like the tiff with Marino in the middle of the trial.

23

Susan sat at Richard's conference table, fidgeting in her seat. Bobby's voice droned on, reporting what they knew to Richard. The account couldn't have been more lackluster. She hadn't done all this work, compromising her relationship with a friend and risking her reputation by openly cavorting with a crime boss, for this idiot to plow through it with the same lack of enthusiasm he'd use to read the obits.

Susan bit her lip. On the verge of interrupting and taking over, she took a deep breath and kept silent. Bobby was taking credit for everything she did and screwing things up for Nicky while he did so. The likelihood that he'd get convicted of murder was keeping Susan awake at night. Damn it, she should be telling this story. She unearthed this evidence. She would've given it some life. Bobby completely failed to convey the promise of the information. Romano had been convincing. Bobby made it sound like Romano was scamming her. Susan had an idea for the way forward on this case. She'd assumed Bobby would ask her to tell Richard what she'd turned up. Instead, Bobby just started talking and didn't even look at her.

Bobby mentioned that Susan knew Rena Posso, and Richard gave her a questioning look, but she kept quiet. Bobby pushed a copy of the photo Susan had taken from Rena into the middle of the table.

Richard grabbed it and his eyebrows shot up. "Who's the guy with Francini and Brady?"

"Eddie Baker," Susan jumped in. "He's Brady's best friend."

"How'd you get this?" Richard asked.

"Susan took it from Rena Posso's condo," Bobby said. "She stole it."

Susan didn't think it was necessary to put it that way, but she didn't really care. She was over feeling guilty about it. How she got it didn't seem to bother Richard. He'd do what he needed to protect his clients.

Bobby finished his report. Richard turned to Susan with open admiration on his face. "You've been busy. And you've turned up some great stuff."

"Thanks, but running into Rena was just luck," she said.

When she'd first sat down at the table, Richard caught her eye and smiled, which triggered a smile from her. She wondered whether he was just being friendly and making her feel welcome, or whether it was flirtatious. Now he was looking at her again. She felt a lightness in her chest. She wanted Richard to like her. She wanted him to think she was smart. And she wanted him to be attracted to her. She'd be embarrassed if anyone knew it, but she'd gotten up an hour early that morning to decide what to wear to the meeting. She tried on half the clothes in her closet, finally choosing a pair of charcoal slacks and a blue cashmere sweater that looked good on her. She was trying to look serious and business-like and pretty at the same time. Richard himself was exceptionally handsome today in a pinstriped suit. She could tell it was hand-tailored from the stitching on the lapels. Her father had given Susan an eye for men's fashion. Her dad seldom was required to dress up, but when he did, he wore

Italian suits. Susan would enjoy running her hand over the soft fabric of Richard's jacket.

She knew Bobby didn't want her to speak at this meeting. He wanted her to play a subservient role in public, but Susan wasn't here to stroke his ego. She wanted to get Richard thinking about why Francini was murdered. Fuck it. She plunged ahead.

"What about this Eddie Baker?" she asked. "According to what Francini said to Rena, Tony was on the outs with him and Brady."

"Yeah," Richard said, "but it's a long way from being on the outs with someone to killing him. This isn't exactly the Boy Scouts we're talking about. There might've been a lot of guys in this crowd who could've found a reason to kill Francini."

Bobby gave Susan a sidelong look. Warning her to keep quiet. No dice.

"There's something important that we don't know," she said. "Why was Francini killed? If it wasn't for stealing from Romano, what was the reason? I think we need to get the answer to that before we can figure out who Brady is covering up for."

"Did Romano ever say anything to you that suggested why Brady might've done it?" Richard asked Susan.

"No," she said.

Richard sat forward in his chair. "Do you know when the relationship between Francini and Brady and Baker soured?"

Bobby frowned. Probably pissed off that Richard was putting questions to her instead of going through him. Bobby looked like he was about to jump in and say something, but she didn't give him a chance. Susan was holding the cards. She'd play them.

"Rena said they'd all gone to the ball game together in the spring," she said. "That's when that picture was taken. Evidently, everything was okay at that time. Then she and Tony ran into Brady and Baker a couple of months later, and they were unfriendly."

Richard picked up the picture again and stared at it, as

though it could tell him something. It didn't and he set it back down on the table.

"We need more information," Richard said, "but I don't know how we're going to get it. Let's think about things overnight and, if it's okay with everyone, we can meet again on Wednesday. We've got the status conference with Judge Morgan at two o'clock tomorrow."

Susan told Bobby she needed to go to class and that she'd meet him at his office before court the next day. Bobby didn't look happy. He looked like he was going to say something, but then he turned and walked away. As he left, she lingered behind in the conference room. Richard came back in.

"I wanted to talk to you about something," Susan said.

Richard got a boyish smile on his face. That's not it, she thought. Her heart was racing. She was about to go behind Bobby's back. The meeting had made her wonder about Romano and she wanted to get to the bottom of it.

"You didn't seem to be surprised when Bobby was talking about Romano coming to see me at Gabriella's. It seemed like you already knew about that."

"Romano and Costa are old friends. Costa asked me to represent him, and he suggested I talk with Romano. Romano told me the same thing he told you. And, yes, he told me he was going to talk with you."

"Why didn't he just talk to Bobby?"

Richard avoided her eyes. "Romano doesn't know Nicky Marino. He'd never met Bobby. Romano does know your father, so he had an entrée with you."

That couldn't be the whole story. Richard was being diplomatic. Romano must have learned the same things about her boss that Susan observed. Bobby was in over his head. He was afraid to take the case to trial. Romano was using her. Now that things were clear to her, that didn't feel so bad. She'd have to take the initiative if Nicky was going to get a real defense.

The problem was that she was only a third-year law student,

and this was a major murder case. She had success in digging up good evidence, but she didn't know how to take it further. Maybe she could work more directly with Richard without having to arrange everything through Bobby. She'd try that. She'd try to remember that it would be better for the case if she and Richard could work together without ending up in bed.

Susan had asked around and found out that Richard wasn't married and never had been. She didn't need a repeat of that fiasco in Chicago. She'd gone out with the guy for months before a friend told her he was married. She'd been more open with him than she'd ever been with a man. She lost confidence in her ability to assess character. She'd regained respect for her judgment since she'd been back in Boston. Still, she wasn't about to let her imagination run away with her. She'd take anything personal slow with Richard.

24

The courtroom was packed for the status conference, with the first row taken up by the press. Judge Morgan opened the proceedings by announcing that he was setting the case for trial in early January. Richard Charles was on his feet immediately, aggressive, clearly upset. "Your Honor, we can't possibly be ready to try this case in a month. With all respect, that's really not fair to these defendants."

Bobby was paralyzed. He wanted to stand up to protest along with Richard, but he couldn't get out of his chair. He'd assumed the day of reckoning was still months away. He'd hoped to figure a way out of this mess. That would take time. Now the trial was scheduled for immediately after New Year's. Marie would go apeshit. Things were still sketchy at home anyway. They planned to go to the Islands for two weeks over Christmas to try to rekindle the spark between them. They couldn't possibly do that now. The whole holiday season was shot.

Susan was glaring at Bobby. She turned her head toward the podium, back to him, and then back to the podium. He couldn't move.

"The trial is actually five weeks away, counselor, and I don't see any reason why you can't be ready," the judge said. "The prosecution has furnished you with all the police reports, grand jury testimony, and scientific evidence. No property was seized from any of the defendants, and none of them have made any statements to the police. There won't be any motions to suppress evidence. All that's left is the trial. Judge Christine Walsh will be sitting in Suffolk for four months starting in January and this case will be the first one out of the box."

At the end of the table, between Susan and Bobby, Nicky Marino sat trembling, his fists balled.

"We're still conducting our investigation, your Honor," Richard said. "We have witnesses to interview and leads to follow up. I request a trial date in March."

"Denied," said Judge Morgan. The judge looked at Bobby with arched eyebrows. "What about you, Mr. Coughlin? Is there any reason why you can't be ready to try this case in January?"

Bobby struggled to his feet. His mind was racing. What could he say? He couldn't very well tell the judge that they needed more time to find the real killer. That would sound stupid. And he wasn't that sure that the defendants weren't the real killers. He'd expected that it would take months to get from arrest to trial. He wasn't ready to face any of this. For an instant, he wondered what would happen if a defense lawyer pleaded insanity. His own insanity. He'd been crazy to let himself get in this position. He could prove it by having a meltdown right here in the courtroom.

He cleared his throat. "Your Honor—" He lowered his head. The room was completely quiet, like a church before the preacher begins his sermon. He had no words of wisdom. The seconds ticked by. The judge began tapping his pencil on the bench. Finally, Bobby looked up. "Your Honor, this seems like an uncommonly short time to prepare for a murder case." So bland. His mind cast about to come up with something better, but before he could think of anything, the judge was on again.

"This is an uncommonly simple case, counselor. The prosecution has a confession from Mr. Brady. He's identified your client as the man who pulled the trigger. Now you'll have a chance to cross-examine him. You'll have until the seventh of January to get ready to do that. You've already been on the case for two months. It's going to trial unless you have some other way to resolve the matter."

The judge was leaning on him to get Marino to plead out. The judge had as much as told him that's what he should do at the arraignment. Bobby hadn't come through. Now Morgan was putting on the pressure. The client was still insisting that he was innocent. Bobby didn't know what the hell he was supposed to do. He began to sweat.

"For the record, your Honor, I join Mr. Charles's request for a March date," Bobby said.

"For the record, your request is denied as well."

The judge turned to the prosecutor. "You don't have any problem with a January trial, do you, Mr. Flanagan?"

The prosecutor nodded respectfully to the judge like a good acolyte. "No, your Honor. The state will be ready to try this case whenever it's convenient for the Court."

Bobby sat back down. The prosecutor was such a little ass kisser. He had no idea what kind of pressure they were under. The FBI and the forensic people delivered the case to the D.A.'s office in a package with a nice bow on top. Fuck him.

Judge Morgan ordered them to appear before Judge Walsh on Thursday, January 3, for a final pretrial conference, adjourned court, and left the bench. The gallery cleared out. The court officers moved forward to take the defendants back to the lockup. They were fanned out behind the defense table in a semi-circle, holding handcuffs they were ready to employ.

"Can you give us a few minutes with our clients?" Richard asked. "Doesn't look like anyone else needs the room right now."

Bobby was nauseous. Too bad they hadn't whisked the

defendants away immediately and rushed them into the van to head back to the jail. Marino's face was red and there was fire in his eyes. He'd want to know what they were going to do. Bobby didn't think he could put on any pretense of confidence.

"You can have five minutes," the head court officer said. "Then we have to get these guys back to the jail." The officers left the room and locked them in.

"What's going on?" Danny Costa wanted to know.

"It's hard to say," Richard said. "I've never been rushed to trial like this on a murder case. If we come back in a couple of weeks and make a record on exactly why we need more time, we might get it. I don't trust Morgan, however, and I'm not inclined to give him a list of witnesses we want to interview. It might not do any good anyway."

Bobby put his papers in his briefcase, Maybe the rush to trial would put enough pressure on Marino so that he'd take a plea. Right now, there was nothing on the table. Bobby would have to talk with Tom Flanagan. And then he'd have to go out to Plymouth. He hated even thinking about it. Without a guilty plea, there'd be a trial. And a conviction. He could feel Jamie's ghost in the courtroom now.

Richard looked at the defendants. "Here's the thing. We need to figure out who Brady is protecting by falsely accusing you. We know he was unfriendly with Francini, but we don't know why. We don't know whether the murder was his idea or somebody else's. I don't want you to start talking about the case in the jail. That's too likely to backfire. Some jailhouse snitch will show up and claim you admitted to him that you were involved. Just think about who might've had a problem with Tony Francini. If you get any ideas about who Brady's partners were, let us know. We'll take it from there."

Bobby wouldn't get any ideas from Marino. Costa might come up with something, but he doubted it. Relying on the clients for information was a real Hail Mary.

Costa was sitting next to Bobby. He put his hand on Bobby's

shoulder. "Are you okay, Mr. Coughlin? You look a little pale." He reached for the pitcher on the table. "Would you like some water?"

Jesus. Even Costa could see he was falling apart. "What are you talking about?" Bobby said. "I'm fine." He was far from fine. He needed to get out of there. He tried to will the court officers to come back into the room.

"What about this Judge Walsh? Is she any good?" Costa asked.

"She's okay. She'll be fair, but we need more to work with," Richard said.

Bobby moved his chair closer to Marino. "We've got to talk. I'll come out to see you on Thursday," he said in a low voice.

"Talk about what?" Marino said, his chin high. "I haven't seen anything so far. What's your plan? I got no idea who Brady did this with. All's I know is it wasn't me."

Before Bobby could reply, the court officers came back into the room. "Okay, time's up. If you need to talk some more, you can do it at the jail." They got the defendants up and started moving them toward the door. "I'll see you Thursday," Bobby called to Marino.

Bobby and Susan walked back to his office. "I'd like to go with you to the jail," Susan said on the sidewalk in front of the building. "I've never had a chance to talk with Nicky, and I'd like to get an idea of what he's like."

Bobby needed to wrap this up before they got into a long discussion inside the office. It would be hard enough talking to Marino about taking a deal without Susan spouting her bright ideas about how to win the case. Bobby was afraid of Susan and the effect she might have on the client. He was sick of her naïve optimism. No way he was taking her with him.

"Not this time, Susan. This short trial date has changed things. I need to talk with Marino about our plans and bringing a new person into the conversation would be distracting. He's very anxious, and I don't want to do anything that will make this harder for him."

"That's not fair. You know how hard I've been working on the case and the only times I've seen Nicky have been sitting next to him in the courtroom, where we can't talk."

Bobby shook his head. "It's really not about what might be fair to you. This is about Marino and his frame of mind. I doubt if you can imagine what's he's going through. It would be more helpful if you'd talk to Patty and tell her about the trial date. I guess she couldn't make it to court today. I want you to get her to come to the office on Thursday so you can do that. I'll see you tomorrow at the meeting with Richard."

Susan was staring at Bobby as though he'd said something offensive. Maybe she thought he considered talking to the client's wife "women's work." Maybe she thought he was avoiding Patty. He was. He didn't see what the wife could offer at this point. He didn't need a session with her sobbing her heart out, which is what she'd do when she learned of the early trial date. Let Susan handle that. He'd have his hands full with Marino. Bobby turned and went into his building.

25

Frank Romano was sipping a glass of grappa in his living room and listening to a very nervous Tommy O'Neill tell him the story of the diamond robbery. He needed men like O'Neill in his business. Brave men stupid enough to walk into a jewelry store with a gun and ask for diamonds. If they got caught, it was no skin off Romano's back. If they got away with the diamonds, they usually came to him to sell them, and he could make a nice profit without running much risk. O'Neill hadn't brought his loot, but for some reason, he was now telling Romano about the theft.

They were sitting in Romano's condo in the North End around ten in the evening. Two walls of the room were taken up with bookshelves and a third featured Renaissance art, including several florid representations of the Madonna. He'd allowed a rumor to circulate among his closest associates that one piece was a Rubens that was stolen from John Ringling's Museum of Art in Florida. This was not true. Romano paid a skilled copyist to spend three weeks in Sarasota producing a replica of the original good enough to fool all but the most experienced art historian. No one who gained admission to his living room fell into that category. Nor were any of his friends likely to notice that the painting in question was still hanging in the museum.

A picture window at the end of the room furnished a good view of the harbor. Not as nice as the view of the ocean from Romano's house in Marblehead, but sailboats bobbed on the water and the dinner launches were all lit up and steaming back from the harbor islands. His wife never set foot in the place. She almost never came into Boston. She loved puttering around their home, tending her beautiful flower garden with prize-winning roses in the summer, and reading in front of the fireplace in the winter.

O'Neill's drink sat in front of him untouched. The guy had shown up at the back door unannounced and said he had something urgent to talk about. He kept prattling on about the stupid robbery.

Robert Caro's book, *The Years of Lyndon Johnson, The Path to Power*, lay on the table next to Romano. He'd read it when it first came out over twenty years ago and was rereading it now. He liked contrasting Johnson's story with that of the current president. Bush was a Texan, but a wimp compared to LBJ. All hat, no cattle, as they say. Johnson was a tough son of a bitch who got things done. Unlike a lot of his associates, he admired Johnson for getting the civil rights and the voting rights acts passed. He had nothing against the blacks and respected their struggle to gain their rights. After all, back in the day, they shared a mutual enemy in the FBI. Romano wanted to get O'Neill out of here so he could get back to his reading.

"Tommy," Romano said. "I don't need the whole story. I really don't care how you pulled the job. For whatever reason, you took the stones to someone else. That was disrespectful, and I don't expect you to do it again. But this time, don't worry about it. I'll overlook it. Maybe you can do something for me to make up for it."

It wasn't hot in the room, but O'Neill was sweating. "That's not why I'm here, Frank. You know that fed, Mike Rizzo? He's on the organized crime squad."

Romano waved his hand. "I know that, Tommy. Get to the point."

"Okay. I don't know why he picked me. I swear to God I don't. But he comes over my house. Late at night. Like, so no one will know he's there. And he says the guy in the jewelry store picked out my picture as the robber. Rizzo says he's got enough to bust me, but he don't care about that. He says he wants the guy who planned the job and who I sold the diamonds to. And he wants it to be you."

"What do you mean, he wants it to be me? Does he think it was me?"

"He don't care who it was. He wants me to say it was you."

Rizzo had bigger balls than Romano thought. The FBI couldn't lay a finger on him any other way, so they were going for a straight-out frame.

"I'm assuming that you came here to tell me you're not going to go along with Rizzo," Romano said.

O'Neill put his hand over his heart. "You know I'm not. But how do I handle this? What do I tell him?"

Romano wasn't sure this poor bastard had a way out. If he didn't cooperate with Rizzo, he'd go away on the armed robbery, and he wouldn't get any consideration from the government. He'd have to figure out if O'Neill could handle that without caving. If he couldn't, Romano would have to take care of that before O'Neill got on the witness stand.

Romano leaned forward. "For now, tell him you'll play ball. Let's get him to lay the whole thing out for us before we decide what our best move is. There's something else, though. How did Rizzo get to you in the first place? How did he learn that you did this job?"

"I don't know. The only people who knew about it were the

guys I did it with and they're not the kind who talk about what they do."

"How about you? You never told anyone about this great heist you pulled?" Romano looked straight into O'Neill's eyes. "Don't lie to me, Tommy."

O'Neill couldn't hold his gaze and looked down. "Sorry, boss. I fucked up. I was an idiot and told my brother. I couldn't help it; you know how it is with a guy's brother, right? Still, I know I shouldn't have. When this came up, I asked him if he blabbed to anybody. He told me it was a good story and he told Eddie Baker about it at Dedham. But Eddie's a stand-up guy. He's always got something going himself, so he's not the kind of guy can be talking to the cops."

Romano sat completely still and stared at O'Neill for several seconds. Romano got up, crossed the room to a credenza where the bottle was and poured another grappa. He slowly returned to his chair and continued to stare at O'Neill silently.

"I'm really sorry, boss. I'll do anything to make this right. Anything. I was stupid, I know that. I'd never do something on purpose to hurt you. You know that, right?"

Romano shook his head. This stupid fuck had created a real problem. Maybe there was a way he could turn this around, but it was dangerous. Rizzo apparently didn't care what sort of risks he was running coming after him. Romano didn't like it, but he might have to go on the offensive. His strategy had always been to be as inconspicuous as possible. With the feds getting this aggressive, that might not work anymore. In any event, he needed more information.

"Like I said, Tommy. Act like you're interested in Rizzo's scheme, whatever it is. Get as many details as you can, but don't let him think you're pumping him for information. Ask him what you're going to get out of this. Anything you learn, you let me know right away."

O'Neill left and Romano was alone with his grappa. O'Neill was wrong about Eddie Baker. He was no stand-up guy. Eddie

Baker was a dangerous little weasel. This was the second time in two weeks that his name had come up. Romano wasn't sure what it meant, but he didn't believe in coincidences.

26

Susan clasped her hands together as she walked side by side with Frank Romano.

"You're asking me about my business. No one asks me about my business." Romano's voice had some steel in it for the first time since she'd met him. He looked grave. Maybe Susan was making a mistake. She didn't know this man. She didn't know how he'd react if she pissed him off.

They were all the way at the end of Hanover Street. She'd gone to the Via Appia at lunchtime on Wednesday and, like the last time, he'd suggested they take a walk. As they went, people averted their eyes when they saw Romano approaching. He nodded to a few people he evidently knew but didn't speak to them. No one stopped him to chat. Several customers from Gabriella's looked away without greeting Susan.

Strolling down Hanover Street with Romano wasn't the best thing for her reputation. She needed another way of getting in touch with him. It was difficult enough seeking him out without broadcasting it to everyone in the North End. It took a few blocks before she got up the nerve to say what she'd wanted to talk about.

Bobby's refusal to let her go to the jail with him to see Nicky could only mean that he was going to try to cram a plea down Nicky's throat. That just wasn't right. She needed to find out who Brady was protecting. There was no way to get to that without Romano. So here she was. She'd told him she understood that Francini hadn't been stealing from him but suggested maybe somebody else had been. That hadn't gone over well.

"Believe me, Mr. Romano, I don't want to know anything about your business," she said. "I really don't. I've got to tell you, though, what I've been thinking. After Tony's murder, someone floated a rumor that he'd been stealing from you. That story started even before Brady was arrested. It accomplished two things. It implied that you were the one who ordered Tony to be killed, and it blamed any thefts from you on Tony. I began to wonder if someone else had been stealing. If someone had been, Tony probably would have been the one to investigate. And if that someone knew Tony was snooping around, that could get him killed. The person who killed Tony and the thief could be the same guy. Brady is covering for somebody. Wouldn't you like to figure out who that is?"

Romano was frowning. "That's a lot of 'ifs.' Let me get this straight. You want to know if we were short before Tony was killed?"

"Yes. If you were, I'd like to know whether you have some idea who was responsible."

Jesus, Mary, and Joseph. She must be out of her mind. It was crazy to walk up to a mob boss and ask him to admit that someone was stealing from him, even nuttier to ask him if he knew who it was. Her knees were shaking, but she was glad she'd leaped into the breach. If Romano didn't want to answer her question, he could say so. After all, he'd sought her out in the first place.

She needed to take a chance. Bobby would never have had

the balls to do this. She didn't know if Richard would. Susan could have run this by Richard before seeking out Romano, but she hadn't wanted anyone to try to talk her out of making the only move she could think of that might get them closer to the truth. So, she'd just plunged ahead.

"Why would I talk to you about this?" Romano asked.

"For the same reason you came to talk to me in the first place. Innocent men, including a good friend of yours, are going to be convicted of Tony Francini's murder unless we figure out who really killed him. I think this is the key to it. If you think I'm wrong, please tell me."

"I don't know if you're right or wrong. You are correct that I'm concerned about Costa. We've been friends our whole lives, and I can't let him go to prison for killing Tony. I know he didn't do it. Listen to me. You can tell Richard Charles and his investigator this came from me, but no one else. Particularly not that idiot you work for. Coughlin might go straight to the D.A.'s Office with it."

Romano stepped closer to Susan and dropped his voice to a near whisper. "Somebody was skimming. No one knew we were short except for Tony, me, and whoever was taking the money. Tony was looking into it, but as far as I knew, he hadn't come up with anything. After he got shot, I changed our systems for collecting and that seemed to solve the problem. Someone pocketed a fair amount of money before that happened, and it wasn't Francini."

A slow smile spread across her face. Romano didn't seem angry. He'd confirmed her suspicions about the stealing. Now if she could just push him a little further.

"Did Eddie Baker ever work for you?" she asked.

27

Less than a minute after Susan entered the Via Appia, Rizzo got a call on his cell.

"You know that girl that you asked me to watch out for?" the agent in the panel truck said. "She just walked into the restaurant. Romano will probably be along any minute."

"Shit. She's popping up everywhere," Rizzo said. "Okay, here's what I want you to do. Put your partner in the backup van, not the one that sits in front of the restaurant. Last time they walked straight down Hanover, so have him set up at the other end. If they go someplace else, he'll have to improvise. Use a parabolic in each van and try to get as much of their conversation as you can. Call me when you have something."

He found Smith at his desk and told him what was going on.

"You want to go out there?" Smith asked.

"Romano would spot us a mile away. Of course, he already knows our guy's in the van in front of the restaurant. I'm hoping once he walks down the street, he might not make the second van and maybe he'll be a little careless."

Smith got up from his chair. "He's pretty careful. Son of a bitch doesn't even have a cell phone. He never talks on the phone at all, unless it's to his wife. Remember the tap we had on him?"

"All they talked about was their grandchildren and her fucking roses. Finally, the judge made us shut it down," Rizzo said.

"Want to try again?"

"Why? You planning on starting a rose garden?"

Smith sat back down. Rizzo knew Marino was innocent, but he was looking at murder one. A life sentence. He could have bargained it down to fifteen years and got out while he was still a relatively young man. Now, this fucking chick is running around like she thinks she's Johnnie Cochran.

Back at his desk, Rizzo got a call from the surveillance agent. "We only got a little bit of their conversation. You know, it's hard with them walking and turning their heads and so on."

"Whatever. What did you get?"

"At one point she said to him, quote, Brady is covering for somebody, end quote. Then it got garbled. A few minutes later, she asked, quote, Did Eddie Baker ever work for you? end quote. We couldn't hear Romano's answer. In fact, we couldn't hear anything he said the whole time."

What did this fucking law student know about Eddie Baker? No one was aware the Bakers were informants except for Rizzo, Smith, the SAC, and higher-ups with access to the top informants. Romano had given no indication that he suspected it—and Willie had worked for him. This wasn't good. This wasn't good at all.

"Tell you what," Rizzo said, "bring your report on this directly to me and I'll file it with mine on the girl. I'm sending this straight to the Director. And keep all this under your hat. I'm not sure how's he going to want us to handle it."

He didn't intend to send anything about Susan Sorella to Washington. The less the Director heard about Susan Sorella and her suspicions that Brady was covering for someone the better. The surveillance report would stay in Rizzo's personal files. That didn't solve the problem of what he was going to do about her.

Rizzo filled Smith in on what the surveillance agents overheard. "Godammit, Mike, where's this going?" Smith asked. "Why the hell is she asking about Eddie Baker? This case is starting to unravel."

"It's the fact that she's talking to Romano that makes it bad. We probably need to have a chat with Eddie about this."

———

Magoun's was quiet at two o'clock on Thursday afternoon. There were only two or three customers in the place, settled in like regulars at the bar. Rizzo made them as the kind of guys who couldn't remember by six o'clock whether their own mother had stopped by earlier for a drink.

Rizzo and Smith grabbed beers and joined Eddie and Willie Baker at a table in the corner. The agents had concluded overnight that they needed to put the Bakers in the picture. They might not have to do anything else.

"A law student who works with Nicky Marino's lawyer has made friends with Frank Romano," Rizzo said. "Yesterday, she was telling him that Brady was covering for someone, and then she asked Romano if Eddie had ever worked for him."

"How did you find that out?" Eddie asked.

"That's not your concern. What you should be worried about is that we don't know how much she knows."

"Did she mention me?" Willie asked.

"What? Now you're just worried about yourself?" said Eddie. "I go down, you go down."

"Don't be like that," Willie said. "I'm just trying to find out what else she said."

"As far as we know, she didn't say anything about Willie," Rizzo said. "We don't know the whole conversation. We don't know what Romano said to her."

Rizzo took a sip of his beer. That's all we need. For the brothers to have a falling out. Willie was fanatically loyal to Eddie, but Eddie was a hothead. Willie was the smarter of the two. Hopefully, Eddie would listen to him. Rizzo had used a pair of brothers as informants once before. Twins. He was working narcotics on the Department in Boston. He and his partner were trying to outdo a couple of other detectives in making big busts. Rizzo gave the twins some money to go down to New York and buy cocaine and plant it on some users in Roxbury. They called him up and gave him the names of the people who were supposedly holding. Rizzo and his partner busted them, and Rizzo was amazed at the quantity of drugs they seized. Since he already knew it was coke, he didn't bother to run a field test, although he told the chief of detectives he did.

The chief called a press conference and claimed the cops had made the biggest cocaine bust in New England history. The chief's photograph, sitting behind a mountain of bags of white powder, ran in all the papers. Problem was, the informants had taken Rizzo's money, bought heroin, shot up, then went to the CVS and bought medicinal quinine in a large quantity. That's what they planted on their friends. The tox report came back negative from the state lab, and the whole thing blew up. Rizzo should've known better. None of the junkies they busted could have afforded that much coke—they didn't know where their next fix was coming from. Rizzo and his partner got sued. The City settled the case and paid off the people they'd arrested. It was a black mark on his record. If this case got fucked up it would be a lot worse than a black mark.

Rizzo looked at Willie. "We gotta put a lid on this somehow. This girl is all over the case. She found out that Brady has a grudge against Marino. And she keeps talking to Romano."

"How could a law student be that dangerous?" asked Willie.

"As far as we can tell, she's the only one on the defense who's developing any real evidence. Who knows how far it'll go? We all got a lot on the line here. The prosecutor thinks he can win the case even without a plea and testimony from Marino. Then again, he doesn't exactly know all the facts."

Rizzo was even more concerned than he was letting on. He didn't want the Bakers to see just how worried he was. He and Smith had gone way out on a limb to get Brady as a government witness and to protect Eddie on the Francini murder. More than their jobs were at stake—they could end up in prison. He needed the Bakers to feel like he had everything under control, and at the same time motivate them to do something. It was a fine line.

"What else can you tell us about this girl?" Willie asked.

"Her name's Susan Sorella," Smith said. "Her father owns Gabriella's on Hanover Street and she works there. She's a student at Suffolk Law." He handed Eddie a picture of Susan that the surveillance agent had taken.

"Cute chick," Eddie said. "What do you want us to do?"

"For Christ's sake Eddie, we can't tell you what to do," Rizzo said. "We're just giving you information."

Unbelievable. What, he had to spell it out for this guy? It's not like he'd never killed anybody before. What's his problem? Maybe Rizzo and Smith should just whack her themselves. It wouldn't be that hard. She didn't know they were on to her.

Eddie started to say something else, but Willie put his hand on his brother's arm and said, "We got this." The brothers got up from the table and started to leave. Eddie turned back and stared at him. "Don't worry, Rizzo," he said. "I'm not stupid."

28

Susan set her pen down and closed the examination book in which she'd been writing. She paid less attention to her courses this semester than since she'd started law school. In the last three weeks, just as everything was heating up on Nicky's case, she was madly cramming to get through the fall semester exams. Thank god, they were finished. She was exhausted. She handed her papers to the proctor and headed to the cafeteria to grab a quick salad for lunch.

Yesterday, Susan met with Patty in the morning and then spent the afternoon in a study group she joined just to get through this course with a passing grade. She couldn't do everything she was supposed to do. She'd only slept five hours a night for the past month. In addition to Nicky's case, and her work at Gabriella's, Bobby assigned her a brief to draft for another client. He'd been appointed by the court to represent someone on an appeal and seemed relieved to hand it off to her. He wasn't the kind of lawyer who got off on the intricacies of legal arguments. Susan enjoyed it, but it took a lot of time. It suited her intellect to operate in the arena of pure law. Appellate issues were confined to legal errors at the trial. In this case, she'd discovered a significant point that the defense lawyer had neglected to raise. If she was right, the defendant could get a new trial. She knew this sort of mistake happened far too often. Some lawyers just went through the motions. Like Bobby. She hoped he'd let her do the oral argument in this case in the Appeals Court.

Susan had filled Patty in on all the developments in the case and then warned her that Bobby was going to try to get Nicky to plead guilty. She'd expected Patty to be upset, or angry. But evidently, Patty and Nicky had already figured out what Bobby's agenda was and were ready for him. Patty said Nicky was innocent and had no intention of pleading guilty. She was worried about the risks he faced by going to trial, but they believed that the truth would come out somehow. That was what Susan had wanted to hear. But it frightened her. The truth sometimes failed to make itself known in a criminal courtroom. She surprised herself by being tempted to advise Patty that Nicky should at least consider the option of limiting his exposure by pleading guilty. But she didn't do that.

Susan had been riding a wave of confidence and excitement that grew stronger with each new discovery she made. The naiveté of Patty's certainty that the trial would get to the truth brought that wave crashing to the sand. For the first time, Susan felt pangs of the fear that had immobilized Bobby.

After lunch, Susan hurried up the hill to get to Bobby's office on Temple Street. Snow was falling. Boston was starting to look like Christmas. The trees on the Common were lit up, and children were skating on the ice in the wading pool. Shoppers were headed back to their offices carrying bags stuffed with presents. Christmas with her father would be a good break.

Romano had never answered her question about Eddie Baker. He'd just warned her again about how dangerous Baker was. Susan wasn't going to tell Bobby about that meeting.

He'd just be pissed she was talking with the crime boss again. Maybe Richard could help her figure out how they could use the information that someone had been stealing from Romano. She had a strong feeling that Eddie Baker was connected to the theft, but no evidence.

She found Bobby in his private office. "How did the meeting with Nicky go?" she asked.

"I gave him another chance to talk about making a deal, but he's not interested."

"So, you think this case will go to trial?"

Bobby stared at Susan with a blank expression on his face. He was violently twisting his wedding ring back and forth on his finger. He picked up some papers on his desk, then put them back down without looking at them. "How's that appellate brief that I asked you to work on?" he asked.

"I put the draft on your desk earlier this week. It needs to be filed sometime in mid-January, but you can probably get an extension of time since Nicky's trial is coming up."

"You know what? I'm going to knock off early today. I'll take the brief home and work on it over the weekend."

Susan was floored. Bobby hadn't asked her about the brief since he first gave her the assignment. It couldn't suddenly be so urgent. And they had a ton of other things to do. Patty needed to be prepared to testify, they needed to get back to the bartender at Magoun's, they needed to talk to Rena about testifying and get the documents to prove she'd bought her condo with her own money, and Bobby had to prepare to cross-examine Brady. Susan hadn't seen anything to suggest Bobby was even thinking about any of that.

"What about Nicky?"

"He's not our only client. We can talk more about him next week."

"But—"

"That's enough, Susan," Bobby interrupted. He grabbed the draft off his desk, shoved it into his briefcase, threw on his coat, and ran out of the office.

"Bobby!" she shouted, but he flew out the door.

She had no idea what to do. Bobby was having a panic attack. This had been building up for quite a while. Failing to talk Nicky into a plea bargain was the last straw.

Susan sat down on a chair and ran her fingers through her hair. Bobby couldn't just ignore a murder trial, could he? She dug her phone out of her pocketbook and got up and started walking about the room. She typed in Richard's office number. She needed advice. The phone rang several times. "Answer already," she muttered. The secretary picked up. Richard was out at a deposition and wouldn't be back this afternoon. Susan knew his cell number but couldn't interrupt the deposition. She'd call him later.

She needed to do something constructive. She'd been putting off talking with Rena about testifying at the trial. Susan didn't know whether Rena understood that she could be an important witness for the defense, or how her friend would feel about it. Now was as good a time as any to bring it up. She tapped in Rena's number and sat back down. Susan closed her eyes and massaged her temples. She'd been up late studying, had the exam this morning, and Bobby's panic attack had thrown her. If she'd been in her apartment, she'd have crawled into bed.

She got Rena who agreed to see her later in the day. In the meantime, she could try to get some Christmas shopping done. She'd have to figure out some way to reach Bobby.

29

It was dark when Susan left the little curiosity shop on Charles Street. As she'd foraged in one Beacon Hill boutique after another, she'd almost put Nicky's case out of her mind. Just as she was despairing of finding anything for Rena, Susan bumped into a cabinet with photographs of famous ballerinas on display. A small volume by Edward Gorey fell to the floor. She'd learned about Gorey a couple of years before, from a customer at Gabriella's who'd achieved some local success as a painter. Susan was mesmerized by the off-beat pen and ink drawings and Gorey's unsettling sense of humor. She started collecting his little books.

The cover of the book she now held in her hands, *The Gilded Bat*, showed a ballerina, encased in the golden wings of a bat, hovering against a black background over three men in Edwardian evening dress who'd fallen to the ground in awe of her. The short story inside was about a ballerina whose success and fame never altered the basic tedium of her life. Susan always assumed that law would make for an exciting life. Nicky's case showed her, though, that a struggle against long odds could be wearing.

On the way to Rena's condo, Susan stopped for the traffic light at Beacon Street and took the gift out of her bag to examine it. The Gorey story was an odd thing to give someone in celebration of Christmas. Her choice told her that she was miserable. Children of the rich families who lived on Beacon Hill were running and playing in the snow. She smiled at their spirit, but her shoulders slumped. She walked through the festive decorations on the Common weighed down by fear. Fear that Bobby wouldn't come through for Nicky. Fear that Nicky's life, and the lives of his wife and children, would be ruined. They'd be poor, living on Patty's wages from the diner. The kids would grow up without their father. Their friends would think their dad was a murderer.

Snow was still falling. The sidewalks were slippery. Susan was preoccupied with her anxiety about her exam that morning and hadn't worn her boots. The leather soles on her flats gave her no traction and she stumbled a couple of times and nearly fell. She barely noticed—she was thinking so hard about Brady. The son of a bitch was a killer. And a liar. Brady was going to get away with it unless they could find out whom he was covering for.

Susan passed the law school on Tremont. At the next corner, the after-work crowd blocked the sidewalk on their way into the Parker House. She was about to step into the street to get around them when two of her favorite professors popped up in front of her and called out, "Merry Christmas!" She could manage only a half-hearted wave in response.

"Do you want to join us?" they asked. "We heard you're working on a murder case. We'd love to hear all about it."

Ordinarily, Susan would've enjoyed doing so. The green leather easy chairs in the hotel bar were inviting. The door opened and the aroma of mulled wine floated out onto the sidewalk. These women, life-long academics, would love to drop into the blood and guts of a real trial vicariously through her. They'd want to know what the defendant was like and whether he was guilty. Not that they'd ask that. Susan couldn't discuss anything except the most superficial facts of the case. Chit-chatting about that in her current frame of mind was beyond her.

"I'm sorry," Susan said, "but I have an appointment." She turned down School Street toward the waterfront.

She'd come this way so she could pick up a bottle at Federal Wines to take to Rena's. Rena said it'd been one of Tony's favorite stores. Susan walked a block past it without stopping, obsessed with the image in her mind of Brady's cruel face. She turned back. A man about half a block behind her suddenly stopped and reversed his direction. He crossed to the other side of the street and stood staring up at the tall office building at Sixty State. He didn't check his watch. He wasn't talking on his cell. He didn't move. She couldn't help but think that he'd been following her. She couldn't see his face. He was a big man, imposing in a navy pea coat and a stocking cap. Susan kept an eye on him as she walked back to the wine store. He scared her, but she wasn't sure if he was a threat.

She entered the store and walked to the back, where she could watch the entrance. She waited for a few minutes. He didn't appear. She wandered around the aisles, anxiously checking out the few other customers. Fifteen minutes crept by. The man in the pea coat might be waiting on the street for her. She tried Richard again. He didn't answer. She left a message on the damn voice mail. She walked slowly toward a set of wine racks near the window and looked for the big man. She didn't see him. It was dark and there weren't many people on State Street. She hadn't even been thinking about what wine to buy and she needed to get moving. She grabbed a familiar bottle of Chianti.

Susan came out of the store. The big guy was nowhere to be seen. She headed toward the Fort Point Channel. She started walking faster but needed to slow down. The sidewalk was so slick. She looked over her shoulder. She saw no one. Maybe no one was following her. She forged ahead.

Across the Congress Street Bridge was the familiar milk bottle in front of the Children's Museum. Immediately in front of her construction obstructed the sidewalk. A sawhorse with a flashing yellow light blocked the way. She stepped into the street to cross to the other side. The pavement was icy, and she lost her balance in the middle of the road and slid. She stumbled backward a little. She took a deep breath and looked down the bridge toward the Seaport.

A car was traveling slowly toward her from the South Boston side. Susan was sure she had plenty of time to get across. Then the car's motor gunned, it leaped forward and bore down on her. Her legs were frozen to the spot. Her heart was pounding. Screaming, she threw up her hands. The car's engine thundered. Its headlights blinded her. She managed to turn away, began to run. Her foot slipped and she started to go down.

She was face down in the snow on the sidewalk before she realized she'd been tackled. A man's body landed on top of her. The car shot by, missing their feet by inches. Tinted windows obscured anyone inside. The tires threw slush over their bodies. She rolled over and looked for the license number, but it was covered with snow.

She turned toward the man who'd knocked her down. Paul Finn.

"My god, that guy was trying to kill me," Susan said, gasping for breath.

"That was close," he said.

"Where did you come from?"

Finn stood and brushed the snow off his coat. He massaged his right elbow and scowled. "Are you all right?" he asked. "Can you stand up?"

Finn took her elbow in his hand. She struggled to her feet. Pain shot through her left hip. A dark red stain ran across the bottom front of her white wool coat. Dizziness overcame her and she leaned against him. He put his arm around her.

"It's just wine," he said, pointing at her coat. "It's only wine." Shards of the broken bottle covered the ground. Susan touched her cheek. It was scratched and bleeding from hitting the sidewalk. She didn't feel any glass. The Gorey was lying in slush, wet and dirty.

"You saved my life. But where did you come from?"

"I'm glad neither of us seems to be hurt badly. I'll have a bruise or two, but I'm all right."

She took a couple of steps. It didn't feel like anything was broken. "Were you following me? I saw someone on State Street. Was that you?"

"Do you have any pain?"

"Goddamit, have you been following me, or not?"

"Alright already. Yes. I've been keeping an eye on you this afternoon, but I didn't want you to know. You'd probably have told me to get lost. Romano asked me to look out for you. He feared you might be in danger. He didn't want to use his guys. He thought—well, he thought their presence might be misunderstood."

Romano hired Finn to protect her. Why would he do that?

"I probably would have told you to buzz off. Did Romano tell you why he suspected I was in danger?"

"Not exactly. He said the last time he saw you, two FBI vans were conducting surveillance as you and he walked down Hanover Street."

The FBI. With two surveillance vans. She'd just been worried what her customers would think if they saw her on the street with Romano. If the feds overheard any of their conversations, they might've picked up Eddie Baker's name.

"Well, thank you."

"We'd better get off the street," Finn said. "Where were you going?"

"I was supposed to have a drink with Rena Posso. It would

freak her out if I showed up like this. I'll call her to explain. Can you take me home?"

"Sure. We should call the police, but we can do that at your apartment."

30

In her agitated state, Susan didn't know where to begin. Richard was standing over her, shaking his head. "What the hell has been going on?" he asked. He didn't know that someone else had been stealing from Romano, or that Romano was worried about her safety, or that he'd asked Finn to protect her. Richard was in the dark. And plenty worried, from the look on his face.

Susan got a call from Richard a few minutes after the police left her apartment. He rushed right over. She barely had time to wash her face and put some disinfectant on her scratches. Her hair was stringy and wet. Nothing quick she could do about that. She looked like crap. Still, she was glad Richard was here. Finn sat across the room. Richard paced back and forth. She went through the events of the past few days chronologically. Richard grimaced at how Bobby was behaving but said nothing.

She related her conversation with Romano. Finn added what Romano had told him about the FBI surveillance. Susan described the attack on the bridge. She finished talking and Richard sat down and loosened his tie.

"This puts everything in an entirely different light," Richard said.

"What do you mean?" Finn asked.

"He's talking about the possibility that there's a relationship between the FBI and whoever Brady is covering up for," Susan said. "What else could it be? Whoever Brady is protecting is the only one with a motive to try to stop me from investigating further. Let's call him Mr. X. And whoever Mr. X is, he'd have no way of knowing what I suspected. Romano is the only one I talked to about my theory that someone else had been stealing from him, and that the same person killed Francini. Romano didn't send someone out in a car to run me over—he sent you to protect me. The agents were the only ones who could've overheard our conversation. Maybe they used long-range microphones or something. If Mr. X came after me, he must have learned about the conversation from the FBI."

"That sounds logical," Finn said. "I just don't see how we can prove it, much less prove that Mr. X is the one who killed Francini. You can't just dangle the FBI in front of the jury without evidence, hoping to create reasonable doubt about the guilt of the defendants."

Richard nodded. "At least now we know what we're looking for," he said. "Mr. X is an informant. They wouldn't go to bat this way for anybody else."

Susan fretted. They were making progress but obtaining something they could use in court was getting harder, not easier. She knew what Bobby would say—that it was impossible to get the names of FBI informants.

"Do you think we have enough to get a court order forcing the FBI to identify any informants working on this case?" she asked Richard.

He shook his head. "Not nearly enough. I wouldn't bring up this attack in court until we have a specific purpose for doing so. Flanagan is a straight shooter, for a prosecutor. He wouldn't like the fact that someone was trying to hurt you, let alone kill you. He knows exactly what Joseph Brady is, so this might make him suspect there's something wrong with his case. Before we press that button, we need to know in what direction we want to send him."

"There must be something we can do," Finn said.

"Let's think about it overnight," Richard said. "Romano will be expecting you to report back. Call him and tell him what happened, and please tell him we'd like to talk with him sometime this weekend. Say we'll be keeping a close eye on Susan in the meantime."

Finn stood. "I'm on it. Susan, you ought to go to the E.R."

"I already told you, I'm okay."

"I landed on you pretty hard."

"Yeah. Next time you save my life, try to be more gentle."

Finn left, reminding them to double lock the door behind him.

"What did the two of you tell the cops?" Richard asked.

"Not much. It would have been a mistake to say anything about a relationship to Marino's case. I didn't want anything I'd learned from Romano to show up in a report that the prosecutor might read. We explained Finn's presence on the scene as a coincidence. I don't think they bought it. On top of that, with no context, they seemed skeptical about whether the driver intended to hit me. They took down the information and promised to follow up, although there isn't much of an investigation they can conduct under the circumstances."

"They might not even turn it over to a detective. You're right, they have no way to figure out who did this."

Richard shuffled his feet. "Susan, I doubt they'll try anything else tonight, but if you don't mind, I'd prefer to sleep on your couch in the living room just to be on the safe side."

Susan did a double-take. The killers might not try anything tonight, but it sounded like Richard wanted to. Nothing like danger to trigger the libido. She could feel it herself. From left field came the idea that they could hang shirts and pants on a clothesline between the couch and her bedroom to preserve her modesty, ala *It Happened One Night*, one of her favorite vintage films. She watched it recently. She'd be happy to play Claudette Colbert to Richard's Clark Gable. She almost started laughing.

Would they have something to eat, sit up talking about the case, then maybe move into a more personal conversation? This wasn't 1934, and she wasn't the frightened virgin played by Claudette Colbert. She couldn't predict how far things would go. The idea of sleeping with Richard had been an abstraction. She'd only thought about whether it would be a good idea or a mistake. Now that she was thinking about it, she wondered what he'd look like with his shirt off.

But this was hardly the time for that. They were dealing with attempted murder. Susan needed to wrap her mind around the fact that somebody wanted her dead. She shivered, just thinking about it. She didn't know if Richard could protect her.

Her cell buzzed, cutting her thoughts short. It was her father. Somehow, he'd heard that she'd nearly been run over by a car. He wanted her to come to his apartment immediately. That made sense. It was risky for her to stay in her apartment alone, and risky in a different way to stay there with Richard. She told her dad she'd be there shortly.

It was long past the time she'd been due at Rena's. Susan called and said she'd been in an accident but was all right. She promised to call tomorrow and explain further. She reassured her friend as best she could without getting into details. That could wait until they could talk in person. She hoped Rena wouldn't be too frightened by this to testify.

Susan rang off and Richard, who'd been sitting on the edge of the couch, came over and took her arms in his hands. "You must be in shock," he said.

"I'm all right. I'm not going to say I'm not scared. I am. If Finn hadn't been there, they would've killed me. I want to get to the bottom of this case more than ever."

"I'm not sure how Bobby's going to react to this news,"

Richard said. "We need him on board. I should go to see him with you tomorrow. We can figure out in the morning how best to handle him."

"That's not a good idea. Better I see him alone. He wouldn't react well if I showed up with you. He's already pissed that I'm doing so much on my own. If he knew I was working directly with you, he'd go off."

"I don't want to complicate things, Susan, but I want you to know that if something had happened to you, I would've been devastated."

Her eyes locked on Richard's. He sounded sincere. Maybe there could be something between them. This wasn't the time to find out.

"My father wants me to spend the night at his apartment. Will you give me a ride over there?"

They drove a few blocks through the North End to her father's. Richard took her up in the elevator and walked her to the door. Susan introduced him to her dad and then Richard left, promising to call her in the morning. He squeezed her hand gently when he said good night.

"Susan, I'm so relieved you're here," her father said. "Are you hurt?"

"I've got some pain in my hip, but it's getting better. I don't think anything is broken. There are some scratches on my face, but they're not serious."

They walked into the living room and Susan started to sit down on the couch.

"Come into the kitchen, honey," her father said. "We have a visitor."

She walked around the corner. Sitting at the kitchen table was the man she most wanted to talk to right now, Frank Romano.

31

Susan's father lived in a small apartment—he wasn't the sort of person to have anything more than he needed. Stepping inside the front door, she always felt transported to Europe. Old, comfortable furniture upholstered in patterned fabrics. Wooden bookcases overflowing with volumes in both Italian and English. Detailed etchings of Roman antiquity on the walls. The only room where anything modern could be found was the kitchen. Gleaming stainless-steel countertops, a massive six-burner stove, and well-seasoned pans hanging from a rack proclaimed that this was where serious cooking took place. The room had a warmth to it, in good part because of the large round oak table where she sat, staring across at her father and Frank Romano.

"Before we talk about anything else, and there's plenty to talk about," Susan said, "I need to know how you two know each other." She'd had it. Her face hurt, her hip ached, Bobby was AWOL, she'd been nearly killed, and she wasn't in the mood for secrets. She needed to know how much she could rely on

Romano.

"Actually, there's one thing I should do first," she said. "Thank you, Mr. Romano, for sending Paul Finn to keep an eye on me. It saved my life."

Romano looked gallant in a black turtleneck sweater and black flannel pants. A sheepskin winter jacket hung over the back of his chair. His eyes crinkled with pleasure. "You're welcome," he said. He looked toward her father, as though he would be taking his cue from him about what to tell her.

"I was hoping we wouldn't have to talk about this," her father said. "But now, given everything else that's happened, I guess I have no choice."

A brief smile crossed Romano's face. "You don't have to be so embarrassed about our dealings, Enzo. It hurts my feelings."

Her father looked up at Susan and frowned. "Your mother and I had very little money when we first came to this country. I was a good cook, and we were willing to work hard, but we opened the restaurant too soon. We got behind in our bills. Suppliers said they could no longer give us credit. Without credit, we couldn't buy food and it looked like we'd have to close. The restaurant didn't have enough history to satisfy a bank and we didn't have any collateral. Then friends told me about Frank Romano. They said he was from Italy and would lend us money."

Her father faced Romano. "Excuse me for speaking plainly, Frank, but they also said there were aspects of your business that were illegal."

He turned back to Susan. "I didn't want anything to do with that. But Gabriella was sick. You were a child, and we needed the money badly. He lent it to me. I made my payments to him on time, including the interest. We were crawling out of debt, but it was going to take a long time."

Susan barely remembered that time. All she'd known of the crisis was her mother's illness. She didn't know that there were money problems. As her father told the story, she could see, even all these years later, how much pain he was in. He spoke slowly and punctuated his narrative by gazing into the distance, rubbing his hand across his brow.

"After I took the loan, Frank's son, Frank Jr., used to come into the restaurant. Sometimes he brought his friends. I'm sorry to say it, but he was loud and rude, and never paid for his meals. I didn't think his father knew about that, but I was afraid to tell him. One weekend, two boys robbed a convenience store in Malden and the clerk was killed. A witness identified Frank Jr. as one of the culprits and the police arrested him. In fact, at the time of the robbery, he'd been at Gabriella's eating with two other boys. Neither of them would testify. The police leaned on them. I guess they wanted Frank's son pretty bad."

Her father took a sip of wine from the glass in front of him. "Frank came to the restaurant and asked if I remembered his son being there that night. I did. I testified in court, but I didn't mention that I owed money to the defendant's father. It felt like I was hiding something, but no one asked me about it. The jury found the boy not guilty.

"After the trial, Frank came to me and asked what I wanted. I said I didn't want anything. He said I had to let him do something for me. I told him what you can do for me is to let me run my restaurant in peace. He said that no one would ever bother me—not him, not anybody. He also said he was canceling my debt. I didn't want that. I continued to send him payments. He sent them back. Finally, I accepted that he wasn't going to take my money, and I stopped trying. Every now and then he drops by for an espresso. We talk—about Italy, about our families. He likes to cook. Sometimes he asks me for advice about how to prepare a dish."

"Why couldn't you tell me this before?" Susan asked.

"Your father is an honorable man," Romano said. "He was embarrassed that he'd been forced by circumstances to deal with someone like me. A lot of people that I've helped don't want it known. You'd be surprised who some of them are. It bothers me, but I can understand it."

Susan put her hand on her heart. Gabriella's was kept in business with a loan from the Mafia. Her whole life she'd believed it was the hard work and the willingness to sacrifice of her parents that made things possible. It was, but it was also money from Romano, from gambling and prostitution and loan sharking, and she didn't know what else. No wonder her dad didn't want her to know what his connection to Romano was. A man like her father must have been mortified that he'd been required to turn to Frank Romano for help. He seemed sort of comfortable with Romano now, though. They were both old men, immigrants. As different as they were, they shared some things in common.

Susan's emotions vacillated between shame and pride. She got her moral code from her father—her ideas of right and wrong. She shared his shame that the money he'd gotten to save the restaurant was dirty. At the same time, she was proud that he'd saved the restaurant and sought to pay the money back even after the debt was forgiven. She couldn't say whether it was right or wrong for her father to borrow money from the mob. Her life and his would've been very different if the restaurant had failed. Her father did what was necessary to protect his family. An immigrant in a new country, there was no place else to turn. He wasn't involved with where Romano's money came from. And yet, it was the people who borrowed from Romano who made his loansharking business profitable.

On top of that, here she was using the same Frank Romano to help her. She'd needed him to get this far on Nicky's case and she needed even more from him to get further. And to prove what? That the FBI, the gold standard for American law enforcement, was covering up for a killer. Probably one of their informants. It was incredible, but it seemed to be true.

Law school trained her to take one side of a case and argue for it with everything she had. To be a zealous advocate for her client. At the same time, the next week she might find herself on the opposite side of a similar case, and her job would be to argue fervently for that client. With respect to the lawyer's job, legal education took no position on which clients were "right" and which were "wrong."

Now that she was in the middle of it, Susan didn't like the idea of being a gun that anyone could pick up and fire. She wanted to be working for the good guys. But it was hard to tell the good guys from the bad guys in the current storm of crime and deceit. Maybe it was too simple to think in terms of good guys and bad guys. Everyone had good and bad in them. Romano was definitely a bad guy, but he'd been good to her. And to her father. Surely, however, at the end of the day, the sum total of what a person did either benefitted society or undermined it. She didn't want to take moral relativism so far that a person wasn't responsible for the harm he caused. But a single action could have both good and bad consequences. Romano lent her father money at a high rate of interest—that was loansharking. And yet, it enabled her dad to keep his restaurant open.

She could go around on this conundrum forever. For now, she needed to deal with the facts of this case. There was a job to do. She had signed on to defend Nicky Marino. If it took help from Frank Romano to get the job done, she'd get as much help from him as she could. She was okay with that. If the FBI was framing people and covering up for a murderer, they were the bad guys. As for her father and the restaurant, they could talk about that later.

Susan looked directly across the table at her father. "Dad, did Mr. Romano tell you about what happened tonight?"

Her father scowled. "Yes, he said you were nearly killed. He said if it wasn't for this Paul Finn, that car would have run you over."

"It would have. Someone desperately wants me to stop digging into this case. As far as I'm concerned, they may as well put up a billboard advertising Nicky Marino's innocence." She slapped her hand hard on the table. "I'm not going to stop. I'm not going to stop until I get to the bottom of this."

"I wouldn't want you to, honey. But this is dangerous," her father said.

"I think we can keep her safe," Romano said. "I'm going to have a couple more men nearby at all times. They'll be guys who are loyal to me and who liked Tony. Susan, I know you have more questions for me. We can talk tomorrow. You should bring Richard Charles and Paul Finn." He jotted an address on a piece of paper. "Come to my house."

"I've got two quick questions for now," Susan said. "First, how will I be able to tell your men from the bad guys?" It would be hard to tell his bad guys from the other bad guys, but she didn't say that.

"If it's all right, they'll come here at nine in the morning and introduce themselves."

She looked at her father, and he nodded. "Okay," she said. "The other thing is that I think I have to tell Bobby Coughlin about what we talked about Wednesday. The attack on me should be enough to convince him that Marino is innocent. Given that, he'll need to know where all this is going, so he can prepare for trial."

"I can see that," Romano said.

Susan wanted to ask Romano more questions, but it would be better to do so with the others there. He said his goodnights and left. Her father returned to the kitchen after showing Romano out and put his arms around her. Susan burst into tears.

32

Romano's men, Louie and Fredo, knocked on Susan's father's door precisely at nine o'clock. They were wearing down jackets. It was hard to tell if they were armed. Susan imagined they were. She said that she needed to go to Newton to see Bobby Coughlin, and they offered her a ride in their Suburban.

Sitting in the car, she wasn't sure if these men made her feel safer or more frightened. Louie took off his watch cap, exposing his shaved head. They were both well over six feet and looked like the tough guys they were supposed to be. Fredo's nose had been broken, maybe more than once. She had no idea what to talk to them about, or whether they expected her to talk at all. She didn't feel free to ask them what their jobs were with Romano. Nor did it seem appropriate to inquire whether they enjoyed working a protection detail. She couldn't ask whether they'd ever killed anyone, even though that's what she wanted to know. She remained silent. Let them make the first move if they wanted conversation.

Louie drove. Fredo rode in the back, so she could sit in front.

He drove precisely at the speed limit, making full stops at all stop signs. Both men constantly scanned their surroundings. Halfway to Newton, she couldn't stand the silence any longer.

"Are you guys expecting trouble?" she asked.

"Not really," Fredo said. "Romano put out the word that we're going to be with you for a while. That should be enough to keep away anybody who wants to harm you."

"You know, we've eaten at Gabriella's a few times and loved it," Louie said.

The menu for conversation became Italian food until they pulled up at Bobby's. Fredo explained how he made his red sauce. "I always start by dropping a chili pepper into sizzling oil before adding the tomatoes."

"Where'd you get that idea?" she asked.

"Evan Kleiman," Fredo said. "I love her book, *Pizza, Pasta, Panini.*"

This was surreal. Her life was in danger and she was talking about Italian cookbooks with her gangster bodyguards. Maybe good food was the answer to everything.

In Newton, Romano's men got out and waited by the car while Susan went to the front door. Once inside, she and Bobby ducked into his den. She began by telling him about the attempt on her life. Bobby sat down and she filled him in on what she'd learned over the past few days. He kept opening his mouth and leaning forward like he was eager to break in. She finished. He didn't speak right away. He looked at one wall and then the other, avoiding her eyes. "Are you all right, physically? Didn't you get hurt when Paul Finn tackled you?" Bobby finally said.

"I'm okay. I have a little pain, but it's nothing that Tylenol can't handle."

Bobby closed his eyes for a moment. "I don't know where to start. I told you not to be investigating on your own. You forged ahead and it nearly got you killed. What you're doing is too dangerous. And now, this whole story that you've dumped on the table. It sounds like you've convinced yourself that it was the FBI that put you in danger."

"FBI agents in the surveillance vans were the only ones who could have heard what Romano and I said. They must have told the person I call Mr. X. I'm assuming he's the one who tried to kill me."

Bobby got up, walked a couple of steps away and came back. "The FBI knows there's a cover-up?"

"Don't you get it? It's the only logical conclusion."

"Marino is really innocent?"

"My god, Bobby, yes, I'm sure of it."

He ran his fingers through his hair. "I'm getting a drink. How about you?"

"I'm good."

He left the room. Pretty early in the day, but he'd better have whatever he needs to get through this. Susan looked around. The den was nicely furnished, a little masculine for her taste, but pleasant, nonetheless. There was room for a small couch and a chair, leather of course, in addition to his desk and bookcases. To her surprise, reproductions of Audubon's paintings of birds adorned one wall. She would have expected pictures of boats or golf courses. There was no television. Bobby was a little more complicated than she'd thought.

So far, this meeting was going better than she'd feared. She'd dumped so much on him at once that Bobby was overwhelmed. She wasn't sure where he'd want to go from here.

Bobby returned with what looked like scotch on the rocks. "Marie says you arrived in a car, and it's parked outside with two guys in it. Who are they?"

Susan got up, crossed the room to a window, pulled back a curtain, and looked out. "That's Louie and Fredo, Romano's men. He put out the word that they're watching me, to discourage any further attacks."

"Jesus Christ. This is a shit storm." Bobby sat back down and took a gulp of his drink. "You really want those men tagging along with you?"

"I guess so. I talked to my dad about it, and he said it was probably the best thing. I'm staying at his house for a few days."

"What does he make of all this?"

Susan wasn't about to go very far into that. She wasn't completely sure what her father thought. He hadn't asked her to abandon the case. That surprised her. He must be terribly frightened. His face was white when she arrived at his house last night and his hands were trembling. Still, he knew her well enough to know that she wouldn't quit. That made her feel good. Her father respected her convictions. She wasn't going to talk to Bobby about the nature of her father's relationship with Romano. There was no point in going there.

"I haven't talked with him about the evidence in the case, of course. As to the attack on me, he was distraught, but he seems to have confidence in Romano's efforts to protect me."

"I wonder if Romano can figure out who this Mr. X is," Bobby said. "Even if he does, it's a whole separate question whether we could ever prove it in court."

There he goes with the glass-half-empty again. Instead of seeing the recent developments as an opportunity, he's focused on their problematic aspects. They did have to come up with a strategy for the courtroom, but Susan suspected they might be closer than they knew to getting to the bottom of things. The other side must be feeling vulnerable to have gone so far as to try to kill her.

"I'm going to talk to Romano about that this afternoon," she said. "In the meantime, I told him we'd keep all this confidential. It's important that you agree to that, so Romano will keep talking to me. He's our only source of information. Finn and I reported the attack to the police last night, but we didn't say anything about the possible relationship to our case."

"You don't have to tell me what's confidential," Bobby said. "I'm concerned about your safety, though. Are you sure you want to keep meeting with Romano?"

Susan was anxious about mentioning confidentiality to

Bobby. It could've gotten him started on how he was the lawyer and she was just a law student, and that whole song and dance. Fortunately, he'd spared her that. Now she just wanted to wrap this up and get out of his house so she could go on about her business.

"I'm the one Romano trusts. It's our best chance of getting something that could prove that Nicky is innocent. As long as I have Louie and Fredo and Paul Finn around, I'll be safe. I'd like to head back to my dad's now if that's okay with you. I'm still shook up from last night. I'll come into the office first thing on Monday and tell you if I've learned anything more from Romano."

Susan headed out to the car, worried about how Bobby would react once the reality of the attack sunk in. He might have another panic attack. Richard said that the judge wouldn't let Bobby withdraw from the case now that there was a trial date. It was unclear how much Bobby could contribute to the defense. He'd have to handle everything in court on Nicky's behalf. Susan didn't know if he had the nerve to prepare for trial, playing chicken with the prosecution, while she worked on figuring out who Mr. X was and how they could prove it. Maybe there was something she could do to build up his confidence. She'd put that on her list.

33

Boston is a remarkably segregated city, given its liberal reputation. The Irish live in South Boston, Blacks in Roxbury and Mattapan, Vietnamese in Dorchester, newly arrived Russians in Allston and Brighton, Brahmins in Back Bay and on Beacon Hill, gays in the South End, Jews in the suburbs of Brookline and Newton, and Latinos in Jamaica Plain and their own special neighborhood, Villa Victoria, carved out of the South End. The Italians own the North End.

Bostonians come from all over the city to the North End to eat. Walking down Hanover Street, one finds a restaurant every hundred feet. There's always a line of people waiting to buy cannoli outside Mike's Pastry. Those who want to buy Italian specialties to enjoy at home step into Salumeria Italiana for prepared meats, olives and olive oil, salted anchovies, fresh sun-dried tomato pesto, and similar delicacies. Several times a year the streets are taken over by people celebrating the feast of one or another Catholic Saint.

The neighborhood exudes *la dolce vita*. Underneath there is another community, a dangerous one, that the weekend diners do not see. The headquarters of the dark side of the North End was located in the home of Frank Romano, where Susan found herself on Sunday afternoon. She was mesmerized by her surroundings—his extensive library, the art, beautiful Persian carpets. Romano was an elegant criminal. She pondered why he hadn't used his obvious talents to put himself in this same position through legal means. Perhaps, in the beginning, his options had been limited. Susan would probably never have a chance to find out for sure. Romano's biography would be mind-blowing, but she doubted there was anyone who could get the information necessary to write it.

Richard and Susan accepted a glass of wine, and Paul Finn, a beer. Romano was nursing his favorite grappa. "You have some questions," Romano said.

"I do," Susan said. "Really, they all revolve around one subject. Is there some way we can figure out who Brady is covering up for? The man who was stealing from you, who killed Tony Francini, and who tried to kill me. Is there anything you can tell us that will help us expose him?"

"There may be. First, I have a question for Mr. Charles." Romano turned toward Richard. "I'd like to consult you as a lawyer. Someone has recently presented me with a situation, one that could expose me to criminal prosecution. I'd like to resolve it in a way that's perfectly legal, and I need your advice to do that. You will need the assistance of a law student, like Susan, and an investigator, like Mr. Finn, to represent me adequately. You'd also have my permission to consult with Attorney Coughlin. Could we proceed on that basis?"

Susan was impressed. Romano wanted everyone to be able to claim that this conversation was covered by the attorney-client privilege. So, he'd said that she and Finn were necessary participants in the consultation. That way no one would be able to repeat what he was about to say in court. It was clever, but she didn't have enough experience to know if it would work.

"Two things," Richard said. "First, we owe a duty of loyalty to our current clients. I couldn't agree to give you legal advice if your interests conflicted with theirs in any way."

"There's no conflict with Danny Costa or Nicky Marino. I can assure you of that."

"Very well. The second thing is that you must be talking about a real threat of prosecution. I won't agree to advise you about an imaginary or purely hypothetical problem."

"I can assure you of that as well," Romano said.

Richard took a yellow pad out of his briefcase. "Okay. You've got yourself a lawyer. What's the story?"

Susan was struck by how quickly Richard identified the potential pitfalls to Romano's proposal. This was where experience paid off. She would have been headed to the library or her computer to do some research.

Romano made a little tent out of his hands in front of him as he spoke. "There's a man in Charlestown named Tommy O'Neill."

"The guy with the long scar on his forehead?" Finn asked.

"None other. He and a couple of others robbed a jewelry store on Washington Street a year or so ago. They got away with a substantial sum in diamonds. I had nothing to do with it. I didn't know about the robbery in advance, and I didn't have anything to do with disposing of the stones. I didn't even know O'Neill was involved until several days ago when he spoke to me about it for the first time."

Romano took a sip of grappa. He related what O'Neill had told him. "I don't know of any way that Rizzo could've gotten to O'Neill except through Eddie Baker. The robbery was a year old and there were no suspects. They still haven't arrested O'Neill. Evidently, they're waiting to see if they can make a case against me."

"What did you tell O'Neill to do?" Richard asked.

"To play along with Rizzo for the time being."

Susan got up, walked over to the bookcase, and faced the

others. "Eddie Baker must be an FBI informant, working with Rizzo."

"It seems like he is," Romano said. "The other interesting thing is that his brother Willie was working for me when Tony was killed. I got rid of Willie shortly after that. He couldn't get along with the other guys. I concluded the thefts stopped because I changed the way we handled collections. Maybe it was because Willie was gone."

"Sounds like it was Willie, or maybe Eddie, or both, who killed Tony Francini," Susan said. "You told me Eddie was Brady's best friend. It makes sense that he'd lie for him. The FBI went along with it to protect their informant."

This was coming together. Her hunch about Eddie Baker was playing out. They knew the truth now, or at least the basics. As Bobby would say, proving it would be a different matter. This whole situation was weird. Sitting here with the head of organized crime in Boston, trying to figure out how to nail the FBI. As a 1L, studying criminal law, Susan would never have guessed that this is what it would lead to. Nobody could have. She'd read enough cases in school to know that agents are tempted by the idea that the end justifies the means. That's why the police cut corners, like conducting searches without a warrant and then lying about whether emergency circumstances forced them to do so. She'd never read a case, though, where government misconduct was this extreme—framing innocent men to cover-up a murder by an FBI informant.

Of course, the cases she read in law school weren't written from the perspective of a mob boss. They were decisions by judges refusing to allow the government to use illegally obtained evidence in court. They didn't cover meetings between criminals and lawyers scheming to expose government wrongdoing. Susan better remember who Romano was and what he did. This alliance was temporary. For now, he was her best chance of getting Nicky off. She didn't go to law school to become a lawyer for the mob. And yet, she had to admit Romano was fascinating.

Look at him sitting there. Calm as ever.

"I gather you want my legal advice on how to avoid getting arrested for this diamond theft," Richard said. "It would be a bonus if we could solve that problem and expose the Bakers as Francini's killers at the same time."

Romano nodded.

"Just how are we supposed to do that?" Susan asked.

Richard tapped his pen on the yellow pad. "That's what we've got to figure out."

34

The Seaport belonged to a different century than the North End. It was part of South Boston, but it wasn't Southie. For years, the area had been a wasteland of parking lots, warehouses, and a handful of eateries along the waterfront. Elderly Bostonians and college students with parents visiting from out of state favored Anthony's Pier Four, dining on baked oysters and stuffed lobster. Locals went to Jimmy's Harborside for fried clams. Eventually, the City demolished the elevated highway that walled off the neighborhood from downtown, and developers moved in, converting the warehouses into condos and opening trendier restaurants, bakeries, and microbreweries. A construction worker from Southie couldn't afford to live in this section of the harbor. Rena was typical of the class of professionals who flooded into the six and seven-figure condos. Susan went to see her after leaving Romano's.

"I can't believe you were nearly killed," Rena said. "Just a few blocks from here."

"It's a good thing that Richard Charles asked Paul Finn to

keep an eye on me. If he hadn't knocked me out of the way, it would've been all over."

Susan wasn't comfortable lying to Rena, but the fewer people who knew how close she'd gotten to Romano, the better. Susan would keep to herself that it was Romano who'd saved her. She'd asked Finn, rather than Romano's men, to drive her to the Seaport. No doubt Rena was worried when Susan didn't show up on Friday. She'd been tempted to let Rena believe that it'd been an accident. Susan hadn't wanted Rena to freak out and refuse to testify. Once again, Susan had been torn between her job and friendship.

Rena motioned for Susan to follow and headed into the kitchen. She poured them each a glass of rosé. "Why would anyone go after you? I mean, I know you're working hard on the case, but, no offense, you're still just a law student."

"It seems crazy," Susan said.

"I thought you just did research and that kind of stuff. I don't mean to pry, but what have you been doing that could drive somebody to such extremes?"

Rena's imagination must be running wild. Her curiosity was normal—her boyfriend was the murder victim. It was more than odd that a student intern would be the object of an assassination. If Rena knew it was Susan's relationship with Romano that triggered it, who knows what Rena might think. Perhaps she suspected Romano of being responsible for Tony's death. If she learned Susan was working with him, she might kiss off the defense team.

"I'm sorry. I can't get into the details of the work I do for Bobby Coughlin. I've interviewed a couple of witnesses, but I never expected anything like this."

Susan hoped Rena would let it go. It might have made her feel better to know that they'd figured out who the real killer was. Some might say she had a right to know. Until they came up with a way to prove that the Bakers were guilty and presented their evidence in court, they needed to keep their suspicions secret. If the FBI agents came to see Rena as the trial got closer, she might let something slip. The FBI might figure out a way to protect the Bakers. It sucked that in the meantime Susan needed to talk to Rena about testifying. Susan could lay the need to do so off on Bobby.

"Speaking of witnesses,' Susan said, "there's something else I have to talk with you about. I know this will be difficult, but Coughlin wants you to testify at the trial."

Rena shook her head. "You can't ask me to do that. I don't want to go anywhere near the trial. It's too painful. I can't do it."

"We need you."

"I don't know anything about the murder, except that Tony's body was left at my front door. The police were there. They must have taken a hundred pictures—why should I have to describe it?"

"It's not that. It's the issue of motive. The prosecution will argue that Tony was stealing from Romano to support you—that he bought the condo for you. You've told me the money was yours. We want you to testify to that, and to the fact that you were self-supporting."

Rena glowered at Susan. "Is this why you've been making friends with me, hanging around over here, just so you can get me to be a witness in your fucking case?"

"Oh, no. Please don't think that," Susan said.

"That's what it looks like. I've had this feeling before. Like I can't tell when you're working, and when you're not."

Susan should never have allowed herself to get so close to Rena. Especially after it became clear that they would need her in court. This is what comes from not keeping your social life separate from your job. Susan had known it, too. This was her fault. If Rena flat out refused to testify, they could subpoena her. Susan had learned in the clinic, however, that people who appeared only in response to a summons rarely made good witnesses.

Susan put her hand gently on Rena's arm. "I'm sorry. I

probably shouldn't have kept making friends with you after I realized that we'd need you as a witness. Or maybe I should have told you right up front that your testimony would be important. I'm new at this. As you said, I'm just a student. I feel terrible. I screwed this up. I like you and wanted to be your friend. But not just to get you to be a witness. I hope you can believe that."

Rena stepped back out of Susan's reach. "I wonder. I wonder if you ever would've made friends with me if I weren't Tony's girlfriend. Some women dropped me when it came out in the press that I'd been seeing him. Maybe for you, that was some kind of turn on."

"It wasn't a 'turn on.' Given my job, I needed to ask you questions about Tony. Even if I didn't think Nicky Marino was innocent, I'd have to do my best to help defend him. That doesn't mean I can't like you for who you are."

Rena glowered at Susan. "What would you do if I said I wouldn't testify? What would you do then? Would you have some process server show up here with a subpoena? Force me to come to court?"

"I hope it won't come to that."

Susan was trembling. She'd told the defense team Rena was a witness, and now she might lose her. Richard would think she was an amateur. She'd been sailing along like everything was so easy. She should have been more careful. Bobby had never wanted her to do her own investigation. He might feel like she'd gotten what was coming to her. Susan would hate to give him that satisfaction. If they were forced to subpoena Rena as an unfriendly witness, she'd be hostile, and the jury would pick up on it. They'd think Rena believed the defendants were guilty. That would be on Susan.

Rena grabbed a bottle of Maker's Mark off the counter, poured some into a glass, and took a sip. Then she got another glass from the cupboard and poured one for Susan. Rena took a deep breath and let it out slowly. "You know, to be honest, I don't think you're the manipulative type. I'm sorry I blew up.

I'm glad we're friends. Isn't there any way you could do the trial without me?"

Susan threw the bourbon down in one swallow. She didn't usually drink like that, but she was glad to have a shot of something stronger than the wine she'd been sipping. "I wish there were, but there isn't. We'll introduce your records to corroborate your testimony, but we need you in court for the jury to understand what they mean. There is a good side to this. Right now, the papers portray you as a kept woman. That's not fair to you or Tony. You can clear that up."

"What exactly would you want me to do?"

"Coughlin will meet with you to go over your testimony. He'll tell you everything he's going to ask you, and you'll tell him what you would say. I'll be there for that. We'll make a list of the records we need to subpoena. We'll give you a summons also, just so you have something you can show the prosecutor. That'll make it easier for you if the cops ask you why you're in court. The trial starts January seventh, but we won't call you as a witness until the defense case starts, probably a few days later."

Rena tossed down the rest of her bourbon. "Someone just tried to bump you off. What will they do to me?"

They'd killed Rena's boyfriend. They almost killed Susan. Of course, Rena was afraid. She was in a very different position than Susan was, though. It didn't make sense for anybody to go after her. Killing her wouldn't change the fact that Tony didn't buy her condo. That could be still be proved through records. Susan wouldn't put it that way to Rena. She didn't want her to think they didn't need her.

"After you've appeared in court, there'll be no reason to harm you. Before then, no one will expect you to give this testimony. You're already on the witness list for the prosecution, but they listed anybody and everybody who has even a remote connection to the case. They won't call most of those witnesses. We'll do the same, and you'll be lost in the crowd."

"I'm not going anywhere between now and the trial. So, if I agree to testify, I could meet with you and Coughlin whenever you want."

"Good. Your testimony is simple and straightforward. I think you'd only be on the stand for about half an hour, maybe a little more. The prosecutor would have a chance to cross-examine you, but I doubt he'll have much to ask since your testimony will be backed up by the records."

Rena teared up. "You know, I loved Tony. We probably would've gotten married if he hadn't been murdered."

Susan looked away to give Rena a moment for herself.

"I couldn't live with myself if I helped his killer get off," Rena said. "How sure are you that it wasn't your client?"

Susan looked Rena squarely in the eyes. "One hundred percent."

"How can you be so positive?"

"I really can't talk about that, but I am."

"There's nothing else you can tell me?"

Susan shook her head. "I'm afraid not."

"Okay, then. I'm on board. I'm only doing this because I trust you, Susan."

Thank god. She wished she could tell Rena what she knew. Susan had kept her as a witness, but she hadn't handled things well. She'd traded on their friendship to get her to testify. Next time she'd be more careful not to mix business with her social life. That wouldn't make this okay, though. Susan hoped Rena would make a good witness.

35

Rizzo drove through South Boston on his way to meet Smith and Tommy O'Neill at Aces High on Dot Ave. The Irish dive bar would be sparsely populated on a Monday night, a good place to do business that you didn't want the Italians to find out about.

The Bakers blew the attack on the girl. Disgusting. Now she knew she was a target. The word on the street was that Romano was protecting her. A couple of his hoods, Louie Moretti and Fredo Rossi dropped her off at his house yesterday, according to the surveillance agent. Then the lawyer Richard Charles and his investigator Paul Finn showed up. A fucking summit meeting. Rizzo should've put an illegal bug in there. No transcripts, no reports. Couldn't use it in court. At least he'd know what was going on. Now, the only thing he knew for sure was that they were onto Eddie Baker. Exactly how much they suspected was anybody's guess. Whatever it was, it'd been confirmed by the botched hit. Rizzo had no idea whether they'd made a connection between Baker and the FBI. If Baker got arrested for Tony Francini's murder, he'd sing like Pavarotti. The Suffolk D.A.'s office would love it. They'd have a couple of FBI agents in their sights.

Taking Romano out of the game would simplify things. This goddam law student obviously needed him. Rizzo's only chance to do that was Tommy O'Neill. Rizzo still wasn't sure if he could trust the diamond thief, but it didn't look like there was a choice. Eliminating the Bakers wasn't an option. Rizzo didn't have anybody who could do it, and on top of that, they'd be on high alert. Too bad. He was tired of cleaning up after them.

Rizzo turned off D Street onto Broadway and recalled how simple it'd seemed when they got Brady to testify. The D.A.'s office bought it and there was no reason why a jury wouldn't do the same. The FBI had never furnished all their reports to the prosecutor, Flanagan. The Bureau took the position that anything relating to their informants was strictly confidential. Rizzo told Flanagan that they'd promised Brady the witness protection program but never said anything about involving the Bakers in recruiting him as a witness. Of course, he never told the prosecutor that he knew Eddie Baker killed Francini, or that the agents had been the first to mention Costa's name. Flanagan was satisfied with the explanation that Brady agreed to testify to avoid a habitual offender sentence.

The Bureau loved how Rizzo and Smith used the Bakers to get Brady to testify. The SAC in Boston recommended incentive bonuses for their creative law enforcement strategy. In addition to the checks, the Director himself awarded them special commendations.

Shit, it might still work. Even if the defense lawyers believed Eddie Baker committed the murder, there was no way for the defense to prove it. If this thing blew up, though, Rizzo and Smith were going to prison. Given how many guys they'd sent away over the years, they'd have to do their time in protective custody. Even there they wouldn't be safe, locked up with a bunch of snitches who'd love to redeem themselves by whacking a pair of former agents.

It pissed Rizzo off even to think about that. It's not like he'd done anything wrong. Illegal yes, but justifiable. The creeps that Brady fingered for the Francini murder were connected. Although Costa didn't do this, he'd done other stuff he hadn't been caught for. Marino was on the fringes, but he would've eventually worked his way up from sports betting to something serious. A little collateral damage was to be expected in war. There was a war on organized crime. That wouldn't matter if the D.A. got wind of their deal with Brady. He and Smith would be in the dock. Failure wasn't an option. They needed to make a move on Romano.

Rizzo got to the tavern and found the others sitting in the back. There was no one else he recognized in the dimly lit room. Tommy O'Neill wore a dark hoodie that obscured his face. He fidgeted in his seat. Rizzo stopped at the bar to grab another beer for O'Neill and one for himself.

"You're going to have to get arrested, Tommy," Smith said. "We'll tell the prosecutor that the clerk has identified you as the one who did the diamond heist. Flanagan will get a warrant out on you. Once you're in custody, the court will appoint you a lawyer. When the time comes, we'll tell you what to say."

Rizzo took a swallow of beer. "We're going to tell Flanagan that we don't think you could've done this job on your own—that someone bigger must have been backing you. We'll suggest that he sound you out to see if you'd be willing to cooperate. When he does, you tell him that Costa came to you with the idea for this job. He told you that Romano would fence the diamonds. After the robbery, you delivered the stones to Costa and he paid you with money he said was coming from Romano. Figure out where you met with him, but don't claim to remember the exact date. Then Costa can't show he was somewhere else at the time. Once you've told your story, stick to it. Don't make it too complicated. That way you won't get fucked up on the details."

O'Neill wiped his brow with his handkerchief. "How much

time will I have to spend in jail?"

"Probably just a couple of weeks," Rizzo said. "Once you've made a deal with Flanagan you'll be released on bail. We'll tell him that when sentencing comes around to agree to probation because you might be useful to us on other cases."

"Hey, I'm not going to be your permanent snitch."

"You don't have to be. We just want Flanagan to think so. You get us Romano, that's enough for us."

O'Neill grimaced. "I don't see me staying alive very long if I send Frank Romano to prison. You gotta give me some protection."

"You want WITSEC?" Smith asked. "We could do that, but you'd never see your family again. You'd have to move away, never contact any of your old friends. It's not easy."

"Well, there sure as shit isn't going to be anything for me around here anyway, not if I testify against Romano. I'm not married, don't have any kids. Way I see it, I wouldn't have a choice—I'd have to leave," O'Neill said with a long face.

"If you go into witness protection, we get you a job, new identity, set you up someplace far from here. It takes a while to organize and that means you'll sit in jail a little longer. Once we move you, you get some money to tide you over until you get established," Rizzo said.

"How much money and how much longer do I have to sit in jail?"

"The money's enough," Rizzo said. "And you'll be safer in jail than on the street. We'll talk to the Marshal's Office. They run the program. We'll give you a week before we talk to Flanagan. In the meantime, don't make it too obvious that you're closing up shop."

"Yeah, well my life ain't that complicated. They're just a few things I have to do, but they won't cause any attention. See if you can get me someplace warmer than Boston."

"Oh, sure. We'll send you to Tahiti," Smith said.

O'Neill clenched his jaw. "There's nothing funny about this."

Rizzo regarded O'Neill carefully. He doesn't like anything about this. Better give him a little something to ease the pain.

Rizzo handed O'Neill five hundred dollars. "There'll be more later." That put a little smile on the asshole's face.

O'Neill left and the agents got another beer.

"Think the Marshals will go for it?" Smith asked.

"If O'Neill gives us Romano? Sure. I just hope we can count on him."

"Once he gets arrested for the diamonds, he won't have much choice unless he wants a good stretch in prison. He can't stand the sound of two weeks in jail—he's not going to risk going to Walpole."

"You're right. Son of a bitch, we might finally get Romano."

Rizzo pictured himself on the beach in Florida, relaxing on chaise lounges with his girlfriend. Her in a bikini, beads of sweat running down her chest between her breasts, legs tanned by the sun. Not a care in the fucking world. He'd only have to work a few more years for the Bureau. Then retire with his pension. Get a little private job to bring in a few more bucks. Some kind of insurance work. He'd talked to other agents who'd done well with that. Nothing that required chasing gangsters or reporting to Washington. It'd be sweet. He deserved it.

36

The windows at the end of Richard Charles's conference room overlooked Boston Harbor. Snow was coming down hard, and Susan could scarcely see all the way to the water. It was beautiful, but hazardous on the streets below. Traffic in the North End barely crawled along. If you were walking, the neighborhood was wonderful. Everyone was bundled up, cloaked in colorful wool scarves, and there was a palpable feeling on the street of, "It's cold, but we can handle this. We're New Englanders." It was a pleasure to stop by a café, have an espresso and chat with others taking a break from the weather. The worse it got outside, the better the neighbors got to know each other. Recent developments in the case were gripping, but Susan wouldn't have minded taking a break for a few days and enjoying the atmosphere around Gabriella's. Unfortunately, there was no time for that.

"Romano's men brought me a message this morning," Susan told Bobby and Richard. "Tommy O'Neill got word to him last night that the FBI is going to talk to Flanagan next Monday.

When O'Neill gets arrested, he's supposed to say that Costa and Romano engineered the job." Susan had previously filled Bobby in about the Sunday meeting with Romano.

Richard sloughed off his blazer and rolled up his shirtsleeves. "I've been thinking about how to turn this to our advantage. It's difficult. I've only got one idea, and it's risky."

"Let's hear it," Bobby said.

"Suppose we go to Flanagan before the FBI does. We tell him that Rizzo and Smith are coming in, they're going to give him O'Neill, and they've asked him to say that Costa and Romano planned the robbery. We explain that it's a parallel to the Francini murder—that the FBI is using O'Neill in the same way they used Brady. When the agents come in and our prediction proves to be true, we'll have credibility with Flanagan, and we can talk to him about the Bakers."

"Maybe," Bobby said. "Or maybe he'll think we're all working for Romano and this is just a ploy to save him from getting indicted."

Susan, for once, agreed with Bobby. They had an enormous obstacle in their path—the acquired cynicism of a prosecuting attorney. "We'd have to come up with a way to convince Flanagan that the FBI persuaded O'Neill to lie about Romano's involvement," she said.

Bobby shook his head. "There's a problem with this. O'Neill would have to take the weight for the robbery. Once he admits to it, he has to give Flanagan something or he's looking at the potential of a life sentence. They went into that store with guns. If we take Romano away, he won't have much. Just naming his accomplices won't take a lot of time off."

"How about this?" Richard said. "What if we get a lawyer for O'Neill who has nothing to do with the Francini case? Someone that Flanagan will believe. And she puts Rizzo and Smith on the table right away. Tells him that O'Neill will cooperate and testify against them, but only if he gets a light sentence for the robbery."

"Why would O'Neill be willing to do any time?" Bobby asked.

"O'Neill's already on the hook," Richard said. "The Bakers probably wouldn't testify against him, but the clerk in the store has identified him. He's got to make a deal: either with the FBI or with us. Not for nothing, but he's going to make the deal that makes Frank Romano happier."

What a double-edged sword Romano represented. Susan was so glad to have his men protecting her that some of the time she'd begun to think of him as a benevolent uncle. If O'Neill had made a deal with the FBI, though, instead of telling Romano about their proposal, it could've been fatal. It fascinated her how one man could be so ruthless, and yet as considerate as Romano was to her. She wondered what he thought of himself. Say, late at night, lying in bed, pondering his mortality. Was he religious, or did he just like Renaissance art? It was part of his Roman Catholic heritage. She'd heard that he went to church. What did he think, sitting in a pew, singing hymns, staring up at Jesus on the cross behind the altar? Maybe it was just for show. Or maybe he did it to hedge his bets. She didn't know if he went to confession. If he did, the priest would get an earful.

Susan turned to Richard. "Talking about the lawyer, you said 'she.' Do you have somebody in mind?"

"As a matter of fact, I do. Jane Friley."

Jane Friley had given a talk to Susan's Women and the Law class at Suffolk. Thirty years ago, as a novice agent in her early twenties, Friley spent every day for two years in a small cubicle analyzing paperwork from construction companies. They were responsible for building a major interstate highway overpass in the Midwest. It'd collapsed on a holiday weekend, causing the death of thirty-five people. Most of the agents had forgotten who she was and what she was working on. She walked into her boss's office one morning and dropped a six hundred-page report on his desk. She documented the use of inferior building materials throughout the project and systematic fraud in the preparation of quality control reports. The government indicted two corporate defendants who were forced to pay millions of dollars in fines, and twenty-eight individuals, all but three of whom went to prison. Those three were the first and only defendants Friley interviewed. She persuaded them to become prosecution witnesses. She then announced they didn't need to make any more deals to prove the case and advised the AUSA handling it to prosecute the rest of the crew to the full extent of the law, which he did.

After that, Friley's career took off. As far as it could. She encountered gender roadblocks. She was a veteran agent, tough, and highly skilled. She'd worked in the Boston office of the FBI for eight years. She'd been the top person in line for SAC twice, and they'd given the job to a less qualified man both times. She got a transfer to New Orleans and ran into the same kind of male chauvinism there. Eventually, it drove her out of the Bureau. She quit and came back to Boston to practice law. Instead of going into the U.S. Attorney's Office, where she would've been welcomed with open arms, she started doing defense work.

"Do you think Jane would go up against Rizzo and Smith?" Bobby asked.

"If she knew that Rizzo and Smith were crooked, it wouldn't trouble her at all," Richard said. "Friley's a stickler for professional ethics. She wouldn't cotton to the idea of FBI agents having the Bakers commit murders for them. I'll tell her I'm approaching her on behalf of a potential client. She'll have to keep it confidential. It would be covered by attorney-client privilege. There's no risk in asking her if she'd be willing to take this on."

The practice of law is not only about what you know, but who you know, Susan thought. Without someone like Friley, it'd be much harder to get Flanagan on board with their plan. Susan would love to have a chance to talk with Friley. All those years with the FBI, then she becomes a defense lawyer. With her experience, she certainly knew what she'd be up against.

Everyone agreed to the plan, but Susan could tell the

lawyers were nervous about it. It was complicated. There were a lot of moving pieces and it depended heavily on people they couldn't control, like O'Neill and Flanagan. They wrapped up and Richard said he would try to see Friley as soon as possible. He invited Susan to go with him. She didn't even have to ask.

37

Bobby was sitting at his kitchen table staring into his third Manhattan. Marie came in through the garage door and he looked up but didn't greet her. "What's the matter?" she asked.

"You know," he said, "I read in the *New Yorker* that according to Nietzsche—when you gaze for a long time into the abyss, the abyss also gazes into you."

"Oh, really. What does that mean?"

"I have no fucking idea."

"Well, while you're working that out, why don't you get started on dinner? You promised to cook tonight. I'm going to shower."

He took another sip of his drink. He'd get to dinner in a while. Marie was good for at least forty-five minutes upstairs and it wasn't going to take that long to get a meal ready. Or, maybe he would just stick his head in the oven. Then he wouldn't have to cook, and he wouldn't have to worry about the goddam Marino case.

Bobby was gazing into the abyss all right. He couldn't tell if anything or anyone was gazing back. At first, he'd been worried about a trial in which Marino would get convicted. Bobby wasn't that worried about Marino—he'd assumed Marino was guilty. Bobby was afraid for himself. Afraid that he couldn't bear the weight of it. He'd planned to solve the problem by getting the client to plead out. No longer. It seemed Marino really was innocent. Bobby's law student intern had turned into Nancy fucking Drew and was on the trail of the real killer. The bad guys actually tried to kill her. Now she had a couple of Romano's thugs as bodyguards. Meanwhile, the defense team was partnered up with the mob boss to run a con on the D.A.'s office.

Bobby couldn't have seen any of this coming and didn't know where it was going. He'd never even heard of a case this fucked up. The therapist he'd seen after Jamie committed suicide would say that he needed to stop dwelling on the abyss and look into himself. If he didn't like what he saw, at least he'd know what he needed to change. There wasn't much mystery about that. Bobby was afraid of a disaster, and so he avoided the reality that he had a client to defend. He wasn't doing the first thing that his job required.

Bobby had to hand it to Susan. She hadn't gotten any encouragement from him, and yet look at what she'd done. Talk about sick lawyer jokes. Susan hadn't even passed the bar and already someone had made an attempt on her life. It didn't slow her down one bit. If anything, she was energized. She might be on the brink of breaking the case wide open. Bobby sure as hell hoped so. He needed to get out of her way. He'd been trying all along to hold her back, putting barriers in front of her, just like the FBI had done to Jane Friley.

He knew about Friley. She was another powerful woman. She was the right person for the job. No question about it. The problem was the job. Maybe it wasn't unethical or illegal. Bobby hadn't thought that through. It was dodgy, to say the least. If it fell apart and Tom Flanagan learned that they'd been behind it, it would sour Bobby's relationship with the prosecutor's office forever. He hoped it would work. Flanagan might get suspicious enough of the agents to delay the trial and investigate further. Maybe they wouldn't have to try the case. That was out of Bobby's hands. What he did have to worry about was the need to prepare for trial in case it did go forward. There was no way out of that. He wondered if he could take it one step at a time and get through it without falling apart.

Bobby needed to get Marino ready to testify. That wasn't going to be easy. Bobby wasn't sure if putting Marino on the stand was a good idea. The guy would be scared to death. His nervousness could easily give the jury the idea there was something to hide. Bobby needed to get Susan to go out to the jail with him to talk to Marino about it. Then there was the incident at Magoun's with Brady. Bobby would have to prepare Patty and the bartender as witnesses. That'd be easier. He'd represented defendants who'd been in bar fights before. Susan could help with that also—she had a relationship with Patty, and she'd met the bartender. Rena Posso was no problem. Her testimony would be like a woman's description of her assets in a divorce case. Bobby did plenty of those when he was younger before the excess of drama drove him out of family law. He still remembered the late Friday afternoon child visitation calls from his women clients. They would say something like, "He's late to pick up the kids again and *she's* in the car." He didn't want to hear it and neither did the judges. In a lot of the cases, he couldn't decide who was acting worse—his client or the spouse. Bobby didn't need that in his life. Still, he knew the routine. Leading Rena through the purchase of her condo would be simple enough.

That left Joseph Brady. Richard Charles would handle that. Maybe Bobby would have to cross Brady on the Magoun's thing. The asshole might be stupid enough to deny it. Instead of trying to beat Brady up about it, Bobby could just rely on calling Patty and the bartender in the defense case to show he was lying.

Bobby got up and poured the rest of his drink down the

kitchen sink. He grabbed a skillet and warmed it on the stove. He put in a little olive oil to heat up. He sliced a shallot and dropped it into the skillet where it began to sizzle. He wiped off some cremini mushrooms, trimmed off the ends of the stalks and cut the mushrooms into thin slices. These went into the skillet as well. As he always did, Bobby wondered what it would be like to gather his own mushrooms in the forest, like in a Russian novel. Maybe he'd have a chance to try it someday. He shook some Borsari seasoned salt into the pan and then poured in a generous amount of Marsala wine and brought it to a boil. As it bubbled, it gave off an aroma sweet enough to call everyone to the table. He turned the burner down to low. He heated oil in another skillet while the liquid in the first pan simmered and reduced. He put two chicken breasts into the second pan, browned them on one side for about a minute and a half, turned them for another minute and then tested one with his knife to see if it was done. He loved the subtle scent they gave off. He let them go for another thirty seconds, then turned the chicken breasts out onto a platter, covered them with the sauce, took the salad he'd made the previous night out of the refrigerator, whipped up a simple oil and vinegar dressing, and uncorked a bottle of Sauvignon Blanc. He'd first tasted this wine during college, on a bicycle tour of Central France. He'd loved it then, and he still did. Dinner was ready.

Just like that. There was nothing on Bobby's plate that he hadn't done before. He wouldn't think about the fact that Marino was charged with murder, and the penalty, if he got convicted, would be life without parole. Sure, no problem. "No problem!" Bobby screamed. He slammed his hands down on the table and sat down to catch his breath.

After a minute, he called upstairs to tell Marie that dinner was served.

38

Susan was too young when her mother died to remember if they'd ever made Christmas cookies. She'd done it a few times with her girlfriends. It helped her get into the spirit of the season. Rena invited her over to bake cookies on Friday night. Susan wasn't scheduled to work at Gabriella's, so she agreed. She wanted to do something normal for a change. She'd lost track of the holiday season this year, focusing on the case all the time. Her life was out of balance and she worried about it. The problem was likely to get worse after she became a real lawyer.

Louie and Fredo dropped her off, walked her up to the condo and waited with her until Rena opened the door. Susan enjoyed their company. Tonight, they'd recapped the Red Sox four-game sweep of the Rockies in the World Series. The men had been at the opening game when Boston trounced Colorado thirteen to one. Louie was needling Fredo. He'd been hung up in traffic and got to the game late.

"So, you missed Pedroia's home run in the bottom of the first?" Susan asked. They were surprised by what she knew. In fact, she could have written out the line score of each game. She couldn't afford tickets to the Series, but she'd seen the whole thing on TV. It vexed her that men just assumed that women would be stupid when it came to sports. Susan enjoyed startling them with the fact that she knew as much, or more, as they did. Particularly when it came to the Red Sox.

Rena took her straight into her kitchen.

"Look at everything you've got," Susan said. "Vanilla, red, yellow, and blue icing, sprinkles of all colors, little red hearts, white snowflakes, rock candy, and cookie cutters to make Christmas trees, ornaments, little mittens. You're obviously a pro." It was hard to believe that someone who didn't have kids would have all this equipment.

Rena immediately got things started. She whisked together flour and salt, then threw butter, cream cheese, and sugar into her standing Kitchen Aid mixer and beat them together. She added eggs and almond and vanilla extract, then beat the flour into everything else. She flattened the dough into disks, covered them in plastic wrap, and put them in the refrigerator to chill. The whole operation just took a few minutes. "Time for Bloody Marys," she said.

"What? No eggnog?" Susan asked.

They headed into the living room with their drinks, flopped down on the couch, and put their feet up on the coffee table. Coltrane was on the stereo. Rena owned the newest Bose speakers and the sound was great. This was the chic, professional single woman, Christmas cookie party. This was how things might be until she and her friends started having kids.

"How's the new play coming?" Susan asked. Rena had gotten the part that she'd auditioned for.

"Too early to tell. Everybody's still learning their lines, and we've just started blocking—you know, where people stand and where they move on the stage. I like the other actors and the crew, and it's great to be working again. How about you? How's everything looking for the trial?"

Susan shuddered. "It's just a little over three weeks away. There's a lot of last-minute stuff to do. I'm glad to be taking tonight off. I don't even want to think about it."

"Okay, it's a deal, I won't make you talk about it. Just one last question. Are you going to give your share of the cookies to those goons who are protecting you?" Rena laughed.

Susan wasn't laughing. "They're not goons. They're friends of Paul Finn. Okay, tell you the truth, I'm not sure what all they do when they're not with me. I don't care. They've been nice to me, and I'm glad to have them around."

"Okay. They just look so *lethal*."

"That's the point."

"I wonder if there are any female bodyguards," Rena said. "I don't know if women can be as tough as men. I don't know if they have it in them."

Susan just assumed that Rena was a feminist, although she wasn't sure what made her think so. Rena was independent, making her own way in the world. Susan really didn't know a lot about her. Like her political views or what sort of people her other friends were. Rena must have been open-minded to be dating Tony. Or maybe it wasn't such a leap. Maybe she was secretly working for Romano too. That would explain why it didn't bother Rena to hang out with her, even though Susan was working for Nicky. Romano would have told Rena that the men accused of the murder didn't do it. Rena was a professional actress—she could pull off a double life. What use would Romano have for someone like her, though? With her background, it was hard to see why she would get involved with the mob. This was silly. She didn't have any reason to think Rena was a criminal.

"You don't think women can be as tough as men?" Susan asked. "Let me tell you about this woman I just met." She didn't see the harm in telling Rena about Jane Friley if Susan didn't mention that Friley had any relation to Nicky's case.

Susan and Richard had met with Friley on Wednesday and arranged for her to represent O'Neill. They'd talked for a couple of hours. Friley wasn't bitter about her experience in the FBI. She did say that a few of the agents in Boston were real pigs, although she was too discreet to name them. She'd vowed, however, not to let her experience ruin the rest of her life. Friley was sad that things weren't changing more rapidly, but for her, it made more sense to leave than to continue banging her head against the wall. She could be an interesting mentor. Mentors were still few and far between for a young woman like Susan interested in criminal defense. She wondered if Friley might be willing to take on a young associate.

"She's a lawyer who used to be an FBI agent," Susan told Rena. "She was with them for a long time and handled a lot of high-profile cases. She told me about this shootout she got into with survivalists in Colorado. She and her partner were checking out a simple trespassing complaint. As soon as she said they were FBI, the suspects started shooting. She was badly wounded but managed to get to cover behind her vehicle. That was the only case where she ever fired her weapon. Bullets were flying back and forth for a long time. She shot and killed two men, and then the third suspect surrendered."

Rena raised her arms and stretched. "From what you're saying, she sounds pretty macho."

"That's the thing. She's strong and she can do everything the men can do, but she doesn't have the arrogance and swagger that a lot of guys seem to think they need. We talked about it. She thinks a woman, or a man for that matter, can be tough without having to act tough all the time. She's fine with people underestimating her as a woman. Then when it's time to get down to business, she's got the element of surprise. Still, it got to the point where she hit the glass ceiling, so she left and started practicing law."

"How did you meet her?"

"Richard Charles introduced me to her. He's working with her on some robbery case."

"Ooh, Richard," said Rena. Her hand fluttered over her

heart. "The way you talk about him, he sounds like McDreamy."

"Believe me, it's purely professional with me and him."

"Sure it is," Rena said.

They went back to the kitchen, rolled out the dough, punched out the cookies and put them into the oven. After the cookies baked and cooled, they tried to outdo each other with more and more colorful decorations. Susan made an ornament in the shape of a bell, on which she used colored sprinkles to create a face with a vague resemblance to the Mona Lisa.

"You're good," Rena said. "Mine don't look any different than the ones I made in third grade. I can't draw. I have to get my artistic satisfaction from acting, and from taking pictures."

Rena led Susan to a small den beyond the living room. Susan had never been in this room before. The walls were covered with photographs, printed on eight by ten glossy paper and stuck up with masking tape. Beautiful landscapes from the Swiss Alps, portraits of vendors at open-air markets in Barcelona, and dramatic black and white shots of street life in the North End of Boston. They were very professionally composed and shot. The portraits demonstrated an uncommon sensitivity to the individual characteristics of their subjects.

"These are amazing," Susan said. "Did you take them?"

"I did. I don't usually show them to anyone, but I wanted you to see them. I thought you might appreciate them."

Susan was touched. They returned to the kitchen. The aroma of the cookies filled the room. Rena had shared something very personal with her, and this had turned out to be a special occasion. They ate some of the cookies and divided up the rest.

Susan wanted to see Rena on the stage and wondered how different Rena would seem when she was acting. The case would be over some day and then they could spend more time together. Although if there was a conviction, there would be an appeal and that would take a couple of years, at least. Susan hadn't known how stressful criminal defense was going to be. She was wrung out every night. She got into bed needing sleep but couldn't make herself stop thinking about Nicky. She'd lie there racking her brain to find a way out for him. The gambit with O'Neill might not work. If it didn't, they'd be back to square one.

Once Susan graduated and got admitted to the bar, she'd have her own clients. Several at a time, if she was going to make a living at it. She was afraid that she might never easily fall asleep again, and that there would never be time to make sugar cookies, or fall in love, or have children, or live a normal life.

The guys arrived to pick her up. "I haven't done anything like this in so long," Susan said. "I needed the chance to just chill out with another girl. Thanks so much."

"I loved it too," Rena said. "Oh, by the way, I'm just curious. What's the name of that woman you were telling me about?"

"Jane Friley. I'll call you to get together next week if I'm not flat out getting ready for the trial. In any event, Bobby's secretary will be calling you to set up an appointment so he can meet with you."

They got to the car and Susan gave half her cookies to Louie and Fredo. *Goons*, she thought. You shouldn't jump to conclusions about people.

39

Tom Flanagan's desk was covered with files for the upcoming Francini case. He shoved a pile to the side, to make a little room in case his guest needed to do any writing. He studied Jane Friley. He'd never had a case with her but was familiar with her reputation. Tough, smart, honest. She handled primarily federal cases, although she'd had a couple of matters with other prosecutors in his office. She looked business-like in a charcoal pants suit. Kept herself in good shape. No makeup, except around her eyes, which were cobalt blue and looked like they could see right through you. If Flanagan were a guilty suspect in her old office at the FBI, he'd probably spill his guts.

Friley said on the phone that she had something to tell him. Other than that, he didn't know what she wanted.

"I have a client who's given me some interesting information," she said. "I'd like to share it with you, but I can't do that without exposing his involvement in a crime. So, first I need to see if he'll be treated leniently if he comes forward."

Flanagan crossed his arms over his chest. "As I'm sure you

can appreciate, I can't make any promises unless I know what we're talking about." Ordinarily, criminals didn't rat out their partners until after they were arrested. He wondered where this was going.

"Of course," Friley said. "Let's see if this works for you. This story is hard to believe, but I'm convinced it's true. My client participated in the armed robbery of a jewelry store, a little over a year ago. They got about a hundred grand in diamonds. No shots were fired, and no one was physically injured. To date, nobody has been arrested.

"Two FBI agents learned of his involvement. I hate to say this, but these agents are crooked. They're guilty of obstruction of justice and subornation of perjury, and probably worse. They leaned on my client and are forcing him to say that two people, one of whom is of great interest to law enforcement, planned the robbery and fenced the diamonds. In fact, those two people weren't involved. The agents have threatened my client with a long prison term if he won't cooperate and promised to put him in the witness protection program if he does. It's a naked frame-up."

Friley might be talking about Frank Romano. He could fence diamonds and he was the person of greatest interest to the FBI. It would take brass balls to put him in a frame. Flanagan would like to know what might make these agents think they could get away with it. If any of this was true. He'd reject the story out of hand if it weren't coming from someone like Friley.

"Your client wants to give us the two agents in exchange for leniency on the robbery," he said.

"Precisely."

If this was for real, Flanagan wanted it. He'd like to see a couple of those arrogant pricks from the Bureau get what they deserved. They treated the people in his office like they were peons to do their bidding whenever they wanted. Like in Francini. Their boy gets a pass on nine murders. Flanagan was still pissed off about that. Off the top of his head, he couldn't think of a case where a state D.A.'s office had prosecuted FBI agents for obstruction of justice. It'd make quite a splash. At the same time, it'd be a painful belly flop if he didn't get a conviction.

The testimony of a thief wouldn't be enough to guarantee a guilty verdict against federal agents. Flanagan would need more. And he'd have to get his boss on board. This would make the D.A. nervous. He'd need to be convinced the politics of it made sense. Flanagan would have to make a strong pitch. Maybe he should take Friley in to see the D.A. Let her close the deal. If the boss dealt directly with Friley and things went south, it wouldn't be his problem.

"I'll need to get the D.A. to approve this. He'll want your client to tell us who did fence the diamonds if it wasn't the men the agents want him to name. And we'd want him to wear a wire and get the agents into a conversation about their deal."

Friley nodded. "That's what I'd want if I were you. He's prepared to do both things."

"How do you suggest we do this?" Flanagan asked.

Friley leaned forward in her chair. "Next Monday, the agents, Mike Rizzo and Harry Smith, are going to come to your office. They'll have probable cause for a warrant to arrest my client. Once he's in custody, we'll sit down with you and he'll tell you the whole story. Later you can tell the agents that he gave you the guys behind the job. I'm sure they'll ask to speak with my client, supposedly to try to get more information. You can wire him up for that meeting."

Friley was talking about the same Rizzo and Smith who got Brady to turn on the Francini murder. Flanagan never had any dealings with those agents before that. Then they show up twice in a row. Friley's story made him highly suspicious. This coming so close to the Francini trial made it likely that there was something more behind it. Flanagan could hardly take what she was saying at face value. Nor could he rule it out.

"Do you know what their probable cause to arrest your client is based on?"

Friley held up her hand like a stop sign. "I'd rather not discuss that. The agents will tell you what they've got."

Flanagan didn't expect her to answer that one. There was no reason for her to furnish specific evidence that incriminated her client. No point in asking for her client's name either. The purpose of her coming in was to test the waters before he was exposed.

"How about the people they want your guy to incriminate?" Flanagan asked.

"Danny Costa and Frank Romano."

It was about Romano. Doubling down on the coincidence made him even more suspicious. Something wasn't right here. He wasn't about to be played for a patsy by this lady, no matter what her background was. Flanagan's eyes searched Friley's face for clues. Her expression was impassive. Damn, he'd hate to play poker with her. He'd just have to go slow and hope she wasn't conning him. Friley enjoyed a good reputation as a successful field agent. She'd made some big cases. Now she was a respected lawyer. At the same time, she was probably nursing a grudge against the Boston FBI Office. This could be payback. He'd know if this was real only when he got a recording of her client talking with the agents. He'd play along for now.

"Are you representing Costa and Romano's interests as well?"

"No. My only client is the man who did the robbery. He tells me that Costa and Romano weren't involved."

"I'll take this to the D.A. today. If he's interested, I'll want you to speak with him directly so he can make the final decision. I've got to be honest with you—I'm skeptical. But if everything you say pans out, I'd recommend a short sentence for your guy on the robbery."

Friley left and Flanagan opened the file with Brady's grand jury testimony and resumed work on trial preparation. He couldn't put Friley's visit out of his mind. It'd been years since anyone had brought a case against Romano. He was the puppet master behind the scenes in the Francini prosecution, even though Romano hadn't been indicted. Now this new case at the same time, generated by the same two agents. It was suspicious either way you looked at it. Rizzo and Smith were on the FBI's organized crime squad. Busting Romano was their primary goal. Still, would they suborn perjury to get to him? Flanagan didn't like them, but he put more faith in the FBI than that.

He closed the file. He'd better talk to the D.A. sooner, rather than later. He headed down the hall to his office.

40

Susan had terrible news to deliver. It was Friday, four days before Christmas, and the defense team was to meet in Richard Charles's conference room. Louie and Fredo picked Susan up that morning and told her that no one had heard from Tommy O'Neill since Wednesday. That's when he last sent word to Romano to let him know that O'Neill hadn't been arrested. They'd been out looking for him. He wasn't at home. They couldn't find him anywhere. Romano said they should assume the worst.

Susan was cold inside, from her forehead to her toes. O'Neill was probably dead. Except for her mother, none of her friends and family had died. A girl at Smith killed herself when Susan was a student—sleeping pills—but Susan hadn't known her.

She'd expected that O'Neill would be arrested early in the week. Nothing happened on Monday or Tuesday. The lawyers figured that Flanagan was busy. Maybe it was taking time to get a warrant. Starting on Wednesday, they'd been getting increasingly worried that something was wrong. Friley was supposed to call as soon as she heard O'Neill had been arrested.

Susan had expected their plan to work. Friley met with Flanagan and the D.A., who'd approved her proposal. Friley reported that the meetings went well. Richard said if they were going to run into problems, they would've been in the D.A.'s office. Richard thought there might be political obstacles to getting them to move against the FBI.

It never occurred to Susan that O'Neill's life might be at risk. She, of all people, should have considered that. After all, they'd taken a run at her when they learned she was talking to Romano about Eddie Baker. O'Neill was an even bigger threat to the agents. The defense should've warned him to lay low until the cops were ready to arrest him. Flanagan could've let Friley know when he got a warrant and she would've arranged for his surrender. Maybe, though, laying low would have been a mistake. It might've made the agents suspicious if O'Neill wasn't at his usual haunts.

Susan was in over her head. She knew too little of how federal agents and crooks behaved. She'd been focused on putting the pieces of the puzzle together. O'Neill wasn't a piece on a board, though. If he'd been taken out of the game, a real, live human being had lost his life.

She walked into the conference room. Richard and Bobby were at the table. "Something awful has happened," she said. "O'Neill's missing." She ran down what she'd learned from Louie and Fredo.

"We've got to talk to Friley," Richard said. He dialed her number and put the phone on speaker. Susan prayed that Friley would know where O'Neill was.

"I just got off the phone with Flanagan," Friley said. "I hadn't heard from him since we met with the D.A. last week and he signed off on the plan. I called him and asked what was going on. Flanagan blew up at me and wanted to know what kind of a game I was playing. Rizzo and Smith never contacted him about any diamond robbery. I said I couldn't understand what had happened and assured him I'd told him the truth, but he wasn't buying it. I called O'Neill but got voicemail."

"No one's heard from O'Neill since Wednesday and we can't find him," Richard said. "When you met with him last week, did you get any vibe that he might not be playing straight with us?"

"No. He seemed sincere, but I don't know the guy. I wouldn't necessarily have picked up on it. What do you want me to do?"

"There's nothing to do right now. We'll get back to you if we learn anything. I'm sorry this made you look bad with Flanagan," Richard said.

"Fuck that," Friley said. "I'm just worried about O'Neill."

Richard hung up the phone. Susan could see on the lawyers' faces that they had the same thought—Tommy O'Neill was probably dead. Richard stood up. "I know what you're thinking. But if O'Neill is dead—and we don't know that he is—we didn't kill him. We couldn't have seen that coming."

"He didn't just freak out and take off," Susan said. "Rizzo and Smith called off their play against Romano for some reason. They probably learned that we were wise to it."

"The trial is just a little over two weeks from now," Bobby said. "We've got to get a postponement." His hands were shaking.

"That's not in the cards," Richard said. "This thing with O'Neill was the only leverage we had to get Flanagan to investigate the Bakers. Flanagan must think that Romano was behind sending Friley into his office. We couldn't get him to look at Eddie Baker now if we showed Flanagan his fingerprints on the murder weapon. We're back to a reasonable doubt defense with the stuff we've had all along. We'll have to do the best we can with that."

Susan couldn't imagine what went wrong. Without evidence that the Bakers were the real killers, all they had was a short series of questions about the prosecution's case. Richard had admitted to her that convincing the jury that their questions amounted to reasonable doubt about the defendants' guilt wasn't going to be easy.

Their plan to turn the FBI's scheme against them hadn't been a bad one. Somehow the FBI knew that they were onto them. She needed to try to figure out how they found out. The problem was she had no idea where to begin.

41

Susan and Bobby were crowded into a small interview room with Nicky Marino at the Plymouth House of Correction on Saturday morning. They'd come to bring him up to date and to discuss his testifying at the trial. Nicky looked gaunt. He'd lost so much weight since he'd been locked up. Susan looked past his drawn face at the gray walls and beat-up furniture of the room. Nicky's cell was probably even more depressing. Susan wondered how this man survived day by day, with little to occupy him other than the charges he was facing.

It was the first time Susan had visited someone in custody. She could call for the guard and leave whenever she wished, but Nicky could not. The jail regulated every moment of his day—when he got up, when he ate, when he could shower, when he was allowed to talk to other prisoners, and, rarely, when he was permitted to go outside. They censored his reading material and monitored his phone calls. The word "confined" took on greater meaning for her as she considered his circumstances in the small, cramped visiting room.

"I owe you an apology," Bobby said to Nicky. "I spent too much time talking about pleading guilty. You said all along you had nothing to do with Francini's death. I'm sorry I didn't trust you."

"So, now you think I'm innocent, Mr. Coughlin?" Nicky asked.

"We think we've discovered who killed Francini with Brady. Two brothers—Eddie and Willie Baker."

"I've heard of them. Everyone says they're mean bastards. Why'd they do this?"

"Seems like Willie was stealing from Romano and might've been worried that Francini knew it," Bobby said.

Susan felt some sympathy for Bobby. Admitting to Nicky that he'd been wrong wasn't easy. Bobby had assumed Nicky was guilty. Most of his clients were guilty. But not everyone. A client should at least get the presumption of innocence from his lawyer. They'd fought about this for the whole case. Was there something she could've done to get him to see the truth earlier? Probably not. He didn't grasp that there was something wrong with the prosecution's case until the Bakers tried to kill her.

Bobby explained how they'd come to believe that the Bakers were responsible. He told Nicky what Susan had learned from Romano and what they suspected about the FBI's role. Bobby described how she'd nearly been killed by a car trying to run her over and Nicky sucked in his breath.

"Patty told me you were working hard on the case, but I had no idea you were risking your life."

"To tell you the truth, neither did I," Susan said. "Not until it happened. Thank goodness I wasn't badly hurt. Since then Romano's men have been protecting me."

"Romano's men?"

"Yeah. I'm secretly a biker chick when I'm not doing the law thing, and I met these guys at a rally."

Bobby and Nicky both stared at her. It had been a poor attempt to lighten the mood.

"I'm kidding, Nicky," she said. "Romano knows you and Costa are innocent. He's been helping us."

Bobby shifted uncomfortably on the metal chair that was bolted to the floor. "There's a problem. We don't have proof that the Bakers were the killers. We can't accuse the FBI of being involved without hard evidence. Unfortunately, there's more bad news."

Nicky was sweating. "What now?"

"Have you ever heard of Tommy O'Neill?" Susan asked.

"No. Another Irish guy? Is he a fucking killer too?"

There was no way to sugar coat this. She described how the FBI was manipulating O'Neill to get at Romano and the defense strategy to turn that back against them.

"That failed," Susan said. "The FBI dropped their plan. O'Neill has been missing for several days."

"What do you mean by 'missing?'"

"We're not sure. No one can find him. He's probably dead."

"Holy crap. They killed Francini, tried to kill you, maybe killed this other guy—"

"These guys are bad," Bobby said. "Worse than I could ever have imagined."

"Goddamit," Nicky said. He stood up and kicked his chair against the wall. "What does all this mean for me?"

"With O'Neill missing, we've lost our only witness with direct knowledge of the FBI's part in manufacturing evidence," Bobby said. "We don't have any proof of a link between the Bakers and the FBI. There's no evidence that would stand up in court that the attack on Susan was related to your case. So, what we've got is the fact that Brady's a bad character who's getting a sweet deal for testifying against you. And that he carried a grudge against you for knocking him down at Magoun's. We've also got testimony from Francini's girlfriend, Rena Posso, that he didn't buy her condo, which contradicts the prosecution's theory that he was stealing from Romano to pay her expenses."

"That's it?" Nicky's shoulders dropped.

"I'm afraid so. The whole case rides on whether the jury believes Brady. You could testify, to deny that you had anything to do with the murder. Costa can't testify. He's too close with Romano. It's up to you if you want to take the stand."

"I got no idea what I should do. I've never even seen a trial, let alone been on trial."

"In general, jurors want to hear from a defendant," Bobby said. "If they like you, it could cause enough doubt about Brady's story for them to vote not guilty. On the other hand, it can be risky to take the stand. One of the main reasons that a defendant might decide not to testify is if he's got a prior record. If the jury hears that someone has been convicted of other crimes, it usually turns them so far against him that he's sunk. You don't have a record. So that's to your advantage.

"The other main reason is the defendant might get so nervous on the stand that he'll look like he's guilty, even if he's not. How do you think you'd bear up?"

"I can't say. I'm not the kind of guy goes around giving speeches. Talking in a courtroom full of people? I'd be scared shitless."

"How about this?" Susan said. "You don't have to commit until the last minute. We've got two weeks before the trial. Bobby can come out here and go over your testimony with you. I'll come some of the time as well. You can practice what you'd say in court. See how it goes. Then decide."

They left it at that. Bobby drove silently back to Boston. Susan asked him what he was thinking about.

"I'm thinking about the only other murder case I ever had," he said. "I was just a young lawyer and my client, Jamie, was a fourteen-year-old kid who killed his abusive father. I couldn't keep the case in Juvenile Court and when it got transferred to Superior Court, the boy committed suicide in his cell. I blamed myself. I'd spent all my time getting close to him and his family and working on a treatment plan. I was so proud of what I was doing. It never occurred to me that the D.A. would want to try him as an adult. I didn't give any thought to the other side of the case. I wasn't ready for the prosecutor's transfer motion. I was so devastated that I went into therapy. I've never really gotten over it."

"Oh, Bobby, I wish you'd told me about this."

Bobby gripped the steering wheel tightly in his hands. "I left my job at the clinic a week after Jamie died. I didn't want to practice law anymore. I got a job tending bar—I'd done that in law school to make my expenses. A couple years later I was working at this gin mill in Southie. Two guys came in with guns. There were only a handful of customers there and they made everyone lie face down on the floor. Right in front of me, there was a shotgun on the shelf under the bar. I was too scared to touch it. I cleaned out the till for them and they were backing out of the place when one of the customers started coughing and came up into a crouch. One of the robbers panicked and shot him in the head. They turned and ran. The cops never found them. I quit the next day. It was a long time before I could even set foot in a bar again." Bobby loosened his grip of the steering wheel and sighed heavily.

"I had a little money saved up and I didn't do anything for a while. When that ran out, I got a part-time job in a divorce firm. I figured if I stayed away from criminal law, I might be able to get back into practice. The whining and fighting drove me nuts. I lasted a year, then I thought crimes might be less stressful than domestic warfare, and I started doing appointed cases. I gradually built up a practice. After a couple of years, I was feeling okay. Not great, but okay. Eventually, I got into a groove and things got better."

Bobby was driving slowly. He moved into the right-hand lane to let other cars pass him. "I never wanted to do another murder. When I got appointed to this case, I just wanted to get it over with as soon as possible. I've done a poor job. Honestly, that's not right. I haven't done any work on this. They tried to run you over, and I promised myself I would do what I could to see this through. Then O'Neill disappeared. That was the last straw. I started drafting a motion to withdraw from the case, but then I didn't think the judge would let me out. I got pissed off. I don't want these bastards to get away with this. I'll do what I can for Nicky, but to tell you the truth, I'm hanging on by my fingernails."

Susan was taken aback. She was completely unaware of what he'd been dealing with. She'd thought something must have happened to make him so fearful, but she'd never sought to find out what it might be. It would be devastating to have a client who was a teenage kid who killed himself. Taking on the responsibility for someone else's life was a dangerous business. Susan had underestimated that. She should have been more understanding. She was glad Bobby had finally opened up.

She put her hand on his shoulder. "I have no idea what to say. What can I do?"

"You've already done a lot. I hate to think where we'd be at on this case if it weren't for you. I'm going to try to do my best at this point. I know you'll give me as much help as you can."

Bobby dropped her off. Susan watched him drive away. It was going to be tough for him to handle what he needed to do. He might fall apart. He'd admitted he was barely hanging on. They were working as a team, so Richard would be there to help him with his preparation. That might not be enough. The idea of him cracking in the middle of the trial scared the shit out of her. And then there was the client to worry about. As for Nicky, when Susan talked with Richard on the phone earlier that morning, he'd said that no matter how much Nicky practiced, they'd never be able to predict how he'd hold up under pressure. Now she really got what Richard meant several weeks ago when he talked about lizard brain fear.

42

The next two weeks, the lawyers worked into the evening every day except Christmas, and up until 5:00 on Christmas Eve. It was unlike any holiday period that Susan had ever known. She'd managed to get through her shopping in a couple of hours on Sunday afternoon. On Monday, by the time she got to her father's, he'd already started the goose. The aroma of the bird roasting in the oven wafted through the whole apartment. The lights were twinkling on the tree they'd put up the week before.

Ornaments they'd had forever brought back memories of childhood. Winding their way around the top of the tree were garlands of colored beads that Susan made at a Christmas party at Gabriella's that her father threw for her fourth-grade class. A hand-blown glass house perched between two lower branches. She'd brought it home from Florence when she'd done a college semester abroad. She'd found it on one of those narrow streets near the Duomo where a person could be wiped out by a crazy onrush of motor scooters while admiring the gargoyles above. In the center of the tree hung a white stocking that meant everything to her father. On it, his sister Gina had cross-stitched the face of St. Nicholas and the words, "Primo Natale di Susan." Gina died in Italy in an automobile accident a few months after making it. He always put it on the tree last.

Susan's father came from the kitchen into the living room with a glass of chilled Prosecco in each hand, limping slightly. Susan took one and gave him a kiss on the cheek. Smiling broadly, she sunk into his big overstuffed couch. She was home, and it was Christmas Eve. This, she knew in an instant, was where life was lived.

"You look happy tonight," her father said. "I've been worried about you. First the car. Then working so hard. Are you okay?"

"I'm glad to be here with you," she said. "Everything has been difficult and takes too much time. It's hard to remember that I'm a person, not just a part of some legal machine. Here, I feel human again. I'm sorry I've caused you so much anxiety."

"I'm fine. I'm proud of you. And you're safe now. Frank Romano told me that either Louie or Fredo would be outside tonight. They're taking turns. It never occurred to me that I'd have his men standing guard outside my house on Christmas Eve."

"I'm sorry it was so hard for you to tell me how you know Romano. Believe me, I'm fine with what you did. You would have lost the restaurant otherwise, and our lives would never have been the same. And I'm proud of you for testifying in court for his kid. Not everyone would have done that."

They finished their drinks and went to the kitchen. Susan threw on an apron and assembled a simple arugula and fennel salad, with a dressing of shallots, lemon juice, and mustard. Her father boiled sweet potatoes, then mashed them with chipotle chiles, maple syrup, and butter. He'd baked an apple pie that morning. It provided a little American flavor.

When everything was ready, her father carved the goose, poured some Nebbiolo, and they sat down to dinner. Long ago, they'd agreed they would avoid talking about work at holiday meals. She happily listened to her dad's news from the neighborhood—who was getting married, who was having babies, who was making a trip to Tuscany. They lingered at the table for a couple of hours, then went back to the living room and exchanged gifts. Susan tore the wrapping off her father's present to her—a handmade leather briefcase from Milan. "You'll need this for the papers of all the clients you're going to have when you finish school," he said. "I only wish your mother were here to see what a fine young woman you've become."

"Oh, Daddy." Susan threw her arms around him and gave him a long hug. She loved the gift and her eyes teared. He'd done everything he could to be both a father and a mother to her. But she wanted a real mother more than anything in the world. She missed having her for simple everyday things, and for the serious advice that her mother might have given her. She wanted to make Christmas cookies with her, to walk about the streets of Boston in the snow, arm in arm, to spend hours decorating the house for the holidays and wrapping presents. She needed to complain to her about Bobby, to get advice on what to do about Richard, and she could really use her help figuring out how to balance the demands of a career and a family. She wished she could crawl into her mother's arms and tell her how frightened she was about this trial. She'd give anything for just a second to glimpse her face. She had none of that. It had been stolen from her by a brain tumor. It wasn't fair. Susan looked at her dad and loved him more than ever for trying to make it all right. He couldn't be her mother, but he'd been the best father she could've hoped for.

Lorenzo unwrapped his present and pulled on the sweater she'd selected. It fit perfectly. "I love the soft feel of the cashmere," he said, as he ran his hands over his shoulders. They sat in the living room, listening to Christmas music, enjoying some more wine, and talking about old times. Neither mentioned the case for the rest of the evening.

She spent the night at her dad's. Lying in bed, she thought

about the different parts of her life. She desperately wanted to be a success as a lawyer. If she stayed with criminal law, though, it would always be about conflict and violence. The work would be stressful. She wouldn't always need a bodyguard. She would, however, have to find a way to protect her family life from the pressures of her job. Not just at Christmas, but every week. That would be difficult. Tonight, it worked just to let herself be a little girl again in her father's house. She pulled the sheet up around her neck and let her body relax into the mattress. She needed this. Her eyelids grew heavy. She thought about how her father used to give her cooking lessons sometimes. She'd loved that. She saw him tasting her sauce in the kitchen, her setting the table, and them sitting there, enjoying the meal. Gradually she lost the sense of whether she was awake or dreaming. Before she knew it, she was fast asleep.

On Christmas Day, Susan worked at Gabriella's. Her father always said that once he'd enjoyed his celebration on Christmas Eve, he should spend the next day serving those of his customers who couldn't prepare their own holiday feast. Susan spent twelve hours at the restaurant, prepping the food in the morning and serving it in the afternoon and evening. It was exhausting, but she loved it and the hard work left no time to worry about the trial. The only reminder of that was the rotation between Louie, Fredo, and Paul Finn, each of whom took a turn sitting near the front door. They were armed but wore suits that were cut generously enough to hide a weapon. Fredo enjoyed himself, sampling one dish after the next while on duty. After his shift was over, he hung out speaking Italian with her father and picking up tips from the guys in the kitchen. A tough guy who could cook. At the end of the evening, Susan went back to her father's house. They shared a final glass of wine together, and the Christmas break was over.

43

Susan's hands shook as she got dressed for New Year's Eve. She wasn't sure if it'd been smart to accept Richard's invitation to dinner. She'd insisted they keep it casual, dress down, and avoid the hoopla at the fancy restaurants. She wasn't ready to plunge into an affair with him. She knew that's what he wanted. Little glances here and there, unnecessary touches. It was obvious. In any event, there was something else about the case she needed to bring up with him, and she was terrified to do it.

The past week they'd all worked hard to get ready for the trial. Finn made sure that Jerry, the bartender from Magoun's, would be available to testify. Finn and Susan went over Jerry's account several times with him, then turned him over to Bobby to rehearse the direct examination. Susan worried about how doing a mock exam would affect Bobby. To her relief, he hadn't fallen apart. He wasn't brilliant, but he got through it.

Richard said Patty's testimony needed to go beyond describing what happened at Magoun's. He wanted her to put a human face on Nicky, to describe in a loving way their family life and Nicky's relationship with the children. Patty could paint a picture of him as the sort of man who couldn't possibly commit murder. That required a lot more finesse on Bobby's part than questioning Jerry. They were still working on that. Patty was sweet and charming, and smart and tough enough not to get tripped up on cross-examination on the Magoun's story. The issue was what sort of atmosphere Bobby could create. So far, he was too wooden. Susan hoped he'd be able to relax when the time came.

Long stretches of Bobby's time were spent at Plymouth working with Nicky. Susan went out there twice. Nicky was so nervous just going over his testimony in the jail, that it was doubtful he could get through it unscathed in the courtroom. Richard said if he didn't testify the jury would be wondering why.

They scheduled Rena to come in after New Year's to meet with Bobby. Susan drafted subpoenas for the necessary records and sent them to the sheriff's office to get them served.

Richard took responsibility for the most important part of trial preparation—getting ready to cross-examine Joseph Brady. He read his grand jury testimony and the FBI reports on his interviews so many times that he had them all but memorized. If Brady said anything at trial inconsistent with his previous statements, Richard would pounce on it. The principal strategy was to show how much Brady was benefitting by cooperating with the government. They conducted several mock cross-examinations, with Finn playing the role of Brady. Susan and Bobby acted as jurors, to give feedback. It was exhausting. They just didn't have the feeling that they had what they needed to make Brady sound like a liar. And they only had a week left before trial.

Susan met Richard at his office. He already had a bottle of wine open and was on his second glass. He poured some for Susan. His room was so orderly. No clutter, just two neat piles of papers on his desk. The books on his shelves were arranged by different areas of the law. His mind was probably just as well organized. His office was the sort of space that invited you to work long hours. Across the room from his desk, a separate seating area with a couch and two easy chairs accommodated more casual conversation. She found it easy to chill there, in jeans and a wool pullover, sitting with her legs tucked up under her on the couch.

She wasn't sure how to start the conversation. He just plunged in.

"I hope you don't mind my asking but are you seeing anyone?" he asked.

She laughed. "I'd hardly have time, would I? Between school, working at Gabriella's, a murder trial. Even if I did have time, no, I haven't been. What about you?"

"I was in a relationship that lasted almost six years. We never lived together, but we saw each other exclusively. She taught English as a second language. Last summer, she got an offer from a school in Hong Kong, and she took it."

"It was over, just like that?"

Richard took a sip of wine. "We talked about it, of course. I guess we both realized there were reasons why we'd never moved in together. It was time for a change. We emailed back and forth for a while. That tapered off after a few months. It was for the best. We had a good time together. It never felt, though, what should I say, magical."

Susan was on the brink of saying, "Oh, you want magic." That, however, would be coquettish. She didn't want this exchange to go further. They were about to start a murder trial. If one or the other of them got disappointed or angry it could create big problems. They couldn't afford that. Given what else she had to tell him tonight, flirting was even more inappropriate.

"I'm looking for magic too, Richard. And who knows? It might be close at hand. Still, I don't want to do any exploring until after this trial is over."

"This is the calm before the storm. It's a good time to talk about what has obviously been building up between us."

Susan put her feet on the floor. "It doesn't feel that calm to me. Have you handled so many murder cases that there's nothing special about this one?"

"No, I'm not like that. This case is special. We've got innocent clients. There's a good chance they're going to be convicted of something they didn't do."

"Let's focus on that, not on our personal feelings," Susan said.

Richard shrugged. "We can't do much about the case tonight."

"Actually, there's something I have to tell you. I think I made a bad mistake."

She'd woken up the last three nights in a sweat. So stupid. She'd just plowed ahead like she knew what she was doing. And she'd screwed up. At least it seemed she had. She wasn't sure. And if so, she didn't know if there was a way to fix it.

Richard moved across the room and sat on the couch, at the other end, giving her some space. "Every lawyer makes mistakes. That's one reason I like having a defense team. There's always someone else to help work things out. I doubt you've made any serious errors. Everything you've said and done has made sense to me. Still, whatever doubts you have, it's important that you share them with me."

Susan gulped. She had no choice but to just come out with it.

"I'm responsible for Tommy O'Neill's death," she said.

44

The moment of truth, or what passes for it in the Suffolk Superior Court, arrived. The courtroom was packed. Susan was barely able to get her father into the gallery. The media were there in full force. The court officers, the clerk, and the stenographer were busily arranging and rearranging their props so everything would be perfect when the curtain went up. The lawyers sat at their tables without fussing with their papers. Their stomachs might be doing flip-flops, but they sat calmly, as though they didn't have a care in the world. The court officers brought in the defendants, costumed in coats and ties. A buzz grew in the room and then gradually died down. It was as though everyone knew they were supposed to be quiet, even though no one ordered them to stop speaking. Susan couldn't sit still. She was at the end of their table, with Nicky Marino between her and Bobby. Costa sat next to Bobby, then Richard Charles. The prosecution table was to their right, closer to the jury box. From Susan's seat, she could take in all the participants with one glance.

Judge Christine Walsh came through the door from her chambers, and a bailiff intoned, "All rise." The judge took her seat on the bench. An attractive blond in her fifties, she'd been appointed to the Superior Court after several years in the District Attorney's Office. Despite her service as a prosecutor, she was widely considered to be impartial.

"Good morning, ladies and gentlemen," Judge Walsh said. "You may be seated. Counsel, we're ready to commence with jury selection, unless there are any motions that I need to hear."

There were no motions. The judge immediately called a recess so the clerk could get a panel of potential jurors from downstairs where they waited to be sent to individual courtrooms. To the consternation of the people in the last three rows, they needed to leave to make room for the potential jurors. Meanwhile, the clerk gave the jurors' questionnaires to the lawyers. They got busy, looking to spot jurors they wanted to accept or reject. Susan helped Bobby organize their copies. There was little information of value, other than the person's address, occupation, whether they ever worked for law enforcement, and whether they had been convicted of a crime. Massachusetts didn't allow lawyers to individually question prospective jurors, like other jurisdictions Susan had read about. Usually, the judges only asked general questions, to identify obvious prejudices. The method was not very scientific. Cynics said you might just as well take the first twelve slices of the bologna.

Jury selection ate up the whole first day. Susan couldn't tell whether the jury they got was good or not. There were eight men, six women; four blacks, seven whites, two Latinas, and an older Chinese man. Judge Walsh said she would select the two alternates at random at the end of the trial; that way all fourteen would be motivated to pay attention.

At Richard's request, Judge Walsh asked prospective jurors where they got their news. Of the fourteen now in the box, ten said "Fox TV." Susan was worried about that, given Fox's law and order orientation. On the other hand, there were two teachers, which was unusual. Defense lawyers preferred intelligent jurors. They were more likely to think critically about the evidence and raise doubts about the prosecution's case. Richard said maybe the teachers would balance things out once deliberations started.

——

The next morning, the courtroom was once again packed to the walls. The judge came onto the bench and the jurors filed into their seats. Patty sat in the first row, together with Danny Costa's wife and Susan's father. Ordinarily, Patty would have been required to wait in the corridor until she was called to the stand. Witnesses were kept out of the courtroom so the evidence given by others would not influence their testimony. Bobby, however, in one of his finer moments, convinced Judge Walsh to make an exception for Patty. Tom Flanagan objected vociferously.

"Are you kidding? It's his wife. You already have everything you need to question her impartiality. Save your ammunition for something serious," Judge Walsh said.

Susan was relieved that Patty wasn't stuck all by herself on a bench in the hallway. Susan was going to like this judge. No nonsense.

The clerk stood and addressed the jury with the language used to open criminal trials in Massachusetts since the formation of the Commonwealth: "Members of the jury, the defendants have been indicted by the Grand Jury on the charge of murder in the first degree against the person of Anthony Francini, on July 7, 2004. Upon this indictment, they have been arraigned and have thereunto pleaded not guilty; and for their trial, they have placed themselves upon the country, which country you are. You are sworn to try the issues. If you find that a defendant is guilty, you are to say so. If you find that he is not guilty, you are to say so and no more. Harken to the evidence."

Judge Walsh turned to the prosecutor. "Mr. Flanagan, you may make your opening statement."

Flanagan stood in front of the jury box with no notes, making eye contact with one juror after another. He spun his tale in a convincing way, transporting the jury to the scene and letting them see what happened. He described how the killers ambushed Tony Francini on the waterfront, and how Nicky Marino shot him. The jurors hung on every word. Several recoiled at Flanagan's description of Brady hacking off the victim's fingers. Mrs. Jackson, juror number ten sitting in the second row, a financial analyst at Fidelity, looked squarely at Nicky. She shook her head from side to side.

Flanagan finished and the evidence began. The Commonwealth called Eric Bates, the young man who'd been Francini's assistant, as its first witness. He testified that Tony worked late on the night he was killed and asked him to take Tony's car to the dealer. Tony hadn't given him a reason for the request, but he'd been happy to do the boss a favor.

"You didn't mind driving his Jag?" Flanagan asked, and everyone laughed.

He's starting with evidence that Francini was anxious that someone might follow his car, Susan thought. He wants the jury to get the idea right away that he was afraid that Romano suspected Tony was stealing. Mrs. Keller, juror number five in the front row, a waitress at the Union Oyster House, was nodding like she got the point.

Flanagan then called a series of forensic witnesses. The crime scene investigators testified about the bloodstains and hair they found in Brady's van, and the fibers they lifted off Francini's suit. The DNA analyst gave the jurors a short seminar about DNA, then presented overwhelming statistical evidence that the blood was Francini's.

The Boston Police trace evidence specialist, a woman in her early forties, took the stand. She wore the nerdiest glasses Susan had ever seen. She may as well have had "Scientist" written on her forehead. She described everything clearly and didn't talk down to the jury. She was likable. She explained that the hair found in the van was consistent with samples of Francini's hair that had been taken at the autopsy. She'd compared the two sets of hairs side by side under a microscope. She projected slides of the microscopic images from a document camera onto a large viewing screen on the other side of the courtroom. She did a similar analysis and demonstration comparing the fibers found on the victim's suit with the carpet from the van. The jurors ate up the CSI quality of this presentation, several nodding as she spoke. The defense was not contesting that Francini's body was transported in the van. There was no point to a searching cross-examination.

The pathologist was the last forensic witness. An older man, with gray hair, dressed in a business suit, he sat up straight in the witness box. The prosecutor took him through his medical qualifications, asked him to describe the autopsy procedure, then paused.

"Do you have an opinion, to a reasonable degree of scientific certainty, about what caused the death of Mr. Francini?" Flanagan asked.

"Yes. It was a gunshot wound through the mouth."

"Are you able to tell us from what distance the gun was fired?"

"Yes. The barrel of the gun was thrust into the mouth of the victim."

"How were you able to determine that?"

"When a weapon is fired, gunpowder, vaporized primer, and metal are discharged through the barrel in addition to the bullet. Some of the gunpowder is completely burned and is black and looks like soot. Particles of burning or unburned gunpowder are also discharged. In Mr. Francini's case, none of this discharge was located on his skin. It was all found inside his mouth, which was burned and blackened."

Juror number six, Julia Martinez, sitting in the front row, demurely attired in a pale-yellow dress with a high neckline and a low hem, blanched and turned away from the witness.

"Did Mr. Francini suffer any other wounds?"

"Yes. They cut off the fingers of his right hand."

Susan watched the jury carefully during this testimony. Flanagan questioned the witness in a cut and dried way. He made no effort to hype the evidence. From the faces of the jurors, it was clear that he didn't need to. The pathologist's testimony was gruesome enough all on its own. The atmosphere in the room tightened up. Susan's skin had goosebumps.

The police officers that responded to Rena's call when she found Francini's body in front of her door described what they'd seen. Flanagan questioned the investigating detective.

"How much blood was there in the hallway outside Ms. Posso's condo?" Flanagan asked.

"Very little," the detective said.

Flanagan held his chin in his fingers. "What did you conclude from that?"

"It was clear that the victim was killed elsewhere and taken to the building sometime in the night after the concierge went off duty."

"Showing you what's been marked for identification as Commonwealth's exhibit 10, detective, what do you recognize it to be?"

"That's a photo of the victim's right hand, as it rested on his chest, on the floor outside Ms. Posso's condo, and of the pocket protector in his shirt pocket."

"We'd like to have this admitted in evidence and I'd like to display it to the jury on the document camera," Flanagan said.

The defense lawyers objected. They contended that the photos were unfairly prejudicial. They argued that the jurors would respond emotionally and might convict the defendants in anger, even if they harbored a reasonable doubt as to their guilt.

"The photos are disturbing," Judge Walsh said, "but murder is disturbing. Your objections are overruled."

All eyes turned to the photo of the bloody stumps on Tony Francini's hand and the severed fingers in his pocket protector as it flashed on the large viewing screen on the other side of the courtroom from the jury box. Several jurors gritted their teeth and narrowed their eyes, while others quickly looked away.

Still no-nonsense. Susan's Evidence professor had shown the class several grotesque autopsy slides so they could see how upsetting such photographs were, but also how important they could be in supporting a prosecutor's analysis of the case. She didn't like it, but she got it. Cutting off the victim's fingers was consistent with a desire to send a message. Given the prosecution's theory that Francini was a thief, the message was clear enough.

Flanagan called a records keeper from MasterCard and introduced a copy of Danny Costa's credit card bill showing that he'd eaten at Lucca on the day that Brady claimed to have met him there to discuss the murder. On cross-examination, Richard got the witness to admit that the bill did not indicate who was with Costa.

Brady was to be the prosecution's last witness, and Judge Walsh said she wouldn't require Flanagan to begin his examination so late in the afternoon. She recessed court for the day.

Susan walked back to the North End alone. Her father had left earlier to attend to his duties in the restaurant. What would Susan think if she were on the jury? It wasn't good. Flanagan did a great job showing how brutal the murder had been. She'd felt the revulsion that the jurors and everyone in the courtroom experienced. That feeling lingered in the room for the rest of the day. The defense lawyers barely asked any questions. She could have done everything they did today, although the overwhelming drama of the trial was more intimidating and exhausting than she'd expected. Flanagan skillfully set the stage for Brady's testimony tomorrow. She couldn't imagine herself cross-examining him. Not yet. But one day she'd be ready for something like that. She couldn't wait.

45

The next morning there was a line of people trying to get into the courtroom that stretched all the way down the hall, past the elevators to the staircase at the end. They came for Brady. Everyone wanted to see the notorious killer. Inside the courtroom, the reporters hovered over their notebooks, pens in hand, like vultures waiting for the blood to start flowing.

Nicky Marino had dark circles under his eyes like he hadn't slept. Patty was back in the front row, with bloodshot eyes and a red nose. Susan's father offered Patty his handkerchief.

Susan had expected the trial to be exciting. Maybe it was for the people in the courtroom who had nothing at stake. She was emotionally drained. The defense lawyers had nothing to work with. The prosecution was roaring along like a European bullet train. On the other hand, other than Costa's credit card records, which didn't prove much, none of the evidence so far tied the defendants to the murder. That would be Brady's job.

Judge Walsh came out on the bench. "Call your next witness," she instructed Flanagan.

"The Commonwealth calls Joseph Brady."

All eyes turned to the door to the lockup, from which Brady entered the courtroom, wearing a navy-blue suit over a crisp button-down white shirt, with no tie. Despite his clothes, he looked like a brute. His eyes were small and deep-set. It was ten in the morning, but he already had a five o'clock shadow. Taking the oath, his voice sounded like a low roll of thunder.

Susan quivered as Flanagan stood to begin questioning the witness. Brady's very presence cast a pall of malevolence in the room. A miasma of pure evil flowed from the witness box in which he sat and collected in the well of the courtroom until it lapped over the bar and spread through the gallery, row by row until it seemed like the Devil himself had announced his presence to the entire room.

Flanagan's direct examination proceeded exactly as Susan expected. She wondered how many times they'd rehearsed it. Brady testified that Costa ordered the hit on Francini. Costa told him that Romano knew Francini was stealing from him to support his girlfriend, Rena Posso. He paid Brady fifty grand for the hit and arranged for Marino to help him.

Brady and Marino had waited on Congress Street in Brady's van. Francini crossed the Fort Point Channel, and they grabbed him. Marino shot him. Then Brady cut off his fingers with garden shears. They wrapped him up in plastic. He was so huge, it kept coming loose. They threw his body in Brady's SUV and dumped him at Rena's condo. Costa told Brady he paid Marino fifteen grand for his part.

Brady told the story without emotion. He could have been describing delivering dry cleaning instead of a dead body. His flat affect was far more disturbing than if Brady had been angry or passionate, or appeared in any way to appreciate the enormity of what he'd done.

Susan and Bobby had advised Nicky to remain impassive, no matter what was said. He couldn't do it. He shook his head vigorously from side to side when Brady named him as his accomplice. The jurors probably didn't notice. Their eyes were glued to the witness box. Brady finished his story, and half the jurors physically turned their backs on him in disgust. That didn't mean they didn't believe him.

On cross-examination, Richard first made it clear that Brady wasn't claiming that Costa was present at the murder. Then he went after the witness, showing what he expected to gain from his cooperation with the government.

"Mr. Brady, when you first spoke with FBI Agents Rizzo and Smith, you were charged with having a gun in a motor vehicle, isn't that right?"

"Yes."

"If you'd been convicted of that charge, you could have been sentenced as a habitual criminal, and could have spent most of the rest of your life in prison, isn't that so?"

"That was just a charge. I was never convicted of that."

"That charge has been dismissed?"

"Yeah."

"As a result of your agreement to testify in this case?"

"It was a package deal."

"And as a part of that package, you agreed to plead guilty to the murder of Mr. Francini, and the Commonwealth agreed not to ask for a sentence as a habitual criminal?"

"Yes."

"As part of that package, you told the government what you knew of gangland murders in Boston?"

"I had to."

"And you told them about ten murders in which you'd been involved, isn't that right?"

"I don't remember the exact number. That sounds about right."

"You've committed so many murders, you don't remember the number?"

Brady just stared at Richard.

"What about Mary Spokane? She owed you two hundred

dollars. You drowned her in her own bathtub. Do you remember that one?

"Yeah."

"How about Howie Stern? The bookie? You burned down his house with him in it. You remember that?

"Yeah."

Richard held a stack of papers in his hand. He flipped a page, read for a second like he was getting ready to describe a third murder, then looked at the jury and shook his head.

"Of all the murders you confessed to, Francini is the only one you're being prosecuted for?"

"Yes."

"After this trial, the government is going to place you in the witness protection program, and you'll get a new identity, a job, and some money, correct?"

"Yes."

"You killed ten people and now you get to go free and start your life over?"

"Most of them were crooks."

"Your testimony is that you got paid fifty thousand dollars to kill Tony Francini?"

"That's what I said."

"If you were willing to kill someone for fifty thousand dollars, you'd be willing to lie under oath for a lot less, wouldn't you?"

Brady raised his voice. "I'm telling the truth here, counselor, and your client knows it."

By then Brady had shown his temper a few times. Susan was afraid that it wouldn't be enough to save the defendants. The jurors were giving them dirty looks.

Richard moved closer to the witness.

"Mr. Brady, how did you know that Mr. Francini was going to have dinner at Rena's condo on the night you killed him?"

"We'd been following Francini and knew that they had dinner together every Monday night."

"How did you know what time Mr. Francini would leave his

office?"

"We didn't. We sat in my van for a couple of hours waiting for him to show."

"You didn't get a call from anyone telling you when he left the office?"

"No."

"Nothing else, your Honor."

Bobby stood and faced the witness. Susan held her breath. "Mr. Brady, you say you got Nicky Marino's name fryyuuom Danny Costa, right?" Bobby asked.

"Yeah."

"You'd never worked with Mr. Marino before?"

"Not that I recall."

"He isn't mentioned in any of your statements regarding the other murders you told the FBI about, isn't that right?"

"I guess not."

Bobby picked up a stack of papers from the table. "Well, so that you don't have to guess, do you want me to show you all these statements so you can be sure?"

"You don't have to. He's not in them."

"So, your testimony is that you were willing to kill Tony Francini, and to rely on Mr. Marino to do the shooting, even though you had no experience with him?"

"Costa's word that I could count on him was good enough for me."

"Do you recall an incident in Magoun's Bar, in Somerville, almost two years ago, where you got into an argument with Mr. Marino?"

"Vaguely."

"You made a pass at his wife, and then you called her a 'bitch,' and then Mr. Marino took a swing at you and knocked you down, isn't that right?" Bobby asked.

Juror number two, Mr. Geckler, in the front row, was coolly appraising Brady.

"I had some words with him. He didn't knock me down. I

doubt if he could."

Geckler screwed up his face. Apparently, he wasn't buying the denial.

Bobby raised his voice. "Mr. Brady, isn't it true that you killed Tony Francini with someone else and to cover-up for your real partner, you picked Mr. Marino because he slugged you? You lost face and you were furious about it, isn't that right?"

"No. Your client was there. Marino was there and he shot Francini as sure as I'm sitting here right now."

Bobby was done. It wasn't a brilliant cross-examination, but Susan liked the fact that he'd done it without notes and without losing his rhythm. He'd done as well as she'd thought he'd be able to do. He'd called her last night to go over it on the phone. He said he wasn't afraid of Brady, just of his own ghosts from the past. Evidently, Bobby was able to conquer his demons. Susan loved that Brady was too macho to admit that Nicky had knocked him to the floor. The bartender Jerry and Patty would contradict Brady, and the jurors were likely to accept their testimony. Whether it would be enough to convince them that Brady was lying about Nicky's involvement in Francini's murder was hard to say.

Flanagan did a very brief re-direct, emphasizing that Brady wouldn't get any of the benefits of his plea agreement unless the Commonwealth was satisfied that he testified truthfully. The defendants objected on the ground that the prosecutor was vouching for the truthfulness of the witness's testimony, which a lawyer is not allowed to do. Judge Walsh overruled the objection. Susan knew the judge was right on the law, but it didn't seem fair. With that, the Commonwealth rested its case. Tomorrow it would be the defense's turn.

46

A defendant in a criminal case doesn't have to offer any evidence. He doesn't have to testify, or call witnesses, or even question the prosecution's witnesses if he chooses not to. The entire burden of proof is on the government. A defendant can sit back and argue that the prosecution failed to introduce enough evidence to prove his guilt beyond a reasonable doubt. Of course, that stratagem is seldom employed. The prosecution must have some evidence to get the case to trial. Ordinarily, it's too risky for a defendant to rely entirely on a critique of the government's proof.

But it can also be dangerous for a defendant to offer evidence. It's particularly hazardous to try to prove that someone else committed the crime. If the jury isn't convinced by the defendant's evidence, they might forget that it's the prosecution that has the burden of proof. If they don't buy the defendant's case, they might convict him.

Susan was thinking about all of that as she entered the courthouse. Everything hinged on what would happen today.

She and Richard had made their plans, going over and over their case, and now it was time to put it in front of the jury. Susan didn't know if their strategy would work. She'd never been in this position before. She didn't have the experience she needed to make an informed judgment about what was going to happen. Richard said they had a good shot at winning. She didn't know how confident she could be in a "good shot." She'd hardly slept the previous night.

There were even more people in the hallway trying to get in than the day before. No doubt the crowd was curious about what sort of defense would be attempted. The lawyers had said very little publicly about their plans. The media was predicting guilty verdicts. The reporters didn't like Brady, but they did find his story convincing.

"Good morning ladies and gentlemen," Judge Walsh addressed the jury. "The prosecution has rested. Defense, call your first witness."

Bobby stood. "The defense calls Rena Posso."

Rena walked slowly from the back of the room to the witness box, wearing a dark blue wrap dress, which accentuated her full figure. Her long black hair cascaded over her shoulders and it was only when she turned her head that one could catch a glimpse of cultured pearl drop earrings in white gold, her only jewelry. She looked every inch the professional model that she was.

Rena made one hell of an entrance. Susan hoped her testimony would go as well as they'd planned.

Rena swore to tell the truth, the whole truth, and nothing but the truth. She sat down in the witness chair and looked up at Bobby.

"Ms. Posso, would you please introduce yourself to the jury," Bobby said.

Rena turned toward the jurors, as Bobby had previously instructed her to do. "My name is Rena Posso. I live in Boston, in a condo in the Seaport, and work as an actress and sometimes as a model."

"Were you acquainted with Tony Francini?"

"Yes."

"What was the nature of your relationship?"

A tear started to fall from Rena's eye down the side of her cheek. Its descent was agonizingly slow and every eye on the jury tracked its path. Finally, just as it reached her neck, Rena took a tissue from her purse and dabbed it away. "He was my boyfriend. I was in love with him."

"How did you meet?"

"He made a donation to a children's theater group that I ran at the time. His niece was one of the students. I invited those who made significant contributions to my apartment in the South End for dinner. Tony was one of the guests."

"How much was his contribution?"

"Five hundred dollars."

"When did you move from the apartment where you hosted that dinner to the condo you live in now?"

"About a year after I met Tony."

"Why did you move?"

Another tear escaped from her eye. It fell just as slowly as the first, but she wiped it away with the tissue while it was still on her cheek. "My father passed away and left me some money. I'd always wanted to live nearer to the harbor and when I could afford to buy a condo there, I did."

"How much money did your father leave you?"

"Objection," Flanagan said. "Irrelevant."

"I'll see the lawyers at the side bar," the judge said.

The lawyers and the stenographer huddled at the side of the judge's bench on the opposite side of the room from the jury. Susan couldn't hear them, but she knew what Bobby's argument would be. The prosecution claimed that Romano ordered Francini to be killed for stealing money to support his girlfriend. Whether she had money of her own was clearly relevant. Bobby finished. Flanagan attempted to continue the debate. The judge just shook her head and waved them back to their tables.

"The objection is overruled," she said.

"May I answer?" Rena asked. The judge nodded.

"He left me approximately three million dollars." A buzz ran through the courtroom and began to get louder.

Judge Walsh banged her gavel and cautioned the spectators to be quiet.

Bobby walked up to the witness box and handed Rena a few sheets of paper. "Showing you what has been marked as Defense Exhibit 3 for identification, Ms. Posso, can you tell us what this document is?"

Rena read the top sheet silently. "Yes. This is a certified copy of the final accounting of my father's estate from the Probate Court in New York."

"The defense offers the document in evidence, your Honor. Mr. Flanagan has a copy."

"It may be received."

Susan noted on her pad that Flanagan didn't object. No doubt he didn't want to try the judge's patience by repeating a spurious argument about relevance.

"What does it show as the amount of money that was distributed to you?" Bobby asked.

"Three million, one hundred fifty thousand, six hundred, eighty-nine dollars."

"How much did you pay for your condo in the Seaport?"

"One million, five hundred thousand dollars."

Bobby approached the witness box again and handed Rena another document. "Showing you what has been marked Defense Exhibit 4 for identification, what is this?"

"That's the closing statement from the purchase of my condo."

"We offer it, your Honor."

"No objection," said Flanagan.

"It may be received."

Susan jotted down that Ex. 4 was accepted in evidence.

Flanagan had changed his strategy. Now he was trying to suggest that the evidence was unimportant by making a point of not objecting. Nice try, but surely everyone in the room, including the jurors, got the point Bobby was making. Some of them were sitting forward on their chairs a little. They looked curious.

This was what originally convinced Susan that they needed Rena as a witness. Susan made friends with Rena to make sure they could get this testimony. Then Susan started to like Rena for her own sake, and things got complicated. Susan had been racked with guilt about mixing business with pleasure. She was over it now.

"Ms. Posso, did Mr. Francini give you any money toward the purchase of the condo?"

"No."

"Was he supporting you in any way?"

"No. I am completely self-supporting."

NICE JOB, Susan wrote on a piece of paper and pushed it over in front of Bobby's chair. She admired the economy of his questions. The exam flowed smoothly, just as they planned.

"Thank you. No further questions." Bobby turned toward Flanagan. "Your witness."

Rena caught Susan's eye from across the courtroom and smiled. Rena was satisfied with herself, Susan thought. Rena had done everything they asked her to do. Now it's going to get interesting. Susan did not smile back.

47

Tom Flanagan gathered his papers in his hand and stood up. Richard rose rapidly to his feet. "Your Honor, before the Commonwealth cross-examines this witness, I have some questions on behalf of defendant Costa."

Flanagan gave Richard a startled look and sat back down. Susan could tell he was confused. Flanagan would have assumed that there was no reason for more than one defense lawyer to question Rena.

"Proceed, Mr. Charles," the judge said.

"Good morning, Ms. Posso, I'm Richard Charles and I represent the defendant Danny Costa."

Bobby leaned toward Susan and whispered, "What's this? Did I forget something?"

"No, you covered everything we talked about."

"Then what the hell is Richard doing?"

"Let's wait and see."

Rena's face remained impassive at this new development. Every time they talked about her testimony, they told her that

Bobby would be the only defense lawyer to ask questions. Susan lied to her. She didn't feel guilty about that. It was necessary. Richard popping up must have made her a little nervous, but Rena wasn't going to show it. She was a professional actress.

"How long were you and Mr. Francini, Tony, seeing each other?"

"A few years."

"After he became your boyfriend, how often did you see each other?"

"It varied, depending on his work and mine. We were both very busy. He worked long hours during the day, and I was often in a play or rehearsals at night, so sometimes it wasn't easy to get together."

Flanagan and his assistant whispered back and forth. They didn't know where this was going and were probably trying to decide whether to object. If they did, and everyone went to the bench, Susan was going up there too. She wanted to hear Richard's explanation for these questions. She didn't know if the judge would allow a student at side bar. The stenographer took down everything they said there, so it was all on the record. They just went to the side so the jury couldn't hear what they were saying. It would be okay. The worst thing that could happen would be she'd be told to take her seat.

"Did you ever have a regular day each week that you would get together?"

Flanagan got to his feet. "Objection."

Bad timing. Some of the jurors were frowning at the prosecutor. They wanted to hear if she was going to confirm Brady's testimony. He'd said they got together every Monday. They didn't like that Flanagan was trying to cut this off.

"Overruled."

"No. We couldn't. Like I said, our schedules often conflicted. There was never any regular day we could both count on being free."

Richard nodded. "So, you made your plans week by week,

depending on what worked?"

"Yes."

"And it was like that the whole time you were seeing each other?"

"Yes."

Richard left no wiggle room on the issue. They hadn't told Rena that Brady claimed to have followed Francini to her place every Monday, so she wasn't aware of the significance of her answers.

Richard looked at the jury, then back at the witness. "Ms. Posso, had you made plans to see Tony on the night he was killed?"

"Yes. As I told the police, I was expecting him for dinner."

"When did you make those plans?"

"That morning. I was supposed to have a rehearsal that night. It got canceled, so I called Tony and invited him for dinner."

Flanagan was operating on the assumption that Brady was telling the truth. For some reason, he didn't call Rena as a witness to finding Tony's body. Susan sure would have. Such pathos. A woman opens her front door and finds her slain boyfriend sprawled across her welcome mat. Flanagan hadn't gone there. So, he didn't bother to check with Rena to see if Brady's story matched her recollection. Now Flanagan would have to argue that the grieving girlfriend must be mistaken on this point. A jury might find that hard to accept.

"What time did you expect him?" Richard asked.

"Originally he said he'd be there around seven. Then he called and said he was trying to finish up something important at work and he was going to be late. He said he'd come as soon as he could."

"Did you tell anyone that Tony was coming to your house that night?"

"I don't think so. Not that I remember, anyway."

Richard looked at the papers in his hand. "Did you meet with any of the lawyers to discuss your testimony in this case?"

"Yes, I met with Mr. Coughlin. His assistant Ms. Sorella was there."

"Did you ever meet with anyone from the District Attorney's Office?"

"I met with Mr. Flanagan several months ago. It was mostly so he could express his sympathy for my loss. His office called, from time to time, to give me an update on the status of the case. A week ago, they phoned and said they wouldn't be using me as a witness."

"What about police officers? Did you ever meet with any police officers to discuss your testimony?"

"No."

Rena was staring hard at Susan. Rena looked irritated. Exasperated. Like, why did she have to answer all these questions? Susan thought about all the time she'd spent at Rena's condo and how their friendship developed. Rena was so charming when she shared her photography with her. Susan maintained a bland expression on her face.

Richard raised his voice slightly. "What about FBI agents? Did you meet with any FBI agents to talk about your testimony?"

"No."

Richard was standing at the other end of the jury box from the witness, holding notes in his hand as he questioned her. Now he crossed the courtroom to the defense table and put his notes down. He walked slowly back to the middle of the room, empty-handed, and looked at her for a few seconds without saying anything. He waited until every member of the jury was looking at him.

"Ms. Posso, do you know an FBI agent named Mike Rizzo?"

"Objection. Relevance."

"I'll see counsel at side bar."

The jurors looked completely confused. Bobby had a look on his face somewhere between irritation and mystification. Susan followed him up to the bench.

Judge Walsh, with a slight smile on her face, addressed her.

"Ms. Sorella, it appears you want to hear what's going on up here in our secret meetings?"

"If it's agreeable to your Honor, yes."

"Students working on a case are always welcome at side bar, or in chambers, in my courtroom. They don't keep medical students out of the operating room, and I don't keep you out of the important proceedings here. Now, Mr. Flanagan, what's your objection?"

"She said she didn't meet with FBI agents to talk about the case," Flanagan said. "There's no connection between the material issues here and whether Ms. Posso knows Agent Rizzo."

"I doubt Mr. Charles would be wasting our time. Would you care to enlighten us about where this is going, Mr. Charles?"

Richard stepped a foot closer to the judge and spoke in a low voice. "Agent Rizzo is the one who developed Brady as a witness, your Honor. I can assure you that I have a good faith basis, including documents I'm prepared to introduce into evidence, for believing that the witness knows Mike Rizzo and that she has information she has never disclosed about the murder of Mr. Francini. I would prefer to develop the details through my next several questions if the Court will allow me to do so."

"Your Honor, this is outrageous," Flanagan said. "Mr. Charles hasn't said anything that indicates the relevance of this testimony."

"No, he hasn't. But he has said that he intends to show the relevance imminently. He's piqued my curiosity, and I'd like to see where this goes. For now, your objection is overruled."

The lawyers returned to their seats, except for Richard who went back to the middle of the courtroom. Bobby gave Susan an inquiring look. She looked down at her yellow pad.

At the judge's request, the stenographer read back the last question.

"I've read Agent Rizzo's name in the paper in connection with this case. I don't know him personally," Rena said.

Richard was looking at the jurors now, although he was

speaking to the witness. "You've never met him?"

"No."

"Have you ever talked with him on the phone?"

Rena paused. "I don't think so. As I said, they called me several times to update me on the case. It's possible he was one of the people who called, but I don't actually remember such a call."

"What about in the last two months? Has he called you during that time?"

"As I said, I can't be sure if he might have been one of the officials who called."

Richard took a couple of steps toward the witness. "Well then, do you remember if you ever called him?"

Rena's hands were pressed hard against the top of the witness box, as though she was trying to keep them from shaking.

"I wouldn't have any reason to call him unless he called me, and I was out, and I was merely returning his call."

Richard turned toward the judge. "Your Honor, I'd like to offer in evidence Ms. Posso's telephone records for the past two months. They've been subpoenaed from her carrier and are now in the custody of the clerk." Richard walked up to his table and the clerk handed him an envelope. Richard took out three copies of the records, gave one back to the clerk, one to Flanagan, and laid one on the defense table.

"Objection," Flanagan said, without even looking at the records. "We're going very far afield from the issues in this case, your Honor."

"Overruled. They may be received as Defense Exhibit 5."

Bobby crouched in front of Costa to examine the defense copy of the records. Richard put the exhibit on the document camera, and it came up on the viewing screen. Rena seemed to be struggling to keep a neutral expression on her face. She was pretty good at it, but the pressure was starting to tell.

"Ms. Posso, 555-964-1632 is your cell number, isn't it?"

"Yes."

"No one else uses your phone?"

Rena hesitated just a fraction of a second. "No," she said.

"These records show that in December and so far in January several calls have been placed from your number to the number 555-854-9570. Whose number is that?"

"I don't know."

"Your Honor, we've also subpoenaed records from Verizon for 555-854-9570, and a certified copy of those records is in the clerk's custody. We offer that as an exhibit."

Again, Richard got copies from the clerk and distributed them. This time, Flanagan looked at the records. He made no objection, and Judge Walsh said that the records could be received as Defense Ex. 6. Rena took a sip of water from the glass in front of her. Then she gulped down half of it.

Richard approached the witness box and handed Rena the exhibit. "Ms. Posso, could you please read, out loud, the name of the subscriber for 555-854-9570?"

She stared at the records for several seconds. "Mike Rizzo," she said softly.

There was murmuring from the gallery. The judge banged her gavel and it quieted. The jurors stared at the screen where Rizzo's number appeared in the records from Rena's phone.

"Let me ask you about one of these calls, in particular, the one on the afternoon of December 7, at three o'clock, for fifteen minutes. You now remember phoning Agent Rizzo at that time, don't you?"

"I don't believe I made that call. I think there must be some mistake in the records—some computer glitch or something."

"You were expecting a visitor that day, weren't you? It was a Friday if that will help you."

Again, there was the briefest of hesitations before Rena answered. "Yes, I was expecting Susan Sorella."

"The woman sitting at the defense table?"

Everyone in the courtroom was staring at Susan. She showed no emotion, but inside her heart was beating fast.

"Yes."

"She didn't come to your condo as you expected, did she?"

Flanagan stood. "Objection, your Honor. It sounds like Mr. Charles is trying a completely different case than the one in this courtroom."

"I don't think so, Mr. Flanagan. Overruled."

"Did Susan Sorella come to your condo that Friday?"

"No."

"And you subsequently learned why she didn't appear?"

"Yes. She called. She was upset. Almost hysterical. She said she'd been in an accident."

Richard stared at the witness. "Nothing more?"

"Actually, later she said that someone tried to run her over with a car," Rena said. "It sounded ridiculous to me."

"Objection, hearsay," Flanagan said.

The judge turned toward the jury. "Sustained as to someone trying to run her over with a car. You will disregard that part of the witness's answer."

It would be hard for the jury to follow that instruction. They probably wouldn't be thrown off what sounded like a hot trail by technicalities. It didn't really matter to Susan. What was important was that Rena made a call to Rizzo shortly before something happened to her. Richard was setting Rena up for his next question.

Richard raised his voice again. "Ms. Posso, on July 7, 2004, you placed two calls to Agent Rizzo, one in the afternoon, and one in the evening, didn't you?"

"That was three and a half years ago. How could I remember— Oh. Oh, my god."

"Yes, Ms. Posso, that's the day that Tony was murdered."

Richard looked at the jurors, then turned back to Rena. He pointed his finger at her. He spat out his next question in a tone of voice that brooked no doubt about what an honest answer would be. "Didn't you call Mike Rizzo that afternoon, to tell him that Tony was coming for dinner that night, and then didn't you call him again during the evening, to tell him when Tony left his office?"

Everyone in the gallery was talking. The judge banged her gavel several times and finally, the room quieted. Rena sat silently. The judge turned to her. "Well, Ms. Posso?"

Flanagan stayed in his chair. He finally got it. The jurors stared at Rena.

Rena looked at the judge. In front of the bench, the clerk held another envelope in his hand, which he was holding out over his table in Richard's direction.

"Your Honor, I have to—I mean—I plead the Fifth Amendment."

Two reporters bolted from the first row to the hall, cell phones in hand.

"Ms. Posso," Judge Walsh said, "it's too late for that. You've already answered enough questions to waive your Fifth Amendment rights on this issue. You can't go as far as you have down the road and then stop. You have to respond."

Flanagan spoke to his assistant, who also ran from the courtroom. Flanagan didn't argue about whether Rena had waived her right to remain silent. Susan figured at this point he wanted to learn what she knew as much as the defense wanted her to spill it.

Rena was visibly shaking. She started to cry. This time, probably real tears. "I can't. I can't answer that question. I'd like to talk to a lawyer."

Judge Walsh looked toward Richard, and then to Flanagan.

"We have no objection to a recess while the witness consults with an attorney, your Honor," Richard said. "Perhaps it will shorten these proceedings."

Yes, Susan thought. A lawyer will tell her to make a deal with Flanagan to avoid being charged with first-degree murder. When she tells him what she knows, this prosecution will be over.

"The Commonwealth also has no objection," Flanagan said.

"Very well. The jurors may retire to the jury room and then be excused for the remainder of the day. The clerk will be in touch with you as to when you should return to the courthouse. I repeat my admonition to you, do not watch the news on television or read the papers until this case is concluded."

The jurors started to file out. "Did you know about this?" Bobby quietly asked Susan.

"Yes, and I'm sorry. I couldn't tell you. It was important that your examination of the witness go precisely as we planned it, so she would have no reason to suspect that something bad was coming."

"I could have handled that, you know."

"I'm sure you could have, Bobby. I'm sorry."

Susan was much more sympathetic toward Bobby ever since he told her about the boy who hanged himself. She wasn't confident, however, that he could have pulled off his exam of Rena so smoothly if he'd known what was coming.

The door closed behind the last juror. Judge Walsh told Rena that if she didn't respond she would be held in contempt of court and jailed until she answered the question. The judge directed the court officers to take the witness into custody and to allow her to make a telephone call to obtain an attorney, but to no one else. Judge Walsh asked the lawyers to meet with her in her chambers. She pointed at Susan and mouthed, "You, too."

The court officers led Rena away in handcuffs. She didn't look at Susan. This woman put Susan through the wringer. All the while Susan was feeling guilty about using her friendship with Rena to get her testimony, Rena was using her. Spying on her for Rizzo. And trying to have her killed. Rena set up her own boyfriend. She was cold, very cold. She deserved whatever she was going to get.

"Was Agent Rizzo in the courtroom just now?" Judge Walsh asked once they were settled in chambers

"No," Flanagan said. "I've sent a message to my office to contact the Special Agent in Charge of the Boston FBI, to ask him to order Rizzo and his partner, Harry Smith, to remain in his office until we can speak with them. I expect that the SAC will cooperate."

"Mr. Charles," the judge said, "I gather it's your position that Ms. Posso told Rizzo that Francini was expected and that he was somehow involved in Francini's murder. I assume you believe Rizzo colluded with someone other than these defendants to bring about Francini's death."

"Yes, your Honor. Not only Francini's death but also the attempt on the life of Ms. Sorella in December."

"I was unaware of that incident until today," Flanagan said.

"I understand," the judge said. "Mr. Charles has been playing his cards very close to his chest. No doubt, with good reason, if the FBI is involved on the wrong side here. Frankly, I'm shocked at the turn that this has taken. Now, Mr. Charles, would you like to tell us what you know?"

"I'm not sure, your Honor, how much the Court should hear at this stage. My colleagues and I will be happy to meet with Mr. Flanagan immediately, to suggest a course of action to him."

"Yes, that's probably the best way," Judge Walsh said. "I can't tell if we'll need this jury back here or not. I suspect maybe we won't. I'll ask counsel to appear here at 9:30 tomorrow morning to let me know what progress you've made. If we need the jury, I'll have the clerk tell them to come in at noon."

The lawyers filed out of the judge's chambers. "Look, give us fifteen minutes to talk with our clients, and then we'll meet you in your office," Richard said to Flanagan.

Bobby went to the lockup to meet with Nicky. Susan went to find Patty. This time she was going to enjoy bringing her up to speed.

48

They met the next morning in the prosecutor's conference room. "The Commonwealth will agree to the court entering directed verdicts of not guilty for all defendants," Tom Flanagan said. Susan was thrilled. Their plans to trap Rena worked. This was Susan's first major trial and she'd helped pull a rabbit out of a hat to get a victory for the defense. She was expecting this result since they met with the prosecutor the day before. It was a relief to have it confirmed.

"Thank you, Tom," Richard said. "Can you fill us in on the details of what happened after we left you yesterday?"

"Rena Posso got a lawyer to represent her," Flanagan said. "He'd been following the case in the paper, and I brought him up to speed on what happened yesterday in the courtroom. While he was meeting with her, I went with Boston detectives to the FBI office in the Kennedy building. The SAC kept Rizzo and Smith in his office, as we'd requested. We arrested them and charged them with first-degree murder. They'll be arraigned this morning.

"I'd told her lawyer that if Posso immediately made a full statement, we'd charge her with only second-degree murder. If she refused to cooperate, she'd be charged with first-degree. I got back from the federal building, and the lawyer said Posso was ready to talk."

Flanagan gestured with some papers he held in his hand. "She made a full confession to her part in the murder of Tony Francini and the assault with intent to murder against Ms. Sorella. Ms. Posso admitted that she'd been having an affair with Rizzo for years."

Susan gasped. She knew Rena was working with Rizzo, but never suspected that he was her lover.

"Rizzo was married until recently, so the affair was secret," Flanagan continued. "Rena met Francini through her theater group, and Rizzo got her to continue seeing him to gather information on Romano's operation. Evidently, Posso never learned anything of importance and was growing tired of the charade, when Rizzo told her they needed to get rid of Tony. Rizzo said one of his informants, who worked for Romano, had been stealing from the boss. Rizzo was afraid that Tony might be getting close to figuring out who the thief was. The informant and his brother planned to ambush Tony. Rizzo got Rena to agree to let him know when he'd be coming to dinner, so they could make the hit on the deserted waterfront at night. Later Rizzo told her it was Willie and Eddie Baker who killed Francini, with Brady's help. Detectives arrested the Bakers late last night and they'll be arraigned this morning as well."

"Why did they go after Susan?" Bobby asked.

Flanagan grimaced. "Rena claims she felt bad about that. Rizzo told her he'd been in Magoun's one night when Ms. Sorella and an investigator came in. He heard them interviewing the bartender about the dust-up between Brady and Marino. Then an FBI surveillance team saw Ms. Sorella and Frank Romano together and overheard part of a conversation about Eddie Baker. Rizzo was afraid that somehow she'd learned what had really happened."

Susan clenched her jaw. Rena *felt bad* about trying to kill her. Poor thing. Susan was pissed that Rena was getting off with second-degree murder. She'd be eligible for parole someday and might be released. With her acting skills, she'd probably convince the Board she was remorseful. Susan got why Flanagan offered the deal—he needed Rena's testimony to make a strong case against Rizzo and Smith. He might not have been able to get to the Bakers without her. Still, it sucked.

"Ms. Sorella, I'm not going to ask you about your conversations with Frank Romano," Flanagan said. "I do recommend you don't see him again."

Susan made no response. She appreciated what Flanagan had done to wrap up the case, but she certainly wasn't going to let the D.A.'s Office tell her who she could talk to.

"What's going to happen to Brady?" Richard asked.

"His plea agreement has been voided, and he'll be going on trial for murder with the others," Flanagan said. "This time he won't be offered any deals."

"There's just one more thing," Richard said. "Jane Friley. She came to see you at our request. Rizzo and Smith were trying to work the same sort of deal with Tommy O'Neill that they'd done with Brady. We wanted to tip you off, so you could see that Rizzo and Smith were dirty. They got wise to the fact that we were on to them, so they never showed up in your office. Friley was acting in good faith. Unfortunately, O'Neill has disappeared, and no one can find him. I suspect that your new set of defendants had something to do with that. You should probably go back to Rena Posso and ask her what she knows about it."

"I've been wondering about that deal," Flanagan said. "Thanks for the information, and thanks for telling me that Friley was on the up and up."

Everyone went down to Judge Walsh's chambers, where Flanagan filled her in on the developments. In open court, the judge entered not guilty verdicts on the record for all defendants and ordered their immediate release from custody. The defendants jumped up and found their wives and they were all hugging and kissing. People from the gallery surged forward to congratulate them and their lawyers. Susan's dad gave her a big hug.

Judge Walsh hadn't called a recess and was still sitting on the bench. She banged her gavel until the room fell quiet. "I'm sorry, but you can't have a party in the courtroom." She grinned. "You should find another place to have one. Court is adjourned."

Everyone looked at Susan. She looked at her father, who nodded. "Okay," she said. "Gabriella's private room, tonight, eight o'clock."

49

"This antipasto looks like a feast in itself," Richard said. The dining table in Gabriella's private room was laden with special dishes. Susan had gone directly from court to the restaurant to help her father get ready for the party. A handmade ceramic platter from Umbria contained a traditional antipasto, with Parma ham, mortadella, capocollo, Milano salami, and buffalo mozzarella, nestled among green and black olives, bell peppers, aubergines, artichokes, sun-dried tomatoes, and mushrooms. The vegetables glistened under a slight coating of olive oil. Loaves of fresh-baked Italian bread lay ready on a cutting board. Platters of bruschetta with figs, gorgonzola cheese, pancetta crumbles, and toasted hazelnuts tempted the guests at one end of the table and Zucchini flowers stuffed with fontina cheese, and asparagus arancini with taleggio cheese lay in shallow bowls at the other. On a sideboard, Prosecco chilled in buckets. Bottles of Barbera d'Alba provided a choice for those who preferred red. A glass pitcher contained lemonade for Nicky's kids.

"Imagine what you'd see if we were serving dinner," Susan said to Richard. "And later there'll be pastries." Richard came early to help her get things set up. The other guests began to arrive. Nicky and Patty Marino and their children were the first. Nicky looked handsome in a jacket and tie. His arm was locked around Patty's waist like he was never going to let go of her again. The kids danced around their father like a maypole.

Susan snapped a picture of them on her phone. It made everything worthwhile to see something like this. The case had been hard, but she'd been surrounded by the lawyers and everyone else in her daily life as she went through it. Nicky was out there alone in his cell, under strict instructions not to talk about the case to anyone other than his lawyer and his wife. Susan wondered how long it would take him to get used to living in the real world. Susan wished she were rich. She'd send the whole family to the Caribbean for a long vacation.

"Hey, Mr. Coughlin, you're looking pretty snappy," Nicky said, as Bobby and Marie appeared. Bobby introduced his wife around. He did look great in his suit. Armani, if Susan wasn't mistaken. Too nice for day-to-day wear in the office and the courtroom. Susan was glad she hadn't quit the internship before the court assigned him to represent Nicky. Nothing else could have compared to the roller coaster ride of this case. She wished she'd known from the beginning why it was so overwhelming for Bobby. He rallied at the end. He had his part to play, setting Rena up with a friendly examination about her finances, and he did it well. Tonight, he appeared more relaxed than he'd been in months.

Everyone filtered in. Costa and his wife laughed in one corner of the room with Paul Finn. Her father poked his head in. He had a full restaurant to take care of outside the room, but he wanted to meet everyone. Susan introduced him around.

"Lorenzo, I've eaten in your restaurant but never had the pleasure of meeting you. It's a thrill to shake hands with the man who makes such wonderful food," Jane Friley said.

"Yes, I believe I've seen you here," Susan's father said. "Welcome to Gabriella's."

Friley put her hand on his elbow and steered him away from the rest of the group. "Listen, if you don't mind, I've got a question about those arancini." Susan couldn't hear the rest. After a few minutes, she saw both Friley and her father laughing as he poured her a glass of wine.

The former FBI agent was flirting with her father! He was eating it up. All these years, she'd never seen her father in the company of a woman. His interest waned after her mother's death. Now in a couple of minutes, Friley rekindled a flame. Her neck was a little flushed. Her dad must be using his Italian charm on her.

Susan clinked the side of her glass with a fork several times. The room quieted. "I want to tell you all what a privilege it was to work with such amazing lawyers as Bobby Coughlin and Richard Charles," she said. "I learned a lot from them. Their clients were lucky to have these men as their attorneys. Let's give them a hand." Everyone clapped and shouted out congratulations.

"I've got a question," Marie said. "What made you suspect Rena?"

"Rena and I were making Christmas cookies, of all things, when I told her about meeting Jane Friley. I wanted to share with her how cool Ms. Friley was." Susan smiled at her. "It never occurred to me that Rena would connect her with our case, or that it would matter if she did. We knew that Rizzo and Smith were coercing a thief named Tommy O'Neill to say that Frank Romano was behind a diamond robbery that O'Neill pulled off. We'd asked Ms. Friley to represent O'Neill and to report the scheme to Flanagan. O'Neill disappeared. At first, I couldn't think of anyone who could've let the agents know that we were on to their scheme. Then I remembered that I'd always wondered how the killers knew that Francini was on his way to Rena's condo, particularly since he'd sent his car in the other direction with his assistant Eric. After the attempt on my life,

I'd also wondered how they knew I was going to her place. It came to me that only Rena could have tipped them off. No one else would have known about both Francini's plans and mine. I saw that mentioning Ms. Friley to Rena might have been a mistake. If she'd passed that information on, somebody could have figured out we knew about O'Neill. I told Richard what I'd done, and he agreed."

Costa stepped forward. "How did you know it was Rizzo she told?"

"At first we didn't. Richard figured that she must have told somebody. So, while Bobby was meeting with Rena at his office, we asked someone to conduct a little investigation at her apartment to get a look at her phone bills."

Everyone turned to look at Paul Finn, who maintained a bland expression on his face.

"Not saying who it was," Susan said. "We got a picture of her records and noticed the same number came up a lot. We called that number from a payphone. A man answered and said, 'Rizzo.' We waited until the very last minute we could, so they wouldn't get notice of it, and we subpoenaed Rena and Rizzo's records from Verizon."

"Couldn't Flanagan have seen those records in the Clerk's Office that morning before court?" Bobby asked.

"Yeah, but I didn't think he'd bother to look," Richard said. "He had no reason to believe that we were going to subpoena anything."

Marie raised her hand. "Why didn't you just go to the D.A. with all this in the first place?"

"We wanted to have this come as a surprise to Rena in open court, where she could dig herself into a hole, and then panic," Susan said. "We needed her to be rushed into making a deal and giving up the others. Otherwise, the case against them would've been a lot weaker."

Bobby raised his glass. "Here's a toast to Susan. By far the best law student intern anyone could ever have, and, obviously, the one who broke this case wide open. I can't wait to see what she does after she passes the bar." Everyone cheered and downed their drinks.

"Time for pastries!" Susan's father said. The door opened some waiters brought in trays of cannoli and other sweets. Everyone got more wine and the party was back in full swing.

Susan went over to Bobby and Marie and thanked him for his toast. "I know your internship is over," Bobby said. "If you want to come back to argue that appeal you wrote the brief on, I'd be glad to file a motion with the court to allow you to do it."

Susan bowed her head. "Thanks. I'd like that very much."

How about that? No hard feelings. Now that she understood Bobby better, it'd be easier to work with him. Not that she'd want to do so full time. She needed someone with a more demanding practice.

Susan found Richard. She lifted her glass and clinked his in a silent toast. Paul Finn came up to them. "I've got to leave. I promised another investigator I'd take the night shift on a surveillance. You were great to work with, Susan. After you pass the bar, call me whenever you need help."

"Oh, Paul," Susan said and gave him a kiss on the cheek and a big hug. "You saved my life. I wouldn't be standing here if it weren't for you."

"I'm glad I was there," Finn said. They stood quietly for a moment, then he shook hands with Richard, and left.

"How long do you think this party will go on?" Richard asked.

Susan felt the heat rise in her cheeks. "I don't know. I have to stay until everyone leaves. Will you wait with me, and take me home?"

50

The next day at noon Susan sat at the bar at Via Appia. Frank Romano came through the door and walked over to her chair.

"I thought I might find you here today," he said.

"Oh dear, I didn't think I was that predictable. I owe it to you to answer any questions you might have about how things ended."

"Paul Finn was good enough to drop by this morning and give me a complete report."

Susan grinned. "Well then, how'd you like to have lunch? I know you don't like to talk business in here, and I'd rather not parade down Hanover Street. What if we went to Lucca?"

"Excellent choice. You must let me pay since your father never gives me a bill when I come to Gabriella's."

They crossed the street and got a table in the back at Lucca. She needed to wrap things up with Romano. She'd enjoyed getting to know him and he'd looked out for her. Now she didn't see any reason to maintain a relationship. Regrettable as it was, he was, after all, the head of the mob.

"Your first murder case turned out to be quite an adventure," he said. "When I talked to you at Gabriella's, I didn't know how things would end. I only knew that the men charged with killing Tony didn't do it. I'm impressed with how much you made out of the meager information I gave you."

"Nicky Marino never seemed to me like he could kill anyone. I know Brady had a grudge against him, but I'm surprised he didn't pick someone more dangerous."

Romano cocked his head. "No one ever accused Joseph Brady of being smart. Ruthless, yes. Not intelligent. A man like that's likely to trip himself up sooner or later. Particularly if he comes up against a worthy adversary. Speaking of Brady's adversary, I'm curious what you learned from this case. How did it change you, if it did?"

Susan took a sip of water. "That's a question worth thinking about. I'm not sure I know yet, at least not completely. When I look back, I think I was terribly naïve at the start. It never would've occurred to me that someone like Rena would betray me, much less try to have me killed. I'm not sure what to make of that. I don't want to go through life not trusting anyone."

"I think you'll work that out. After all, there were people you trusted on this case, who didn't disappoint you. By the way, Louie and Fredo asked me to say hello for them. They enjoyed spending time with you."

"Please thank them for me." Susan furrowed her brow. "That's another thing. Everything was upside down. FBI agents were murdering people and planning crimes, and you and your men were on the side of justice. Oh, that didn't come out very well. Please don't take offense, I just meant that—"

"Don't worry about it," he interrupted. "I know who I am. I chose my life a long time ago. Sometimes I wonder if things could have been different. But they're not. You're quite right to assume that there are many times when I'm not, let's say, on the side of justice. I've also learned, though, through long experience, that things are never as black and white as we'd like. The older I've gotten, the larger the gray area has grown."

Romano was philosophical. Susan wondered, not for the first time, what crimes he'd committed to get where he was today. Perhaps she was better off not knowing. As far as trusting him was concerned, what she'd learned was that you can count on someone to have your back when his interest is aligned with yours. The problem with Rena was that Susan was mistaken about what Rena's interests were. In the future, she'd be more careful about making assumptions about people.

"What will you do after you graduate?" Romano asked.

"I'm definitely going to practice criminal law. I've been thinking about what Rizzo and Smith did. That kind of thing must happen more than we know. After I get some experience, I'd like to specialize in cases where it's possible to expose that kind of misconduct. Maybe I'll work with the National Police Accountability Project, or maybe I'll do it on my own. I don't know yet exactly how things will shake out. One thing though, I'll be on the lookout for more Agent Rizzos."

"I'm sure you'll find them. I've enjoyed seeing you in action, Susan. I'm afraid, however, that our paths may not cross again for a while."

She grinned. "Well, you never know. I hope you'll never need a lawyer. But if you do, I'll probably have my license by October."

They finished lunch and left the restaurant. They were on the sidewalk before she realized they hadn't paid. "Mr. Romano, they never brought us a bill."

"No," he said, "they didn't." He winked at Susan and turned and walked down the street.

Acknowledgments

A great many people supported me in the writing of this book. I can't name all the people who encouraged me to keep working at times when I felt it might never see publication. My biggest debt of professional gratitude is to my teacher, the novelist Stuart Nadler, from the Bennington College Master of Arts in Writing program. I had gone to Bennington after retiring as a law professor to improve my skills in writing non-fiction. One semester I switched to fiction, just for fun, and fell in love with it. I was lucky enough to have Stuart and the writer Jill McCorkle as my teachers that semester and I continued to work with Stuart for the next year and a half. His patience with a lawyer who knew next to nothing about writing fiction and his insight into just what I needed at various stages of the process are what enabled me to produce a book. Other Bennington teachers, Susan Cheever and Dinah Lenney, helped me shed much of the baggage I had accumulated over forty-five years at the bar that kept getting in my way as a writer.

I was fortunate to be surrounded by a great group of

students in the January 2017, MFA class at Bennington. The inspiration, affection, and support that the people in our group showed each other was unique in my experience in any academic institution. I would be happy to return to living in the college dorms twice a year forever to learn from them and be in their company.

Many of my friends were kind enough to read occasional chapters, or in some cases the entire novel, as I went through one revision after another. Their advice and encouragement were invaluable. My thanks to D.D. Allen, Karen Blum, Heidi Boghosian, Jeanne Carol, Chip DeWitt, John Duggan, Page Kelley, Jean Johnson, Gary Morton, Kevin Nixon, Marley Stuart, Charlie Rankin, David Rudovsky, and Garland Waller. If you were kind enough to read a chapter and I left your name off this list, my deepest apologies. I owe a special debt to Dan and Sam Avery, and my children, David, Katie, and Samantha Avery, for indulging their brother and father when I foisted various parts of the manuscript upon them.

You can't get a book published without a publisher, and I am particularly grateful to Susan Brooks and Literary Wanderlust for taking me on. Susan was generous enough to take on the job of editing the manuscript when the original editor became ill and could not take the assignment. Susan's advice was instrumental in fine-tuning the manuscript in ways that had previously escaped me and I learned much from her.

Finally, one person not only read these chapters numerous times, but also suffered me to read them aloud to her. Her advice on how women think and what readers want to see on the page was invaluable. Her love and support throughout the entire process was what kept me going. Regardless of how this book may be received, Jill Abbott Comeaux has made the rest of my life worth living.

About the Author

As a civil rights lawyer, Mike Avery spent over forty years representing the victims of police abuse and racial and sexual discrimination. In criminal cases, he defended people charged with everything from peaceful protesting to murder. He knows the law and the people who break it, including those who are supposed to enforce it. As one of the leaders of a team of attorneys representing four innocent men framed for murder, he obtained the largest judgment ever against the FBI for illegal actions by agents. Politically active as well, he has served as the President of the National Lawyers Guild, and the National Police Accountability Project.

Avery has written several books and articles about law and politics. Most recently, he co-authored The Federalist Society: How Conservatives Took the Law Back from Liberals. He is a graduate of Yale College and Yale Law School and spent a year as an exchange student in the former Soviet Union at the University of Moscow. After retiring as a professor of law at Suffolk University in Boston, he obtained a Master of Fine Arts from Bennington College. He now makes his home in New Orleans. The Cooperating Witness is his first novel.